A STAGE

FOR
Harriet

A STAGE

for

Harriet

MARY-CELESTE RICKS

• SWEETWATER BOOKS •
An imprint of Cedar Fort, Inc.
Springville, Utah

ISBN 13: 978-1-4621-3892-0

Published by Sweetwater Books, an imprint of Cedar Fort, Inc.
2373 W. 700 S., Springville, UT 84663
Distributed by Cedar Fort, Inc., www.cedarfort.com

Library of Congress Control Number: 2020948526

Cover design by Shawnda T. Craig
Cover design © 2020 Cedar Fort, Inc.
Edited and typeset by Valene Wood

Printed in the United States of America

10 9 8 7 6 5 4 3 2 1

Printed on acid-free paper

For my one true love

Prologue

The road back to London
September 20, 1813

Virginia wrestled the carriage window open and took a gasping breath of fresh air. She wasn't sure which made her feel more ill—the carriage's unstable motions or the baby growing inside her. Perhaps the only thing worse than either was realizing that once the motions of travel stopped, she would be living in a nightmare far worse than the ride.

Her normally chatty maid, Mandie, sat next to her in uncharacteristic silence and squeezed her hand. That was far more kindness than Virginia's mother had expressed in the letter confirming her return.

The fields and grounds they passed became smaller as the houses and buildings became taller and closer together, and a rosy hint of dawn brightened the edges of the structures still looming ahead. They blocked the warmth and light of the sun from reaching her. *How fitting.*

"We're nearly there, my lady," Mandie softly said.

Virginia squeezed her eyes shut and twisted the old handkerchief in her lap. She had tried and failed to grasp the life of her dreams and now a harsh reality called her back. She'd thought she had no more tears to give, but two or three fat drops rolled down her cheeks as the dusty road gave way to the worn cobblestones of London streets. She missed him so much her chest ached.

She said a silent prayer for a savior from what she was about to endure, but it was half-hearted. After all, who or what could save her now?

Chapter One

Burnham-on-Sea, Somerset
September 12, 1813

Miss Shore, you are a perfect dancer!" Mrs. Reed exclaimed to a breathless Harriet just coming out of a dance with rosy cheeks. Harriet curtsied to her obliging dance partner before turning to Mrs. Reed.

"Thank you, ma'am! I do love a good country dance."

Mrs. Reed took her hand. "My dancing days are long over, but I still cannot miss an assembly knowing I will see your performance on the dance floor, my dear. During a quadrille you are as stately as a queen and during a jig you are as light on your feet as a nymph! Perhaps you were made for the stage." The older woman squeezed her hand affectionately before leaving her side.

Harriet smiled to herself, but felt a familiar twinge of odd longing at her words. The stage was far from a respectable place for a young lady of gentle birth, but she had always privately yearned for a chance to perform before an audience despite her mother's disapproval.

"Harriet!" Her best friend Maria rushed to her side, interrupting her reverie. "Have you seen him yet?"

Harriet shook off her theatrical daydream with a laugh as she walked over to the punch table, Maria behind her. "And which 'him' is this, Maria?"

"Mr. Grimsby, of course! He's fresh from Oxford and I've heard he'll be here tonight."

Harriet prepared a cup for herself in surprised silence, trying to calm her pounding heart.

"What's the matter, Harriet? Cat got your tongue? *That's* unlike you," Maria teased, taking a cup of her own.

Harriet tried to smile and glanced over at the door as she took a sip, but her cup of punch never quite arrived at her mouth. She couldn't believe what she saw. She took a deep breath and blinked several times, but he was still there when she opened her eyes, smiling and talking with those standing near the entrance to the assembly room. *Stephan.*

He had slipped in with a small wave of newcomers and had immediately been greeted by old neighbors and friends. He smiled, and Harriet could feel his warm, calm countenance from across the room. It was really Stephan. There was no mistaking it. It had been years since they'd seen one another, let alone attended the same function, but it was not possible for her to forget her dearest childhood friend. Harriet glanced at the floor and recovered herself just enough to finally take a sip.

"*Harriet!*" a voice hissed near her. "Have you seen who just arrived?"

Harriet's already pounding heart throbbed a bit harder at the thought they could be overheard. "Of course I have, Maria—lower your voice!"

Maria giggled and leaned close enough to Harriet that a whisper could reach her ear. "Well? Are you going to speak to him?"

Harriet shook her head. "I can't. He is a gentleman, Maria. And not just any gentleman, but the son of Squire Grimsby! And I was lucky to be invited to the assembly in the first place."

Maria sighed and shook her head. "Any two guests in the same ballroom may speak to one another, Harriet, especially if they are already acquainted."

Harriet tried to quash the hope and excitement rising within her, but she could already tell she was losing the fight. "But I am far from an eligible candidate for him. And besides, I am leaving for London in less than a fortnight!"

Maria drew herself up to her full five feet and attempted to look down her nose at Harriet, even though Harriet was several inches taller than she was. She tutted loudly. "You *are* eligible! Your father may not exactly be a gentleman himself, but he's a gentleman's *son*. And why would you ever wish to go and be a governess in London when you can stay home and marry Mr. Grimsby instead?"

Harriet couldn't hold back a nervous giggle and sneaked a glance at Stephan only to catch him looking at her. His face lit up when their eyes met and Harriet took a steadying breath as she turned to Maria.

"Lower your voice, Maria. Please! I . . . you know how much my mother wishes me to go."

"But what do *you* want, Harriet?" Maria whispered.

Harriet glanced back at Stephan and smiled despite herself. Stephan never broke their gaze as he walked straight toward them. Harriet nervously smoothed her long white gown as he approached.

"Miss Shore." He was a bit breathless as he arrived before her, and his whole face smiled along with his mouth.

Harriet couldn't stop her smile. She hadn't thought it possible for her heart to pound any harder or faster, but it proved her wrong. She dropped a hasty curtsy. "Mr. Grimsby." When she looked up into his eyes, the look there waiting for her was so intense that she felt her cheeks flush even more, if that were possible.

"It is so good to see you, Ha—Miss Shore."

Harriet felt warm down to her fingertips as she glanced back up at him. Had he nearly called her by her Christian name? She suddenly felt transported back to her childhood, sitting side by side with Stephan in a leafy, sun-warmed oak tree.

"It has been a very long time, Mr. Grimsby."

"Yes, it has! And I apologize for my absence. But I have finally completed my studies at Oxford and have come home. Just in time to come of age and into my estate." He finally looked away, glancing at his shoes with a smile before turning back to her.

Harriet's face fell at this reminder of the inequality of their stations. As she remembered his comparative importance, her gaze flickered anxiously across the room, searching for a face that had always sent a shiver of fear down her spine.

Maria loudly cleared her throat, and Harriet hurried to follow her cue. "Oh, excuse me! Mr. Grimsby, this is my friend Miss Maria Wallbridge from the village school. She is one of the daughters of our dear vicar. Maria, this is Sir Stephan Grimsby."

"How do you do?" Maria asked cheerfully.

Stephan seemed distinctly uncomfortable at the introduction, but he smiled genially. "I am well, thank you. It is lovely to meet any friend of Harriet's." His face immediately flushed and his eyes squeezed shut. "Forgive me! Any friend of Miss *Shore's*."

Harriet's heart seemed to skip a beat. It wasn't every day that a handsome young man accidentally used her given name!

Maria smirked. "I believe the Quadrille is next," she said casually, "and I have seen Miss Shore's card and can answer that she is not yet engaged for it."

Harriet's mouth dropped open and she stared at Maria.

Stephan only gave a little nod and smile to Maria before turning to Harriet, his hope clear in his eyes. "I would be honored if you would stand up for the next with me, Miss Shore."

Harriet closed her mouth and dropped another curtsy. She swallowed. "I would like that very much," she managed.

His hand closed around hers and he led her onto the floor and into position. She easily turned her attention to the dance. She knew it and many others altogether too well, though was not in the habit of having a male partner. She had remained at Mrs. Wyncham's Village School for Gentlewomen far longer than most young ladies did because she had wished to. She had no brothers or sisters, and as a farmer's daughter and gentleman's granddaughter, she occupied an unusual and often lonely place in society—to low to be a full member of genteel society, but not allowed to associate with servants, tradesmen, or laborers.

She stepped lightly and focused on losing herself in the dance and moving as gracefully as she could. However, each time that Stephan's face came back into view and her brown eyes met his blue ones, she felt a surge of happy nerves rush to her chest and she needed to begin the process of calming herself all over again. She wondered how long it would take before her heart would stop cheerfully pounding in his presence.

They danced the rest of the quadrille together, and then a cotillion and two country dances. Each time one dance ended, Stephan would escort her to the side of the floor and talk to her for a minute or two as the next set formed, and then shyly ask her to dance the next, constantly certain she would be claimed by a previous engagement. But she was always free to accept him, and she ignored the prim little voice inside of her that said she should dance no more than twice with any one gentleman. Just as their fourth dance was about to end, however, she caught sight of a skinny older woman in a lavender gown who glared at her through narrowed, hawk-like eyes.

Harriet's breath caught in her chest and she felt ice trickle down her spine. Suddenly she was a child again, her knees knocking together before the woman's cold-eyed gaze. She barely managed to finish out the dance before breathlessly excusing herself, her bravery spent.

"I am sorry—I must go. Thank you for the lovely dances, Stephan." She was so flustered it took her a moment to catch her error. "I mean Mr. Grimsby!" She shook her head, embarrassed.

He smiled at her error, but his expression remained concerned. "Must you leave?" he asked.

Harriet gave a little sigh as she nodded. She caught sight of the hawk-eyed woman coming toward her out of the corner of her eye and quickened her pace toward the door.

Stephan followed her and caught her hand before the servant sent to fetch her pelisse could return with it. "Miss Shore," he said.

She barely resisted the urge to sigh as his voice intoned her name. "Yes?"

"I will call upon you this week, if you tell me I am welcome."

Harriet's mouth formed a little 'o' of surprise, and she shyly glanced up at him, unable to hide her smile. "You are always welcome, Mr. Grimsby."

Stephan's chest expanded as he gave her another broad, warm smile. "Until we meet again then, Miss Shore."

Harriet could not contain her grin, but when the frightening woman in lavender arrived behind Stephan, she was glad to turn and be helped into her pelisse by a servant.

Stephan caught the woman by the shoulder before she could speak to Harriet. "What is it you need, Mother? As you can see, Miss Shore was just leaving."

The woman stopped and turned reluctantly to Stephan. "All right. It would appear, then, that my assistance is not required after all."

Her words stung Harriet's ears as she hurried out the door into the cool evening breeze, not caring whether or not her horses were ready for her.

Burnham-on-Sea, Somerset

The next day Harriet was on a bumpy carriage ride of emotions. One moment she would feel elated, daydreaming about Stephan's hand clasping hers as they danced. The next moment all she could see was the angry, disapproving face of Mrs. Grimsby, and all she could feel was the sting of a long-ago slap on her cheek.

Harriet shook her head, taking another sip of tea. Her hand was trembling slightly. Mrs. Grimsby's words, both those from the evening before and those from her past, replayed mercilessly over and over on the stage of her mind.

Maria shook her head as she dipped a biscuit in her tea. "I don't see why *you're* so melancholy—you clearly have a prospect in Stephan Grimsby!"

"His mother does not approve," Harriet responded quickly.

Maria rolled her eyes and shook her head. "Harriet, he is *of age*. Let the man choose for himself. Besides, I cannot see why she ought to be in such a sweat to disapprove of you."

Harriet could feel her cheeks flush as she looked down at her hands, studying an uneven fingernail. She would need to repair it later.

Maria paused and glanced at Harriet over her teacup with some suspicion. "Is there something I don't know?"

Harriet finally looked up. "Have you not heard any of the gossip, Maria?"

Maria's eyes lit with excitement. "Gossip? What gossip?"

Harriet bit her lip and gazed up at the ceiling before sharing her report. "Mr. Kemp—The Grimsbys' groom, who's a good friend of my father—told me that the estate is in debt, possibly due to Mrs. Grimsby's spending habits since Squire Grimsby passed away three years ago. And from what I hear, the squire himself was something of a spendthrift."

Maria grimaced. "In debt, you say? Well, debt *would* keep him from being considered a prize on the marriage mart—so you still have a good chance, then."

Harriet, groaned. "Don't you see? If the estate's in debt, he'll need to marry into a fortune."

Maria frowned. "But you don't lack a dowry, Harriet."

Harriet gave a humorless laugh. "My little dowry is nothing to what they will require. If I understand the damage done, he won't be able to repair the estate for less than seven or eight thousand pounds of ready money, and my mother told me I'll not get more than two."

Maria grimaced. "What a mess! But it's not as though *marrying* a fortune would work for your Mr. Grimsby, anyway," she added as an afterthought.

Harriet smiled at Maria's persistence. "Whyever not?"

"Apart from being unlikely to attract a young lady of sufficient fortune, he's far too much in love with you to consider marrying anyone else!"

Harriet could not hold back a little laugh before correcting her friend. "That's not true, Maria. There is no understanding between us, you know."

"He said he wanted to marry you," Maria interjected.

Harriet's face flushed. "I was twelve! We were children!"

Maria laughed at Harriet's indignation.

Harriet gave a little groan. "I am not even certain I *wish* to marry Stephan, Maria."

Maria nearly choked on her tea. "But are you not in love with him?"

Harriet bit her lip as the honest truth hit her from within. "Of course I am," she admitted. "But, truth be told, I am terrified of Caroline Grimsby."

If Harriet had not been so distressed, she would have laughed at the consternated look on Maria's face. "But Harriet, you aren't afraid of *anything*."

Harriet smiled weakly and gave a heavy sigh as she gathered her thoughts into words.

"Stephan and I . . . have been friends since we were children. And for as long as we have been friends, his mother has disapproved of me. A secret meeting to climb trees as ten-year-olds is one thing. Proposing marriage to a young lady one's mother heartily disapproves of is quite another."

Maria frowned, and Harriet continued. "One of my earliest memories of playing with Stephan is accompanied by the memory of the slap his mother gave me that same day."

"She *didn't*," Maria whispered.

Harriet nodded. She could still hear Mrs. Grimsby's voice echoing in her mind words she had long tried to forget. "Running about the countryside with a common little snip of a girl, Stephan! Don't you *know* that she's only a farmer's daughter?" Harriet shuddered a bit as she recounted a couple of stories to Maria, including the time Mrs. Grimsby had struck her after her weak attempt to protect her friend Stephan from undeserved punishment as a child. She'd been only eight years old.

"That's awful," Maria murmured. "Harriet, I cannot blame you for not wanting her for a mother-in-law, but I still . . ." she sighed, and unceremoniously swallowed the rest of her tea before continuing. "I still cannot see why you won't at least *consider* marrying him anyway."

Harriet's heartbeat quickened as it did every time she thought of Stephan in a romantic way. "It's only a dream, Maria. Even should he wish to marry me, he *ought* to choose someone with a fortune so that he need not divide up his estate. Can I truly say that I love him while allowing him to ruin his estate? He and I would do better to forget about one another. It is hopeless. Especially since I'm due to depart for London in barely ten days."

Maria glared at the biscuit crumbs on her plate and remained silent for a moment. Harriet sipped at her tea.

After a moment, Maria sighed. "Harriet, *why* must you go? I know why I'm seeking work as a governess—I've no fortune, no dowry, and no marriage prospects to speak of. But why should *you*?"

Harriet forced a smile. "It is my mother's wish, and therefore it is my father's as well," she laughed at her own joke. "I cannot have a season in London and there are no marriage prospects for me here. I may as well, Maria. Besides, they have promised that if my position is less than ideal, they'll welcome me home with open arms after a year."

"Oh, Harriet. Why is it that all the excitement passes by me and lands on you?" She sighed. "*London*, though! How exciting. For two young ladies?"

"Yes, aged ten and twelve."

"Charming! I do hope you'll enjoy them."

"I am looking forward to it," Harriet said with a smile, shoving aside the sudden longing to remain close to Stephan and Burnham-on-Sea.

Chapter Two

Burnham-on-Sea, Somerset

"Harriet!" her father smiled as she entered the dining room for breakfast the next morning. He looked up from his newspaper expectantly and she walked over and kissed his cheek.

"Good morning, Father," she said, sitting at the place set next to his and buttering a scone. "Where has mother gone?"

"She's gone to visit Mrs. Chambers."

Harriet nodded and nibbled on her scone.

"What shall you be up to today?" he asked.

Harriet smiled. "I am not sure. I suppose it's still too early to begin packing a trunk."

Her father's face fell, and Harriet hurried to cheer him. "Is there anything you would *like* me to do today, Father?"

The past few weeks her father had organized a dinner or an evening visit from nearly every eligible bachelor for ten miles in any direction. There were precious few, and her father had seemed even less disposed to like any of them than Harriet had been.

Her father's face seemed even more heavily lined than it had been the morning before.

"Father, there aren't many . . ." she paused and sighed as she tried to gather her words. "There aren't many young ladies quite like *me* out there, are there?"

Her father peered at her over the rim of his spectacles as he set down his newspaper. "I'm afraid I don't understand your meaning, my love. You are unique, of course. I would not have you be the same as another." His voice had a question in it, as to her real meaning.

Harriet could not meet eyes with him, instead fiddling with a curling brown wisp of hair that had escaped the knot on the back of her neck. "Well, you are a farmer, and yet . . . are not quite like other farmers."

"Oh, *that* is what you mean." Her father nodded, clearing his throat lightly. "Yes, you are quite right to point that out." His expression grew very grave, and he suddenly appeared much older than his robust forty-five years. "I am sorry to have made things difficult for you with my chosen profession, my dear."

Harriet stumbled over her words in her hurry to explain herself. "I don't mean at *all* that you ought not to have become a farmer, father! You enjoy managing land so, and Uncle Robert inherited the estate when grandfather died so what else were you to do? It isn't as though you could purchase your own estate with the amount left you. I don't blame you in the least, papa!"

Her hurried words did nothing to appease her father's sudden guilt. "I suppose we *all* could have remained on the estate at Berkforth," her father was rueful. "Or at least in the cottage on the eastern part of it. Your uncle offered it, you know."

Harriet shook her head, her nose wrinkled. "And share a home with Abel and Jesse? Visiting my cousins once in a year is ample enough for me! Indeed, I do *not* blame you, Father—I ought not have mentioned it at all. You would have been miserable as an attorney or a politician. You aren't one for sermons, either. It's simply rotten luck that Uncle Robert was born first, is all."

Her father laughed. "And perhaps it is unfortunate that the estate was so small to begin with!" He reached over and took Harriet's hand in his, meeting her eyes. "Do not concern yourself overmuch with these affairs, little Harriet. You are more than lovely enough to find a suitable husband in spite of the difficult situation I have created for you." His eyes twinkled, but there was real worry behind his smile.

Harriet smiled, sympathy filling her warm brown eyes. "Papa, I am certain my future will find me soon enough and all will be well. Perhaps Mama is right."

Her father leaned back his chair, the concern returning to his face. "I still do not see why you need to leave so soon."

Harriet stood and walked over to embrace her father. "Think of it this way instead—the sooner I leave, the sooner I can also return."

Her father forced a little smile and patted Harriet's arm.

Harriet could not bear to see her father looking so miserable. Swallowing her own worries, she shook her head again. "Oh, stuff! I am sure everything will be all right! We are being far too grave for eight o'clock in the morning."

Her father gave a sincere chuckle and seemed to relax. "You never answered me, my dear. What do you intend to do today?"

Harriet gave a little sigh as she returned to her seat and her breakfast. "I ought to visit Mrs. Owley and see if her foot is feeling better. And I might work in the garden."

Her father nodded approvingly. "If you've an interest in raspberries, I have heard that the bushes are laden with the last of the season and cook would like to put up more jam this week."

Harriet smiled as she continued eating her breakfast. "I shall begin with the berries, then."

After finishing breakfast, Harriet put on her bonnet, apron, and half-boots, and set out for the garden with a lined basket on her arm. She sang as she filled her basket, enjoying the sunshine. After a few minutes, she removed her somewhat itchy bonnet and cast it aside. She finished one song, then another, and continued singing whatever came to her.

"It is such a lovely day and I am not at school," she warbled cheerfully, plopping another fat berry into the basket. The next berry went straight into her mouth, and her song continued at a hum.

She was about to burst into another refrain when she heard rustling behind her and turned around. It was only a rabbit speeding from one bush to another bit of foliage. She smiled to herself.

"Why Stephan," she said to it, "I didn't expect to see you here."

There was no one there, of course, but this wasn't the first time that she'd indulged herself by imagining he was.

An imaginary Stephan took her hand and gracefully kissed the back of it, looking up at her with the calm, contented expression he always wore that did funny things to her heart. Even as she pictured him in her mind, the image of her plain but wonderful friend Stephan grew younger, until he was little more than a boy.

The stage of her mind opened onto a memory she had relived countless times. She had just decided that she was going to run off to London and become a famous actress one day. It was a fleeting, girlish desire she might have forgotten about had it not been for Stephan's reaction to it. He had begged her with surprising vehemence not to leave home.

His words from that day echoed through her mind yet again. "If you stay here, Harriet . . . Stay here and don't go to London and I *promise* I sh-shall court you someday. Should you wish it."

She sighed and returned her attention to the raspberries, shaking her head. Stephan had only been fourteen years old. Surely things had changed too much for him to keep such a promise to a young lady of her station.

Her basket slowly filled with berries as old memories replayed in her mind.

"Hello, Miss Shore," a man's voice said by the gate.

Harriet looked up in surprise and nearly dropped her basket of berries.

"S-Stephan." Was she dreaming? Suddenly she was not sure.

"I am sorry not to have come sooner." He gave a slight bow, removing his hat to reveal a thatch of fine tawny hair. "I have not been at liberty to do so until now."

"Of course," she said quickly. "It has barely been two days. And you are certainly occupied with important matters of business . . . now you are come into your estate."

Her heart thudded. It wasn't a dream. She was talking to Stephan. *Stephan.* She'd daydreamed this moment so many times that finally living it was quite surreal.

"It is very good of you to come, sir," she finally managed. Then, realizing for the first time that she was wearing a dirty gardening smock, she hurriedly untied it and pulled it off over her head, mussing her simple coil in the process and leaving a halo of golden brown frizz over her head.

Stephan smiled at her. She had always liked his smile. It was the most genuine one she'd ever seen. His face was so honest and easy to read—he could not possibly be anything but happy when he smiled. His hair was a pale, dusty color and was thinning slightly on top of his head. And he had more than usually expressive blue eyes that frequently sparkled with amusement. He wasn't renowned for his looks—no one ever said he was—but he was by far the handsomest man of Harriet's acquaintance.

"It's . . . been a long time since we've really spoken," Stephan took a hesitant step toward her through the gate. Harriet stood still, her heart already racing. She could not think of anything to say. It had been nearly a year since the last time she'd seen Stephan in passing, let alone spent any time with him. After all, why should a squire's son move in the same circles as a farmer's daughter?

Stephan walked over to Harriet with a slight question in his eyes. He took her hand in his and bowed over it. She winced in embarrassment—her fingertips were brightly stained with berry juice. She came to herself and dropped a curtsy in response. Her heart was pounding so hard she thought it might bounce right out of her chest. One of the last social engagements they had both attended had not gone very well and she could not help but remember it.

It had been one of the rare occasions that Stephan was home from school for a holiday, and both Harriet and Stephan had attended one of the same local assemblies. The entire evening they had been inseparable, and had danced nearly every dance together, until he went to dance with Eleanor Collins at his mother's insistence. She was a gentleman's daughter whom everyone knew stood to gain at least four thousand pounds on her marriage. Once Stephan left Harriet's side, his mother had approached her.

"There, that is as it should be," she'd hissed. "You are a farmer's daughter, not a lady. You two are no longer children, and it is time he seeks his equal in rank and fortune!"

"Miss Shore?" Stephan's voice brought her back to the present. "What's the matter?"

"Nothing at all." Her gaze was still on her basket. She shook his mother's words from her mind. "How have you been, Mr. Grimsby?"

Her throat tightened and she looked back up at him. He was now of age—his birthday was May 17th. He'd only just returned home from Oxford, but was he courting Eleanor already? Was he courting someone else entirely?

Stephan hadn't said anything. He was looking at her with an unreadable expression. When he finally spoke, he seemed hesitant. "Am I imposing on you, Miss Shore?"

"Of course not!" she exclaimed. She was so flustered that she would not have been surprised if he had started to laugh. And perhaps a younger Stephan would have. But this Stephan only smiled, inclined his head, and asked if she would like to accompany him on a walk down the lane.

Harriet hastily smoothed her hair and skirt and complied, walking beside him in the direction of Stephan's estate.

"I heard from John Kemp that you are finished with your schooling," Stephan said.

"Indeed. At long last!"

"What are you going to do now, Harriet?" His smile was teasing, but there was a real question in his eyes. "Take London by storm? Become a famous actress?"

Harriet scoffed, but an embarrassed little laugh escaped. "Of course not! I put that silly dream away years ago, St—Mr. Grimsby."

Stephan grew serious for an instant. "It is *difficult*, is it not? To address one another properly? To follow these . . . *conventions*? We've known one another since we were children, climbing trees together! You were only ever Harriet to me then."

Harriet nodded, enjoying the shiver of pleasure she felt whenever he said her name. "It *is* difficult."

He did not pursue the subject, but instead asked her questions about her time in school. She in turn asked him about his challenges as the new owner of the estate, which he deftly avoided answering. After a few minutes of conversation, however, the initial awkwardness faded and they laughed as easily as they always had together.

"I'd wager that you always managed to keep the upper hand over your instructors."

"Are you referring to the time I corrected Monsieur Dubois's French?

Stephan laughed. "Indeed! You must tell me all about it! Or perhaps when you out-sang the music instructor."

"I did no such thing."

Stephan turned to meet her gaze and stopped walking a moment. "With a voice as beautiful as yours, I'm certain you did."

Harriet's cheeks flushed with pleasure. "Stephan, you always did like my singing better than anyone else did. And I am still terrible at the pianoforte."

"I would invite you to play and sing at any party," he insisted, "and I would never tire of hearing you."

Harriet smiled, but her face fell when she could not help but remember that these parties Stephan spoke of had never happened, and likely never would.

They walked in companionable silence for a few minutes, enjoying the first tinges of yellow on the edges of the oak leaves. They had nearly reached Stephan's house on their short walk—where had the time gone? Surely he'd be escorting her back home before long, but it felt too soon. When Stephan stopped walking again, Harriet turned to face him. He was staring off into the distance, biting his lip. Her hair was lit by the sun's warm glow behind her.

"What is it, Stephan?"

"Harriet, do you remember our last conversation in our tree? Seven years ago?" He glanced up at the mighty oak between their properties.

Harriet's heart skipped a beat and pounded faster to make up for it. "Yes," she breathed.

He took a step closer. "I told you I'd like to court you someday."

She swallowed. She could not believe he remembered! "I remember. I was only twelve."

He smiled. "And I was only fourteen."

She didn't speak. After a moment, he continued. "That was long ago. We have both changed and grown."

Harriet looked at the ground as her heart beat faster. Was he going to formally reject her? Suddenly she could not bear to listen, but knew she had no choice.

"But Harriet . . ."

She closed her eyes, bracing herself for the sting. It didn't come. Instead she felt Stephan's hand on her cheek. She opened her eyes to see him standing right in front of her, looking intently back at her with a question in his eyes.

"I still feel the same way," he whispered.

Her eyes felt wet, but she smiled. "B-but you—"

He leaned forward and stopped her mouth with a kiss.

She froze in surprise but thawed almost instantly, melting into his embrace, her mind blank, her whole world wrapped up in that kiss.

"Outrageous conduct!"

The sharp voice seemed to physically tear them apart. Harriet was disoriented but recognized Caroline Grimsby's voice and felt her blood run cold. She stumbled backward in her hurry to put distance between Stephan and herself.

"Mother," Stephan nodded, his voice tight.

Mrs. Grimsby's skinny, wilted cheeks were an ugly shade of fuchsia as she hissed at the pair of them. "How *dare* you!"

Stephan grew louder. "*Mother*!"

"What are you thinking by dallying with this upstart fortune-hunting *hussy*?"

Harriet recoiled at these words, glancing at Stephan for his reaction. She had never seen him so angry before. "That is *enough*. You will *not* speak about Miss Shore that way, Mother." His voice remained calm but was laced with ice. His hands were clenched into fists and his face flushed red from the edges inward.

Harriet wanted the earth to rise up and swallow her. Blood was pounding in her ears and she felt like her stomach was trying to climb up her throat. Before Caroline could say another word, Harriet picked up her skirts and ran as quickly as she could toward her home.

"Harriet, wait!" Stephan called.

She did not stop. She was less than a mile from her house when she stumbled on the road, sprawling on the ground. She bit back a yelp of pain and climbed to her feet to begin running again, never looking back, blood pounding in her ears and autumn air stinging her lungs.

Chapter Three

Curzon Street, London

Virginia's return to London had been as awful as she had worried it would be. Compared to the happiness of where she had been . . . she blinked as tears rushed to her eyes and nausea returned to the pit of her stomach. The nausea was never-ending. No matter what food Mandie brought to her or what distraction she plied herself with, she felt ill. And being hidden away in the guest apartments at the back of the house made her feel unwelcome even in her own childhood home.

And she *was* unwelcome.

"Oh, I wish I were *anywhere* else," she muttered, as a wave of nausea forced her to drop her paintbrush. Her seascape would have to remain unfinished for now.

She closed her eyes and took deep breaths, willing her stomach to settle, but she reached for her chamber pot, just in case. She had at least managed to get dressed today, although for what reason she wasn't sure. She wasn't allowed out of her apartments at all, let alone for a walk outdoors in the sweet autumn breeze—or as sweet as a breeze in the densely populated London streets *could* be.

She wished she were back in Brighton, where the smell of the sea and the sound of the waves would wash over her with every salty breeze. With Ralph. But he isn't there, she reminded herself. He had left even before Mandie had come to take her back home.

It seemed as though she had been nauseated for an age. When would it pass? Her mother had said that it always passed after a few months. Well, it had been at least two. She had to thank the nausea, though. The midwife said it meant her baby was healthy.

She patted her soft midsection. Her stays had begun to make her life miserable weeks before, and they were already impossible to wear. She felt swollen and plump, although she was far from displaying the same large, round belly she remembered her Aunt Victoria having while in confinement.

The nausea subsided long enough for her discomfort to shift from her stomach to her unceasing boredom. She stood up and walked over to the window, sitting in the window seat. The guest room only displayed the back of the house—alleyways for rubbish collecting and servants' entrances. Virginia was certain her mother had engineered it that way. The only ones aware she was even in the house were her mother and her trusted lady's maid, Mandie. She wasn't even sure that her father knew. She smiled as she thought of her cheeky maid. Mandie could always be relied upon to keep her from feeling *too* sorry for herself.

But Mandie had been given other duties now that the rest of the household was largely unaware of Virginia's return, and she couldn't spend too much time keeping Virginia company lest she arouse suspicion. At least she kept Virginia well stocked with fresh novels and painting supplies.

Virginia's mother, the Duchess of Dorset, couldn't be relied on to be good company. Virginia's nausea worsened dramatically whenever her mother was near. Her mother never visited without either offering a harsh lecture or bursting into angry tears and leaving her room in a huff.

And Virginia still couldn't think of Ralph without crying. He had told her to return to her childhood home, knowing that it was a prison to her. And then he'd . . . left. He had told her he loved her and would always be with her . . . and then he had gone. The worst part was that she knew that he had to. She understood. But that didn't ease the pain of having a child set to arrive in half a year, no husband in sight, and little hope for the future.

"He has to return," she whispered, her eyes greedily taking in the splash of sunlight coming through the curtain, "he *has* to."

She sat at the window for hours like a ghost, nearly motionless. Watching the servants scurry around the back entrance from behind a sheer curtain. Laughing, working, beating carpets. Enjoying their freedom, oblivious to the supposedly privileged young woman jealously watching them from above. She would give almost anything to trade places with them.

Burnham-on-Sea, Somerset

The word *hussy* echoed in Harriet's mind until she thought she'd go mad. What had she been thinking? Bare-headed and bare-handed, without a chaperone . . . she shook her head. If the gossip hadn't made its way around yet, it was only a matter of time.

That *kiss*. What had he been thinking? She had been agonizing over it since the moment it had happened. What did he think of her? It would be better for both of them if he could forget her. She hadn't managed to tell either of her parents about the kiss. Her mother might disown her, or worse—arrive at the same conclusions as Mrs. Grimsby. Instead of confessing to them, she'd passed off her excitement and unease as nerves for her upcoming position in London.

His lips had felt so soft against hers, softer than she'd ever imagined. He was tall and thin and angular, so the fact that any part of him could be as impossibly soft as his lips had felt against hers had taken her by surprise.

Tempted though she was to see him again, she knew she would have no peace in Burnham unless Stephan married a young lady of fortune as his mother wished him to. And yet, if he could not court her, she did not think she could bear to stand by and see him court another.

It was all for the best she had a position waiting for her in London. She began packing her trunk immediately.

When Mrs. Shore had first announced she thought Harriet ought to try her hand as a governess before seeking a husband, Harriet was surprised, but not necessarily disappointed. She liked children and Her mother had been a governess herself in her youth and things had turned out well for her. Her father was another matter. He had frowned and it had taken months of whispered conversations behind closed doors before he finally agreed that it was a good plan. Harriet had overheard them talking of it once.

"She *is* a good girl, my love, but she has a bit too much . . . oh, you know. A bit too much of the *theatre* in her, no thanks to you! She will never be happy settling down quietly until she's had a little taste of adventure and independence."

Harriet had smiled when her mother had said that. When the three of them had pored over the papers and finally come across the position with the Donahue family in London, it had almost seemed too good to be true.

"London! How wonderful! And never fear, Mother—I shall be a perfectly respectable governess." She had smiled innocently. "Who occasionally attends the theater."

Harriet grinned to herself at this happy thought as she selected one or two of her prized childhood possessions and placed them into her trunk.

Her memories took her back to the first time she'd ever seen a play. Her father had heard there were players passing through town and going from village to village. Their village had no theater, but the troupe had met enough friendly people at the tavern that they had decided to rent the village hall to perform an abridged version of one of Shakespeare's comedies.

She remembered relatively little of it—only how much she had adored it. Her father told her later that she had remained spellbound the entire duration of the performance, her eyes wide. She had frequently dissolved into gales of laughter, even when the jokes were beyond her understanding. Whenever she had heard people laughing around her, she'd laughed too.

"You loved it, pet," her father said.

"The theater is no place to bring a child," her mother had scolded the both of them.

But Harriet's father loved to see her happy and had never ceased to take Harriet anywhere they could find a little bit of the theater in Burnham-on-Sea. He had borrowed or purchased copies of Shakespearean tragedies for her to read, and she had grown up reciting out of Macbeth and pretending to be Hamlet as Stephan filled in the other roles alongside her.

She had smuggled a play or two into the schoolroom, as well, and some of her happiest memories were of escaping between the pages to find a role to bring to life for her fellow classmates. She had never had a sister or brother, but between Stephan and her friends from school, she had been perfectly contented and never alone.

Now, though . . . where *did* she belong?

Too genteel to talk and laugh with servants or laborers. Excluded from all but the most generous invitations from the local gentry. Leaving the schoolroom a few months ago had been miserable. Being paraded about by her father for the few eligible bachelors the area boasted for a young lady of her station had been both humiliating and disappointing. Perhaps she *would* find something wonderful in London. Perhaps the work of teaching and training would make her happy. Perhaps she would sneak away and attend an audition and become a famous actress! Her ending had yet to be written, and Mrs. Grimsby had given her an even more urgent wish to exit stage left from Burnham-on-Sea and find her way to a bigger story on a larger stage.

Harriet finished her packing for the time being and skipped down the stairs. "Mama?"

"In here, darling."

Harriet walked into the hall to see her mother sitting in a dining chair next to the credenza, polishing silver and staring off into the distance.

"Mama? What are you doing?"

Her mother glanced up at her. "Oh, I thought it could use a bit of touching up. We're lucky to have it, you know. My grandmother's. This set was missing a serving spoon and that is why my older sister did not take it—my younger brother took the spoon out into the garden to dig with it and lost it. Mother was so very angry . . ." She chuckled to herself and finished polishing the spoon with a sigh.

"I'm always amused by the pleasure you seem to find in menial household chores, Mama."

"Perhaps you'll understand when you're older."

Harriet took on a lofty, pretentious tone. "Perhaps. Or perhaps I'll be a fine lady that never needs to work."

Mrs. Shore let out a scoff and scrubbed at the silver with even more determination. "This sort of work has never been forced on me, my love. I'll take my work-worn hands over a fussy dowager's lily-white ones any day. Nothing so pleasant as work, I say."

Harriet smiled as she watched her mother work. Mrs. Shore had always prized common sense above every other virtue. Harriet could see, looking at her, that she'd got her stubborn little chin and small nose from her, but her laughing amber eyes and chestnut hair she'd got from her father.

"Are you going to miss me at all, Mama?" she asked quietly, suddenly needing to know.

Mrs. Shore didn't say anything.

Harriet took a deep breath. "Mother, I promise I will not do anything to displease you while in London. And I will write often."

Dorothea set down the spoon she was polishing and turned to wipe her hands on a cloth. After a moment she raised her gaze to meet Harriet's. Her eyes were filled with tears, but the corner of her mouth halfheartedly lifted into a smile. "Of course I shall miss you, you silly girl. More than anything."

Harriet closed the distance between them with a bound and drew her mother into a tight embrace.

The Road to London

One week later, Harriet was on the stagecoach to London, clutching a valise with a few books she had not managed to open and read. She squeezed the letter with the job offering in her gloved hand before securing it in her pocket. She had a headache as the coachman drove on, and she suspected she was nervous. Her mind was racing from thought to thought without pause, leaving her exhausted and more than a little apprehensive. Against her will, the scene from more than a week earlier replayed itself again and again on the stage of her mind.

His lips on hers, his gentle hand on the back of her neck, whispering her name . . . she shook her head. It did no good to dwell on it. When her memory replayed Mrs. Grimsby's rude entrance to the scene, a wave of fear and anger swept over her.

"I can't blame her," Harriet thought to herself. She forced herself to think as charitably as she could of Stephan's mother. "If I were in her position and Stephan were my son, I would feel every bit as protective of him—he is so impossibly kind. So gentle."

"So . . . impulsive and dashing," she murmured aloud, her fingers brushing her lips. Her fellow travelers glanced at her and resumed studying the passing scenery. She looked up at the ceiling of the coach and sighed. Her frenetic mind went back and forth after each replay of the scene. On the one hand, an impossible vision of a life married to her childhood best friend, the new squire of Burnham-on-Sea. And on the other, a life in which she was alone and disgraced, ostracized from the entire community and forbidden from ever seeing Stephan again.

She did not know what would have happened had she stayed, but she, like her mother, had to remain occupied to keep from feeling anxious about things. She chose a third option: the unknown, far away from Burnham-on-Sea. The older she got, the more like her mother she became. She smiled to herself. Life as a governess would be hard work, and she was eager to begin. Besides, if time permitted, she may occasionally be allowed to attend the theater, and that was solace enough.

And Stephan. Her thoughts jumped back to her best friend and again her heart wrenched inside of her chest. He was the primary reason she had decided to abandon her childish dream of becoming an actress. Her mother had always been opposed to the unseemly plan, of course, but her mother's disapproval hadn't been enough to deter her.

"Actresses are *not* respectable young ladies!" her mother had insisted.

"Why should I care if unkind people think I am not respectable?" Harriet had shot back, "I shall respect *myself*. I know in my heart what I am and that is enough for me—and it ought to be enough for you too, mother!"

Harriet's stomach twisted at the memory of her words. She may not have cared what other people thought of her virtue as a young girl, but Caroline Grimsby's voice still echoed through her head, calling her a fortune-hunting *hussy*. She knew she was no fortune hunter—here she was, running a hundred miles away so that Stephan could be free to marry a young lady of fortune . . . but *was* she loose? Was that what people thought of her? Was that what *Stephan* thought of her? Her stomach twisted at the thought. Mrs. Grimsby's words rattled around in her mind, and she felt her breathing begin to hasten and grow more shallow. Stephan was the son of the squire and she was a farmer's daughter.

She would have loved to marry Stephan, but was disgusted at the thought that people could think her a fortune-hunter. She loved him for himself alone. Ever since the summer he'd returned from Eton he had been different. Instead of racing her and always winning, he had slowed just before the finish line so they could win together. Instead of always wanting to pretend to be pirates and privateers, he was willing to walk with her and talk with her about anything she liked, even if other boys laughed at him. She remembered thinking that Stephan was beginning to look quite grown-up and handsome even then. He was kind, and she found herself wishing they could be together again the moment they parted, every single day.

She had never stopped feeling that way. When Stephan had asked her to abandon her dream of acting to instead grow to be an ordinary, respectable young lady, her commitment to decorum had suddenly become every bit as strong as her mother's.

"But apparently after all my efforts, I'm *still* not respectable," she thought to herself, and inwardly sighed. "What's the use in continuing to try?"

When Stephan had kissed her, a beautiful, fleeting moment of hope had risen in her chest. Hope that she could have a future with her best friend. That they could overcome all of the obstacles standing between them. But Mrs. Grimsby's arrival had crushed those hopes before they could gain any strength. She felt foolish. At the end of the day, he was a squire—a powerful landowner. And she was a farmer's daughter and a nobody. He might like her, or even love her. But even if he did, how could it possibly be enough to overcome the difference in their stations? She could stay in Somerset and marry a farmer, a steward, a tradesman or even a widowed gentleman. But the thought of marrying anyone but Stephan made her miserable. And any imaginary path she and Stephan could follow to be together would be such a long, uphill climb that she felt tired at the mere thought of it.

She finally surrendered to the drowsiness that had threatened to overtake her for half the drive. If sleep were willing to give her a temporary respite from her whirling thoughts, she would gratefully accept its offer.

Chapter Four

Burnham-on-Sea, Somerset

It was no use. The markings on the ledger had long been disheartening, but now they were blurring into meaningless patterns and shapes before his eyes. Stephan set down his pen.

He leaned back in his chair, away from his desk. *Two weeks.* It had been more than a fortnight since he had last seen Harriet, and he still could not stop thinking of her. And what she must be thinking of him! Each time he thought of Harriet he also thought back to the kiss he'd bestowed, uninvited, on her, and to the tongue-lashing his mother had given the pair of them.

"Poor girl," he groaned into his hands. "Whyever *would* she choose me? What possessed me to kiss her like that? I was a fool—am a fool. She must *hate* me now."

Stephan heard his mother's shrill voice coming up the hallway and clenched his fist on the ledger he'd just been attending to. He narrowly avoided smudging the ink, and looked up to the doorway in time for his mother to darken it.

"Stephan, my love, I'm afraid I'll need a bit more than the paltry amount you gave me at the start of the quarter. The bill from the milliner's has arrived and I cannot pay it."

Stephan forced himself to respond calmly. "Mother, I do hate to keep saying this. You have *already* exceeded your allowance for this quarter. You must *stop* spending money that simply isn't there!"

Mrs. Grimsby seemed taken aback. "I beg your pardon? Allowance? How dare you speak to me as though I were a child? I am your *mother*, Stephan."

He stood with an exasperated noise, and gestured at the estate ledgers and account books littering his heavy oak desk. "Do you know what these are, Mother? Have you ever looked at them?"

She glanced at them fleetingly. "The estate ledgers, of course."

He took a deep breath and tried to remain patient. "You have garnered more debt for the estate than I think you realize, Mother."

Her eyebrows rose and her face reddened, but she did not respond.

Stephan took a step toward her. "Where is the bill?"

"For the milliner's?"

Stephan nodded, and his mother gave him a withering look before handing him the bill.

He unfolded the letter, skimmed it quickly, and looked up at his mother. "Ostrich feathers in Burnham-on-Sea? Why on earth would you need a dozen new bonnets in the space of a month?"

"I was so tired of my mourning clothes, Stephan. I'd only just come out of light mourning and wished for some *color*!"

Stephan pinched the bridge of his nose and took another calming breath before looking back at her. "Mother, the estate is already in debt and I am doing my all to bring us out of it. If you wish for me to succeed, *please* do your part. If you do not . . . I'm afraid I shall be forced to contact all of the businesses that you solicit and forbid them from accepting your credit!"

She looked taken aback, and her nose and mouth wrinkled as though she'd just swallowed a lemon. "I . . . what would you have me *do*, Stephan? Carry a purse jingling with coins wherever I go?"

"If you wish you make any purchases, Mother, then *yes*."

Mrs. Grimsby paused, inhaling through flared nostrils, before appearing to relax slightly. "If I am to do my part, Stephan, you must do *yours*. I fully expect you to sever any ties with that inappropriate farmer's daughter I saw you with and begin courting young ladies of *means*."

Stephan abruptly stood and looked down at his mother with cold eyes. "How dare you? You make baseless accusations of Miss Shore being a fortune hunter while urging me to become one myself."

His mother's mouth puckered even more than before. Stephan shook his head with a light laugh and tutted disapprovingly before reaching down to kiss his mother's hand. "My dear Mother, I am astounded by your hypocrisy."

He swept out of the room without another word. He was down the stairs and across the hall when his mother called after him, but he pretended not to hear her, and slammed the front door shut behind him. He was going to visit Harriet. Hang what his senseless mother thought. Harriet may not choose to forgive him, but he would not allow his mother or his own pestering self-doubt to keep him from seeing her any longer.

Palace Court, London

"It is clear that my daughters like you."

Harriet smiled. She had not expected the terror of a formal interview upon her arrival at the Donahue's elegant home, but that is more or less what had greeted her. "I am happy for it, madam. I like them, too."

Mrs. Donahue looked back down at the piece of paper she kept glancing at. "But I found that tired Mozart piece you performed a moment ago to be rather lacking."

Harriet bit her lip to remain silent. Harriet may have had a quick temper, but she also controlled it well. She was a respectful, and respectable, young woman. She reminded herself of this continually, as often as Stephan's mother's insults repeated themselves in her mind. She bobbed a small curtsy.

The woman sighed and stood. She could not afford a much more expensive governess for her daughters, that much Harriet knew. Mrs. Margaret Donahue's father had been a wealthy gentleman, but she had married a second son, an attorney. In spite of this, she still clearly enjoyed a comfortable place in fashionable society, and her marriage seemed a happy one.

"Well, for a governess to be a true artist at the pianoforte is unusual. I suppose I shall have to bring in a maestro to tutor them once they have surpassed your teaching abilities. Yes, you shall stay on, Miss Shore."

Harriet dropped another curtsy and continued to hold her tongue as Mrs. Donahue proceeded to explain the rules of the house.

"You shall have Thursday afternoons off and every third Saturday. You may have a few days to visit your family once per year, at the end of the social season. Do you find this reasonable?"

"Quite, madam." She decided that informing her employer that she only intended to stay for one year was unwise.

"Please instruct them in history, French, penmanship, drawing, dancing, and the pianoforte. I would like regular evidence of their continued progress from you however you should like to supply it."

"If you please?" Harriet waited for approval to continue. When Mrs. Donahue nodded, Harriet spoke. "May I teach them how to sing?"

Mrs. Donahue looked skeptical. "Do you sing better than you play?"

Harriet bit back a retort. "I do, ma'am."

The older woman smiled briefly, quirked an eyebrow, and nodded. "Very well. Sing a song for me, and I will decide. But only teach if the girls show some natural aptitude for it. There is nothing more painful than being forced to listen to someone or other's tone-deaf daughter singing for half an hour at a party and to clap politely afterward. I refuse to subject others to such torment."

Harriet managed to stifle her snort of laughter at this speech, but it was difficult. She took her place behind the piano to accompany herself as she sang, but she was interrupted before she could begin her performance.

"If you please, madam," the housekeeper interrupted, "you have a visitor."

"Who is it, Mrs. George?"

"Her Grace, The Duchess of Dorset."

Mrs. Donahue smiled easily. "Oh, dear Ruth! Do tell her to come in, George."

A tall, elegant woman with an elaborate hairstyle impatiently crossed the threshold before Mrs. George could lead her in. She had a generous but stately figure, wore a dark green riding costume, and carried the largest fur muff that Harriet had ever seen. She narrowed the distance to Mrs. Donahue in an instant, her hands outstretched and her cheeks flushed from more than exertion.

"Margaret! Oh, my dear cousin Margaret. I hardly know where to begin."

Mrs. Donahue cleared her throat and nodded at the housekeeper. "That will be all, George."

Mrs. George nodded and disappeared through the doorway.

"Margaret, all has fallen to ruin. I am in such disgrace. You are the *only* one I can speak to."

"There now, my friend. I am certain all will be well." Mrs. Donahue's eyes twinkled, but there was true concern for her friend behind them.

Harriet suddenly felt embarrassed. She knew she shouldn't begin playing and singing for Mrs. Donahue if she was entertaining a guest, but she also had not been dismissed. She felt she was intruding and had been awkwardly forgotten.

"You are the only friend I can trust—you know to hold your tongue. Far more than I can say for Mrs. Fletcher. Why, did you know that after I told her—"

Harriet couldn't take it anymore. She lightly cleared her throat, and the duchess immediately looked up in her direction with a frown.

Mrs. Donahue herself had clearly forgotten Harriet's presence. "Oh, my—terribly sorry. Excuse me. Ruth—sorry. Your *Grace*, this is Miss Harriet Shore—my daughters' new governess. Harriet, you may be excused."

Harriet abruptly stood from the pianoforte's bench in relief and attempted a quick, graceful curtsy.

The duchess was staring at her as she did so. There were lines in her face and her hair had the beginnings of silver streaks starting from her temples and working toward her elegant coiffure. She had clearly once been strikingly handsome, but looked as though she had spent too many years disapproving of too many things. Harriet instinctively felt that it would be unwise to cross her.

Harriet stood from her curtsy and turned to leave the room.

"No, no. Wait." The duchess flapped a careless hand to stop Harriet. She hadn't stopped staring at her, and Harriet was starting to grow extremely uncomfortable. She shifted where she stood and swallowed.

"Margaret, I am getting an idea. You said this is your new governess?"

"Yes," Mrs. Donahue said slowly. "Why do you ask?"

"She is not from town?"

"No. She is just arrived from Somerset this morning."

"In town only a day? Who can she have seen?"

Mrs. Donahue's face betrayed all of the confusion she felt. "I'm not sure what you mean by all this . . ."

"Can she be trusted?"

"Ruth!" Mrs. Donahue burst out, "What *are* you talking about? I cannot follow your meaning at all!"

"*Look* at her, Margaret." The duchess spoke in a hushed tone. "Do you not see the resemblance?"

"Resemblance? To whom?"

"To *Virginia*."

Chapter Five

Palace Court, London

Mrs. Donahue looked back at Harriet then, and her eyes widened. "Oh, yes! Why yes, I suppose there is a certain something they both share, now you mention it. A similar nose, and eyes almost the same shade and shape. Quite remarkable—they could be twins! But what does that have to do with—"

"Margaret, I told you a few months ago that Virginia, er . . . had not been seen of late, and we were terribly worried for her. Well, that wasn't quite the truth."

"What do you mean?" Mrs. Donahue asked. "Is she all right?"

"Virginia is *ruined*."

Mrs. Donahue's face turned white and she gasped. "*No.* You cannot be serious! You must be joking, except I know that you would never joke about such a matter, and . . . oh, how terrible. Oh, my dear friend. I am so terribly, terribly sorry."

"She has been found, and she is with us again, although most *shamefully* unrepentant."

Mrs. Donahue said nothing. It was clear that she felt deeply for her cousin in this difficult time and that she clearly understood the implications of her daughter's little adventure.

"Is she . . ."

"Married?" The duchess shook her head. "No, thank heaven. I never could have taken her back had she disgraced her name by marrying a common *sailor*. It would be better to have her dead! As it is, I only hope we can somehow pretend the *whole* affair never happened."

Harriet grimaced. Her own mother may have been a strict moral teacher, but she would never speak with the same unforgiving vehemence this woman did. Mrs. Donahue bit her lip, and Harriet felt so uncomfortable it was all she could do to refrain from fleeing the room.

"Well, can you simply reintroduce her into society and pretend nothing happened?" Mrs. Donahue suggested. "That would solve everything, I'm sure of it. Was she much missed?"

"I'm afraid that is impossible. Her absence did not arouse much suspicion—I told all our acquaintance that she was staying on with a cousin of mine near Brighton for those months she was missing. However . . . now I must find a new solution."

Mrs. Donahue put a hand up to her mouth. "Oh, no. She isn't with *child*?"

The duchess glanced out the window, her mouth a hard line. "I'm afraid she is."

"Oh, dear." Mrs. Donahue wrung her hands together and started pacing back and forth.

The duchess inhaled sharply through her nose. "Calm yourself, Margaret!" she barked. "I am upset enough for both of us, and there is no need for *you* to be quite so bothered."

"It's simply . . . oh, dear. What are you going to do?"

The duchess waved a careless hand. "What else is there to do? I'll find someone to take the child away once it is born."

"But surely Virginia will object?"

"Virginia doesn't need a child," the duchess snapped. "She needs a second chance to live her life correctly."

Harriet was filled with horror. Toss away a baby like refuse? This was a different world from Burnham-on-Sea, that was certain.

"But what does the Duke say about all this?"

The duchess sniffed. "He knows none of this. He was also told that Virginia was staying with my cousin."

"Don't you think you ought to tell him and have his assistance in the matter?" Mrs. Donahue wheedled.

The duchess stood and began to pace. "Assistance? He would never offer *assistance*! He would likely say that all hope is already lost, and would have her sacrifice all her future prospects and disappear from public life." The duchess shook her head. "No, he would be no help at all."

Harriet glanced longingly toward the door. She shouldn't be hearing this private conversation, surely. She felt she had suddenly become invisible. Was this what it meant to be a governess? Harriet wasn't certain she'd ever accustom herself to it. When Harriet was considering slinking silently from the room before she could hear any more embarrassing family confessions, the duchess looked directly at her.

"Now, Margaret, I've had the strangest fancy."

Harriet raised an eyebrow. The duchess was looking directly at Harriet, though clearly still speaking to Mrs. Donahue. "I . . . beg your pardon?" Harriet asked.

The duchess did not look away from her. "I was not talking to you." She turned to Mrs. Donahue again. "My dear, she is quite Virginia's double. I am shocked by the resemblance, in fact."

Mrs. Donahue looked doubtfully back at Harriet and raised her eyebrows. "I *do* see the resemblance, but—"

"What if . . . oh, my dear. I do not know what I intended to do when I called this morning beyond confess to you the whole of the horrid affair and bask in your consolation. But now, I have the most awful and *wonderful* idea."

"What are you thinking of?"

"Have this, er . . . what was your name again, child?"

"Harriet," she breathed, feeling the awkwardness so strongly that she thought she might burst.

"Have *Harriet* take Virginia's place in society. In Virginia's gowns, and with Virginia's mannerisms, no one could possibly know the difference!"

"Are you mad?" Mrs. Donahue asked, but she laughed in astonishment. "I cannot imagine that would do at all. Harriet is a *governess*, not the heiress to a duchy."

"Harriet would not be an heiress. *Virginia* remains the heiress. Harriet would be her . . . double. Her stand-in. Her understudy!"

At the word understudy, Harriet suddenly stood up straighter. Any reference to the world of theater, however small, was guaranteed to capture her attention. The Duchess of Dorset wanted Harriet to pretend to be her daughter? An heiress? It would be a difficult role, to be sure, but Harriet found herself tingling with excitement at the prospect of such a daring challenge. Auditioning for an ordinary play in an ordinary theater seemed positively dull by comparison.

Mrs. Donahue looked over at Harriet with extreme hesitation. "Aside from the quite obvious fact that Harriet may not *agree* to participate in such a ludicrous scheme, she is only a governess—what would she know of high society?"

Harriet felt her cheeks turning pink, but did not slink backward.

"That is absolutely perfect, Margaret—she is nobody at all, but speaks and acts as a young lady of quality. You, there. Harriet, was it?"

Harriet was going to do this right. Thinking quickly, she took a step forward and performed the most elegant, formal curtsy she had ever learned. She held her head high, as she imagined the daughter of a duchess ought to. "Yes, Your Grace."

Mrs. Donahue's jaw dropped in a most unladylike way at Harriet's instant transformation from mousy governess to fine lady and a broad smile began spreading itself across the duchess's face.

"I really think she could do it," the duchess whispered.

"If I may be so bold," Harriet was still standing tall and looking both of them in the eye as a lady of equal rank would, "Your Grace, I would be happy to assist you in the manner you suggest." Her heart pounded as she awaited a response.

Mrs. Donahue closed her mouth again, but looked confused and displeased.

The duchess looked far from displeased, but her grin did stiffen slightly and her brow wrinkled warily. "Er . . . yes, my dear. I am happy to hear it. May I ask, however, why you are interested in being party to a scheme that involves considerable risk to yourself? I confess I had thought you would require more convincing."

Harriet's mind raced from reason to reason—because it was a great adventure, because it would allow her to be an actress in the most interesting of ways, because she would not have to spend all her time teaching the pianoforte to young ladies, and because she would likely be able to attend the theater and have an excellent view! She thought for a moment how best to express a reason the duchess would believe, and finally said, "Since you have confessed something very private before me, madam, I will share with you, as well. The idea of being an actress has always been appealing to me."

Mrs. Donahue looked appalled, and Harriet quickly explained herself. "Naturally, I realized while still very young that it was not a respectable position for a young lady and never pursued the matter. However, for obvious reasons, this venture does pique my interest."

The duchess seemed pleased with the response. "Indeed. I can see already you have a natural gift."

Mrs. Donahue finally intervened, "I still cannot think this is a good idea. There is far too much at risk!"

The duchess frowned at Harriet. "She is right. How can we trust you with a secret like this?"

Harriet bit her lip. Another thought crossed her mind—one that was never far away. Stephan. He had to marry well—a woman of high birth or fortune, and preferably both. She may not be able to do anything about her birth . . . but perhaps she *could* change her fortune.

"If I may speak frankly?" she looked up at Mrs. Donahue, as if for permission, before continuing. "I am honored by the position Mrs. Donahue offers, but if I had a more sizeable dowry, I think I would prefer to marry well instead." She dropped her gaze to her feet. Her heart was pounding in her ears.

"And *there* it is." The duchess sounded like a cat who'd found a puddle of cream. "Now I see. Well, Harriet. What do you say to making a little arrangement with me? If you take Virginia's place in society convincingly until she has her child and is able to return to her usual engagements herself, I will see you receive a dowry of . . . shall we say five thousand pounds?"

Harriet's eyes bulged. That was a larger dowry than any other young lady in Burnham-on-Sea! "I—I—"

The duchess pulled a calling card from her reticule and handed it to Harriet. "Harriet, I *do* hope you will call on me later this week so that we may discuss the matter further. For now, I ought to go."

Harriet took the card, still speechless. She managed a somewhat clumsy curtsy and watched as the duchess swept out of the room. Neither Mrs. Donahue nor Harriet spoke for a few moments. It was difficult to say which was more flabbergasted. Finally, Harriet cleared her throat.

"Er, would you still like me to sing for you, madam?"

Mrs. Donahue turned to her, her expression still stunned. After blinking a couple of times, she nodded and sat heavily on the sofa with her hand over her face.

Chapter Six

Burnham-on-Sea, Somerset

Stephan was surprised to see Harriet's father open the front door himself. He stopped short and immediately pulled his hat from his head as he bowed.

"Mr. Shore! Sir, I . . . must confess you took me by surprise."

Still a robust man of forty-five and a tolerable shot, Harriet's father was a well-respected man, not the least by Stephan himself. The effect he had on the young Mr. Grimsby was astonishing. Somehow, Harriet's humble farmer of a father managed to overturn Stephan's composure more than anyone else did.

The older man smiled. "I can see the road from my library and saw you arriving. I took the liberty of answering my own front door. Do come in, Mr. Grimsby."

Stephan nodded politely and followed the other man into the library. It housed hundreds of volumes, in no particular order, and a large, heavy desk covered with ledgers, papers, notes, and open books. The only unusual thing about the room was that the desk faced the window instead of the door. Stephan took a seat at the chair Mr. Shore gestured to—the finer one, reserved for the owner of the desk. He hoped he did not appear as uneasy as he felt.

"I . . . had meant to ask if Miss Shore might be in?" he asked as he sat.

Mr. Shore smiled as he took a seat in a chair opposite Stephan. Although Stephan was sitting in the finer seat, he found himself feeling small and stupidly overdressed compared to the comfortably informal Mr. Shore.

"I'm afraid she is not here," the older man said.

Stephan realized he had been holding his breath, and forced himself to inhale. "Oh? Perhaps I ought to return . . . at another time. I . . ." Stephan could not remember feeling more awkward. "I am sorry to impose on you, sir."

Mr. Shore surprised Stephan by chuckling lightly. "Nonsense. I was thinking of calling on you myself, and your visit has spared me the trouble. And you need not call me 'sir,' you know. You rank far higher than do I."

Stephan could only incline his head in a slight bow. "You must know, Mr. Shore, that I respect and think very highly of you."

Harriet's father smiled indulgently. "I am honored. And I will tell you now, to save future questions, that Miss Harriet is not here at the moment, nor will she be for quite some time."

"Where has she gone?"

Her father's face grew sad and appeared to age several years in the space of one second. "She has gone to London," he finally answered. "To be a governess."

Stephan worried that his expression did nothing to mask the horror he felt, but he could not force himself to change it. "A governess?" he whispered.

Mr. Shore nodded, the lines in his face deepening. He reached over to the desk and plucked a pair of spectacles from it, placing them on the end of his nose. "I'm afraid so. She would not tell us her reasons for doing so, but her determination began about a fortnight ago. After . . . well, after your last visit with her, Stephan."

The suspicions on his face were clear, and Stephan shifted in his seat. "I did not know that . . . Yes, I visited a couple of weeks ago. And Miss Shore and I went on a short walk together."

Mr. Shore did not speak. He waited for Stephan to continue.

"And when we came near my house . . . we were seen by my mother."

"Ah," Mr. Shore gave an understanding nod. "Say no more. I believe I understand now."

Stephan could feel his cheeks flushing and he sank a little lower in his seat. He didn't know of another person alive who could make him blush, but Mr. Shore did not have any difficulty doing so.

"Mr. Grimsby, as we talk of my daughter, and before we arrive at the bit of business I would like to discuss with you, I trust that you aren't unaware of how highly my daughter thinks of you?"

Stephan could not speak. She thought highly of him? After a moment, he only managed an, "oh?"

Mr. Shore nodded. "And it's as clear as day that *you* are besotted with *her*." Stephan made an odd choking sound, but Mr. Shore pretended not to notice. "What I cannot understand is why she should refuse to accept a visit from *you* before she left. One would think she would want to bid you farewell."

"I am not certain either." Stephan was dismayed to hear his own voice crack.

Mr. Shore nodded sadly, staring out the window in thought. "Well, you and I must find a way to convince her to return home, Mr. Grimsby. She is my only child, you know."

Stephan could only nod. He wasn't certain what Mr. Shore was going to suggest, but if it would bring Harriet back, he was ready to agree to just about anything.

Mr. Shore snapped back to the present, offering Stephan a sincere smile. "Now then, Mr. Grimsby. I have heard all the rumors about your estate's being in trouble, and I am indeed sorry for it. On that note, however, I had wondered if I might interest you in a proposition."

Stephan's thoughts whirled, but he nodded. "What sort of proposition?"

Palace Court, London

"Miss Shore! Miss Shore!" Susan held up a little pencil sketch. "Look at what I have drawn! Is it not quite the prettiest little thing?"

Harriet smiled. The two girls were ten and twelve, and were famously well-behaved with warm manners. Mrs. Donahue had been accused, by other ladies of fashion, of being a slave to her children's education. She was the exception—Harriet knew it was more common for wealthy women to leave the education of their children entirely to others, expecting for their children to magically grow into interesting people to befriend and entertain them later on. It had never seemed a reasonable expectation to Harriet, but it remained common practice.

The more Harriet learned about Mrs. Donahue, the more she admired the woman. Mrs. Donahue was fair, practical, and economical. She hadn't had a governess for her girls when they were very young—only a nursemaid—because it did not yet seem necessary to her. When they were old enough, the lady began to educate her daughters herself, until some of her elder daughter's skills began to surpass her own limited knowledge.

Katherine and Susan were respectful toward all adults, not merely those of status or position. She couldn't help but be grateful that Maria's dour outlook of governess life did not extend to *every* situation. She appreciated her good fortune, but easily recognized how very awful things would be if they were only a little bit different.

"It is lovely, Susan. A little house, with a garden?"

"Yes. It is a cottage on our aunt Jacobs' estate. At Apperly."

"And where is Apperly?" Harriet asked.

"Near Gloucester, I think," inserted Katherine, still working busily on her own sketch.

Harriet found that she enjoyed being a governess to Katherine and Susan. They needed little coaxing to do as they ought, and genuinely enjoyed their studies. They lived for praise. That much was clear already.

"I think it is a very pretty cottage, and you've done a lovely job with it. Would you like to paint it now?"

"I do not know." Her brow wrinkled. "I do not paint so prettily as I draw. I do not want to ruin it."

"I have an idea," Harriet said, "Here is another piece of paper—one suitable to paint on. Go ahead and try drawing your sketch lightly over again on this paper. That way, if something goes awry with your painting, you will have your favorite sketch safe."

Susan smiled a little. "I shall try it."

The door opened then. Mrs. Donahue was checking in on her daughters again. Harriet smiled.

Mrs. Donahue entered and came over to look at her daughters' sketches.

"Try adding some shadow on this side of the vase, Susan—but not too much. It is coming along well." Her younger daughter glowed at the praise.

"Mama, look at my drawing!" Katherine chirped, "I am going to try to paint it!"

"That looks lovely, darling. Only try to put some more detail in those trees—they do not look real as you have drawn them."

"I shall, Mama." Susan seemed only mildly deflated, and returned to her work with a vigor. Harriet's heart squeezed in her chest and she felt a sudden strong desire to be a mother one day. She frowned. It was unlikely she would have the opportunity, although perhaps she eventually may find a nice farmer like her father and . . . she sighed a little. The man she truly wanted felt so very far from her reach. Even further now that she was all the way in London, surrounded by people miles above her station.

Mrs. Donahue turned from inspecting her daughters' artwork. "Miss Shore, may I speak with you a moment in private?"

Harriet's heart fluttered a little with nerves. "Yes, madam."

Mrs. Donahue led Harriet down the hall and into her private parlor. When they arrived, Mrs. Donahue turned to face Harriet and sighed. "You perhaps know why I wish to speak with you."

Harriet frowned, but listened with excited apprehension. "Is it about what the duchess said when she visited?"

Mrs. Donahue nodded. "Indeed. I am quite at a loss. I've never heard of such a scheme. I do not know that it will work, but I do know that Her Grace is my dear friend."

Harriet willed herself to remain calm, even though thoughts of dowries and Stephan Grimsby were flitting through her mind. "If I may say . . . I would not mind at all helping the duchess in this venture, but I would not wish to do so at the expense of losing this position."

Mrs. Donahue smiled. "I was hoping you might say that. I hope that you will continue on with the girls. Your position will remain here for the time being—this . . . this *venture* is a temporary arrangement, and should not take up *all* your time."

Harriet nodded vigorously. "Indeed, ma'am. I am already so fond of Susan and Katherine. I would not wish to leave them." Her heart was beating faster and she squirmed guiltily at the half-truth. She would rather be Stephan's wife than anything in the world. If he still wanted her.

The older woman gave her a sad smile. "I shall need to reduce your pay to reflect your time spent away. And I shall expect you to arrange with the girls' nursemaid each time you leave, to ensure they are cared for."

"I shall." Harriet nodded eagerly.

"Then it's settled. I shall bring you with me to call on the duchess this morning."

"So soon?"

Mrs. Donahue nodded. "A note from her arrived this morning to beg you to consider her offer. And to beg me, by extension."

Harriet nodded. "And shall I . . ."

Mrs. Donahue's eyes flitted to Harriet's plain day dress. "Leave your things here. I do not expect you will need any of your own clothes. You will continue boarding here and teaching the girls when you have no engagements with Her Grace."

Harriet bobbed her head in acknowledgment and walked upstairs for her spencer and reticule in a daze. She'd read Shakespearian comedies less improbable than the plot she now found herself embroiled in.

Chapter Seven

Curzon Street, London

"I have found a solution to all our difficulties," Virginia's mother declared triumphantly upon entering the room, "and she is coming here directly."

Virginia stared out the window, irritated at being dragged out of a rather splendid daydream. "What are you talking about, Mother?" she finally asked.

"There is a young lady who looks very much like you, I think, and she will be taking your place in society until you can come out of confinement."

An irreverent giggle escaped Virginia's mouth, but she quickly grew serious at the look on her mother's face. "Mama, you cannot seriously think that such a scheme could ever work! I realize you're upset about . . . my condition, but perhaps it is best to reconcile yourself to the situation. If you would only let me remain at our house in Brighton, or even the one in Exeter, then no one need . . ."

Her mother's nostrils flared. "And leave you without my supervision?"

"If it were that important, you could remain in the country too, Mama."

"And miss the season?" The thought clearly had never occurred to the duchess. She shook her head. "No, no. *This* is the best course of action, my dear. Trust me. We do not wish you to lose the connections we've worked so hard to build, now do we?" Her chin tilted upward as it always did when she felt she needed to assert herself.

Virginia pursed her lips and raised an eyebrow.

The duchess ignored her. "Virginia, you ought to at least *meet* the girl before dismissing the scheme entirely. The resemblance is striking."

The last thing in the world Virginia wanted was to be rid of the child and reintroduced into society as though nothing had happened. That was what her mother wanted, but she was already feeling quite affectionate toward what was currently only a small lump in her midsection.

"Virginia?" Her mother prompted, impatient for a response.

"Very well."

"Because it's really not asking too terribly . . . oh. You *will* meet her? Excellent. She should be by with Mrs. Donahue any moment now."

Virginia had to chuckle at this. "She is already on her way? Well, it is lovely to know I had a choice in this matter, Mother."

The duchess scoffed in annoyance at her daughter's sarcasm, and they heard a soft but determined little rap at the door before it swung open. "Hello, Your Grace. Mrs. Donahue and Miss Harriet Shore," Mandie dropped a careless curtsy as she led Mrs. Donahue and Harriet through the door.

Virginia caught herself staring at Harriet, who stared right back at her. Mrs. Donahue and the duchess were looking back and forth from one to the other as well.

Harriet's hair was a couple shades lighter than Virginia's, and it held enough natural curl that Virginia felt a twinge of envy, remembering all the time she'd spent covered in pins or using hot irons. Her figure was similar to Virginia's, but was slightly more delicate. Her lips were slightly more full, her eyes a lighter brown, and she had a few more freckles, but the shapes of their eyes, pert noses, and oval faces were startlingly similar.

"Gracious," said Harriet.

"You weren't mistaken at the resemblance, Mother," Virginia breathed, "although she is quite a bit lovelier than I."

"Nonsense!" barked the duchess. "You are both beautiful girls. I'll just leave you two to get to know one another, then. Come with me, Margaret. There's something I'd like to speak to you about."

With that pronouncement, the duchess flounced out of the room, Mrs. Donahue in tow.

Harriet looked nearly as awkward as Virginia felt, and she gave a deep curtsy.

"That won't be . . ." Virginia began. She trailed off and cleared her throat. "Make sure you keep your spine straight during a curtsy. I only bend at the knee and lower my head slightly."

"How is this?" asked Harriet, trying again.

Virginia nodded. "Better," she said, and fell silent.

After a moment, Harriet began shifting where she stood. The poor girl looked uncomfortable. It was likely that she didn't feel she could speak to Virginia, or ask questions without invitation. Virginia gestured to the sofa she was sitting on.

"Please sit."

Harriet did so. She waited another few seconds before speaking.

"Forgive me, I—"

"I suppose we—"

Harriet laughed nervously when they both started speaking at once. "I am sorry to interrupt you, Lady Virginia. Please go on."

Virginia sighed and smiled. "I thought my mother's idea was fit for Bedlam."

Harriet nodded in agreement, although she seemed disappointed.

"However, now that I am meeting you, I feel it just might work."

Harriet's head popped up. "Do you really think so?"

Virginia nodded. "I may not always *like* them, but I've spent a fair amount of time in front of looking glasses. And I feel as though I am in front of one now—a flattering one."

"I think it'll work, too," a voice chimed in suddenly. Harriet jumped and her hand flew to her chest. Virginia chuckled lightly. Harriet had clearly forgotten about Mandie, who had collapsed into a chair in the corner soon after introducing Harriet.

"You can call me Mandie." She stuck out her hand to shake Harriet's.

Harriet took her hand, still seeming a little startled, and Mandie jerked her up to a standing position from the sofa. She started physically rotating Harriet, inspecting her figure.

"Mmm, yes. I believe it could work, miss."

Virginia smiled. "Do go on, Mandie."

"But miss, there are simply *so* many more interesting things I could be working on downstairs."

"Well, I'd hate to keep you . . ." Harriet said quickly.

Mandie and Virginia both laughed at Harriet's awkwardness until her cheeks turned pink.

"What is it?" she asked.

Virginia's eyes sparkled with mirth. "You assumed Mandie was saying what she meant."

"So . . . she does *not* have more interesting things to do?"

Virginia smiled. "Mandie may be my lady's maid, but she is a full *two* years older than I, as she frequently likes to remind me. She is the daughter of my father's steward and has been near me for most of my life. She may do what I ask her to, but never without sharing her thoughts on the subject first."

Mandie stuck out her tongue at Virginia, and immediately feigned innocence. Harriet smiled hesitantly, as though not yet sure she was allowed to.

"Mandie, you were saying?"

"Right. As I was saying, miss, this chit looks enough like you that it ought to work. Remember that scheme a couple of years ago? Lady St. Clair managed to turn her protégé into the talk of the season all because she managed to get Lord Rodney to dance with her at her coming-out."

"Yes, I remember," Virginia said slowly.

"What's this?" Harriet asked.

Mandie smiled patiently. "Listen, Miss . . .?"

"Shore."

"Miss Shore. Everyone in town was willing to treat Lady St. Clair's niece like a princess because the right people started out treating her like a princess. So . . . If everyone—starting with the duchess—treats Harriet like she's you, the rest of the *ton* will follow along like a herd of sheep. I'm also fairly certain no one's memorized every inch of your face, my lady. Few people are capable of it, and to be frank—which I always am—you look even more like Virginia's portrait than *she* does."

Virginia laughed at this, and Harriet smiled at the image. "How do we accomplish this?"

"Start with the important people! If the duchess dresses you like Virginia, addresses you as Virginia, and treats you as she would treat Virginia, no one's about to argue with *that*, now, are they?"

Virginia giggled. "I'm imagining the stir it would cause if someone *did* dare mention any differences they noticed after a full summer away. I would not envy the one who dared to cross my mother."

"And because you two look alike enough, and there's clearly no proof of the switch . . . no one would dare say anything, even if they did suspect!"

Virginia shot Mandie a little smirk. "As disgusted as I am with this whole scheme, I'm inwardly congratulating my mother. It looks like she will win this battle." She sighed then, and sat back on the sofa.

Curzon Street, London

Harriet was caught somewhere between awkwardness and fascination. She had never been in another house—if you could call this *palace* a house—even half so lovely, let alone in the company of a truly glamorous member of London's high society, the *haut ton*. Virginia wasn't exactly what she'd expected her to be. She didn't seem haughty or self-important, but she did have a quiet, graceful confidence about her that made Harriet a bit envious.

"I . . . your home is lovely," Harriet said to Virginia, seeking to change the subject.

Virginia looked at Harriet and gave a little scoff and looked around the room. "I suppose it *is* lovely," she said reluctantly, "But I wish I were nearly anywhere else."

Harriet did not know how to respond to this, and was beginning to grow frustrated with Virginia's excessive reserve.

"Go on, miss," Mandie coaxed, "can't you tell the girl wants to talk openly to you? I don't think she'll bite."

Virginia laughed ruefully and looked over at Harriet. "You're right. Harriet, please call me Virginia. I may not like my mother's plan, but there's no reason to make *you* the object of my displeasure."

Harriet smiled. "I am still Harriet," she said, holding out her hands. After a hesitant pause, she added, "What is it you dislike about your mother's plan?" She wanted to avoid bringing up Virginia's indelicate state if it was a source of pain to her, but she had no way of knowing whether or not it was—or how she had gotten herself into it.

Virginia turned her gaze back to the window, to the shaft of light penetrating the white curtain. "It looks as though my mother intends to keep you near. What could be the harm in telling you my story, I wonder?" she murmured.

"Well, it *might* kill you," Mandie said, "but pray do not let that stop you."

Virginia laughed, which made her sharp tone harder to take seriously. "My, but your tongue is wicked today, Mandie!"

Harriet bit her lip to keep from laughing, and finally Virginia gave another almighty sigh, her cheeks glowing cheerfully.

"Right. Where to begin?" Virginia continued. She leaned forward and looked Harriet in the eye. "Have you ever been in love, Harriet?"

Harriet could feel her cheeks heat up at the thought of Stephan and his kiss. "Y-yes," she said, taken aback.

"*Truly?*"

Harriet stumbled over a response. "I do not . . . oh, *please* continue, Virginia. I would much rather hear your story than share mine."

Virginia gave her a sly smile. "I did not know you had a young man. I hope you will tell me all about him later."

Harriet remained silent, smiling expectantly and waiting for Virginia to continue.

After a moment, Virginia settled back into the sofa and began to speak. "My story begins last summer, at the end of the season."

Chapter Eight

Curzon Street, London

The season ended in mid-May, and as soon as my father's parliamentary responsibilities finished, we all traveled to Brighton."

"Nice place, that," Mandie remarked.

"What happened at Brighton?" Harriet leaned forward slightly in her seat.

"Well, it's by the sea," Virginia's eyes were unhappy and far away as she continued. "I have never been as fond of company as my mother is. She is still the center of attention at every ball, even at her age, and that is as she likes it. She tends to dominate every social circle she enters, and is never short of friends. We could not be more opposite. I have always been solitary. I enjoy reading, walking, painting, and fostering intimate relationships—few of which have been with members of the *ton*, to my mother's disappointment. It is impossible to tell who among them would continue to be kind to you if you hadn't a penny. The fluttering around expected of a young, wealthy lady never appealed to me. I was always terrible at it."

"I beg pardon, but you can't have been at it for *very* long," Harriet said curiously.

"I've now been out more than four years—my mother introduced me to society at seventeen."

"Oh. I'm nineteen," Harriet supplied. She felt a little foolish, but as she'd never really been "out," did not know what else to say or how to relate.

Virginia straightened her skirts and reclined slightly to make herself more comfortable before she continued. "I used to walk by the harbor every morning. Our house was right in the center of town, close to the shore. I would walk down and look at all the boats in the mornings, when the light was still gray and the mists were still out."

Mandie sighed, and fluttered a hand next to her face. Virginia quirked an eyebrow at her and pursed her lips.

"What?" Mandie asked, seeming embarrassed for the first time since Harriet had met her. "It's all terribly romantic, you know."

Virginia smiled, but Harriet could see some pain behind her eyes. "His name was Ralph. Ralph Clifton. I met him walking near the water. He liked to walk along the docks, as I did. I never dressed formally on my morning walks—my walking dresses are all very plain and modest at my request, and I was such a dull charge to Mandie and footman that half the time neither was in sight at all. Ralph never knew I was from such an imposing family. He wore simple clothes and no coat, as the weather was warm. We began walking together in the mornings, and became friends."

Harriet felt herself drawn into the story, imagining a bronzed young man with tousled brown hair and a roguish smile. Virginia, in her imagination, wore a yellow walking dress with small flowers printed on it. Or perhaps the dress was white. She continued listening to Virginia's story, not wanting to miss a word of it.

"Weeks passed before we even learned one another's situations in society. I saw him one day in uniform. He'd needed to don it earlier than usual in the day and hadn't had time to change before coming to meet me. He was a naval officer—and not the fashionable variety, who purchase their commissions, but a recently promoted lieutenant from a poor family. I knew then, although a part of me had always known it, that I would never be allowed to marry Ralph. I didn't care about his low status myself, but I knew my family would. I nearly told him that day that my father was the Duke of Dorset, but I couldn't muster the courage. I told him two days later, instead."

There was a smart rap at the door, pulling the three of them from the trance created by Virginia's story.

"Virginia?" her mother's voice queried as she charged into the room, not awaiting a response. "Mrs. Donahue must leave. If you are willing to assist Harriet in this venture, she will stay, but I will leave that up to you. You know full well what I would *prefer* you choose, but you must cooperate if it is to—"

"All right, Mother, she may stay. I will cooperate."

The duchess stopped mid-sentence and glowed with pleasure. Her pause was brief. "I shall have her measured for suitable attire this afternoon, and will meet with the both of you before your supper to discuss further expectations. Oh, everything is going to go *famously*, Virginia." She clapped her hands together in satisfaction. "Excellent, excellent. All will be well, Virginia. Now that Harriet is here, I am actually glad to see you home."

Three steps later, the duchess was out of the room, and the door closed behind her with a smack of finality.

Harriet's face must have shown the horror she felt, because Virginia gave a small, humorless laugh.

"Yes. That . . . is my mother."

Mandie gave a huff, "Cheery thing, ain't she?"

Harriet stared at Virginia, who was avoiding Harriet's gaze. She was outwardly very calm, but Harriet noticed a slight shudder to her breath—the only betrayal to a perfectly controlled countenance. "Mandie, would you mind seeing about luncheon for us?"

Mandie heaved a dramatic sigh. "Miss, *you* may not seem bothered by your condition, but it makes life blasted inconvenient for me—I never used to need to see to your luncheon, you know."

Virginia smiled at this and feigned sympathy. "Oh, my poor, dear Mandie. What would I know about inconvenience? It's not as though I am kept prisoner in my own home."

Mandie chuckled. "Touché. Your sarcasm is coming along famously, my lady. My training has had the desired effect."

Harriet suppressed a giggle. She suspected she was going to get along just fine with these two young ladies.

Mandie left to have a tray prepared.

"It's a wonder no one has noticed the food disappearing yet. I've been here three weeks," Virginia told Harriet.

"So the servants don't know you're up here?"

She shook her head. "No one gossips more than the household staff. We can trust Mandie, and my mother's maid knows, but in the meantime I've been trapped up here very much alone."

Harriet looked horrified. "Virginia, that's . . ."

"It's not ideal," she said with forced calm, "but let's not dwell on it. I *am* glad for your company, though I had not expected to be. I hope that you can adjust well to this highly unusual situation, and that all goes well for you. I also hope Mandie and I have not frightened you overmuch with our . . . informality. But if you are to become my duplicate, we cannot afford to stand on ceremony with one another."

Harriet smiled. "I agree, and I often feel as much in need of friendship as you describe."

Virginia turned her full attention to Harriet. "You are a governess, are you not? I imagine that *is* lonely. I remember my own governess confiding to me once how awkward a situation it can be."

"I've felt this way all my life," Harriet admitted.

Virginia frowned. "Lonely?"

Harriet nodded. "I haven't any brothers or sisters, and my father is a farmer and a gentleman's second son."

Virginia frowned. "That *is* an awkward situation."

Harriet bit her lip. "Do you require anything to make you more comfortable with your present . . ."

"Oh, out with it. My pregnancy. All this senseless beating about the bush the upper classes insist upon is part of the reason why I wanted to have done with it entirely and run away with a sailor!"

Harriet smiled. She and Virginia were from very different walks of life, but she couldn't help feeling that they were two of the same kind notwithstanding. Lonely and unable to achieve a real intimacy with their equals for one reason or another. "I can't help but agree with you, at least in part. I have always been rather forthright, myself."

"I'm glad to hear it," Virginia said, "I hope to see more of it as I come to know you better. I do not want to re-enter society at all, so this plan to perfectly mask and erase this chapter of my life was never my idea. However, I am glad to participate in this absurd scheme if only because I shall have another companion aside from Mandie and my mother. And I'll admit I have a bit of morbid curiosity to see if this plan could possibly work."

"The things we do to please respectable society," Harriet sighed sympathetically.

Virginia's eyes narrowed. "I sense a story about you, Harriet. Speaking of which, you have not yet mentioned—why on *earth* would you agree to submit to a scheme such as this one?"

"Clearly your knowledge of the lower classes is lacking if you are unaware of the draw money can have."

Virginia narrowed her eyes and stuck out her chin. "You do not seem mercenary to me."

Harriet's gratitude shone in her eyes. "Thank you. As to why I agreed . . . the man I would prefer to be with above anyone else is of a higher rank. His mother disapproves, and I go back and forth between hope and despair. But if my dowry were larger, she might be persuaded to accept me. Perhaps."

Virginia nodded slowly. "I see. Yes, that unfortunately makes sense. I know how overbearing and entitled women of quality and position can be. You are already perfectly genteel, however—your manners are nearly flawless. It's quite impressive for anyone from the country, let alone a farmer's daughter. With a tidy fortune at your side, no matter your lineage, you are bound to attract some excellent offers."

"There's only one I want," Harriet mumbled into her lap.

Virginia sighed, and when Harriet looked up, she saw Virginia grinning at her. "You *are* in love," she said.

"Yes," Harriet said.

"And is he in love as well? Is he of age? If so, why hasn't he proposed yet?"

"It's complicated," Harriet grimaced as she spoke. "But in short, he needs to marry a young lady of fortune if he is to keep his estate intact."

"Hmm," Virginia said, a stormy expression overtaking her eyes. "And my mother promised you money?"

"Yes."

Virginia nodded. "Well, my new friend Harriet—I hope I may call you my friend—I'll be happy if this absurd scheme can be made to work, if only for your sake!"

Curzon Street, London

Later that day, once the duchess had returned from several social calls and finished her afternoon tea, Mandie scouted the upstairs hallway, and when it was pronounced safe, the three of them made their way over to the duchess's rooms.

"There you are," the duchess said when they arrived. "Now, where to begin? I'll assume the two of you have been coming to know one another better?"

"Yes, Mother," Virginia said.

The lady nodded. "Excellent. I'll want to start some trial runs soon. Harriet, could you go with Mandie to try on one of Virginia's gowns to see how it fits you? I may need to have some of them altered to better suit you."

Virginia did not change her placid facial expression, but her mother turned to her as though she had and snapped, "it's not as though *you* would be wearing them anyway, Virginia."

Virginia blinked rapidly, and Harriet turned away to give her privacy. Harriet was glad to follow Mandie out of the room. The duchess was so utterly *unpleasant* to her daughter that it made Harriet feel uncomfortable. Mandie opened Virginia's armoire, selected a jade green gown that complemented Harriet's eyes and skin, and helped her into it. Once the gown was over her head and fastened, Harriet gasped at her reflection in the glass.

"I've never worn anything half so nice before," she whispered, running her finger along some of the gold rope trim and admiring the fine lace at the bottom.

Mandie grinned. "Feels good, don't it? Virginia's passed on some of her old gowns to me, and it's always a pleasant change from the uniform. I've been her maid so long, we've become more like sisters. She's never treated me like I'm less than she is, which is why I'm like to give her the lip I do—though, I'm sorry if it's frightened the wits out of you, lass."

Harriet smiled. It was easy to smile when Mandie was around, and she liked Virginia already. Her brow furrowed as she remembered the question she'd been dying to ask all afternoon. "What is . . . what is going to happen to the child?"

Mandie looked truly unhappy for the first time all day. "Don't know, miss. Honestly, I wouldn't put it past the duchess to have it . . . you know . . . done away with. But without Virginia's cooperation she could never. She'll more likely give it away to whomever will take it off her hands. I've heard stories of wet nurses who take unwanted children and raise them to be sold to chimney sweeps."

"That's horrible," Harriet whispered.

"That's the *ton*. Appearances are more important than life. Why do you think Virginia dislikes it so much?"

Harriet gave a little shudder as Mandie finished clasping the gown. "There you are, miss. You look quite the fine lady, you know."

Harriet glowed with the compliment. "Thank you, Mandie. You've been so kind to me."

Mandie waved off the compliment. "It's only because you're new here. Once you've settled in, I'm sure I'll abuse you as much as I do the others." She patted Harriet comfortingly on the back and made her laugh.

"Well, miss, shall we go back in?"

"Let's," nodded Harriet.

They made their way back into the duchess's sitting room, where Her Grace immediately stood and walked over to Harriet to appraise her at close range.

"Mm, yes," she said with pleasure after a brief examination, "it suits you. Was not this dress too snug for you to wear to your last ball?" the duchess asked Virginia.

Virginia pursed her lips. "Yes, Mother."

"Well, it doesn't seem as though *Harriet* had any difficulty getting it on."

The tension was so high that Harriet started to feel slightly light-headed. She mentally chided herself, and willed her heartbeat and breathing to return to their regular paces. If she kept up these nerves, she was bound to faint at her first social engagement, which would produce a highly awkward situation. She stared at a point on the ground as she relaxed. The duchess noticed and lifted her chin.

"Do not stare downward, Miss Shore. The floor should not take your attention when there are people to know and conversations to be had."

Harriet looked up at the duchess, butterflies fluttering around her empty stomach, and curtsied once more, as she tended to do when she did not know what else to do.

"And do not offer so many curtsies! Gracious, we have a lot to learn. You shall stay with us tonight—I shall notify Mrs. Donahue—and you shall practice walking and talking as you ought. Both Virginia and I shall coach you. I on proper behavior, and she on . . . *her* behavior."

Harriet nodded. She had the sinking suspicion that it was going to be a very long evening.

Chapter Nine

Curzon Street, London

The next morning came far too soon. They had stayed up late and Harriet spent the better part of two hours lying awake in Virginia's palatial bedroom. The room was extremely comfortable and fitted in the first style of elegance, the bed of the softest materials. But she felt frighteningly alone—the room was too large for her, and unfamiliar shadows kept her feeling unsettled for much of the night. Her room at home was modest, and the family cat, Hubert, normally slept by her feet. At the Donahue home, her plain little room was connected with the children's rooms—she could hear them making noises in their sleep, and once Susan had cried out because of a bad dream. She had not felt alone there, either.

In the Duchess of Dorset's house, however, she was rattling around in an enormous and lonely gilded cage. She felt so sorry for Virginia, hidden away, living a shameful existence in which a child—what should have been her greatest joy—was reduced to a source of shame so great the family would not even acknowledge it.

To be unmarried and with child . . . Harriet shuddered. She did not envy Virginia in the least. And yet her story sounded so romantic. To feel trapped in her own life, and to find a man who loved her enough to rescue her from it all. Virginia had not said what had happened to Ralph—*was* he going to return? But if he was going to come back to her, why was she *here*? Her stomach churned in sympathy for

Virginia. And what of Harriet? She felt as trapped as Virginia had before she'd met Ralph. She was a governess, and a farmer's daughter. All she wanted in the world was permission to be Stephan's best friend again, and perhaps one day even . . . she tried not to think of it. Marrying Stephan was still so far out of reach, even with a hoped-for dowry, that she did not dare dwell on the prospect. Her mind flitted back to Virginia.

Virginia's story was so dashing! To walk by the seaside, watching the sun rise day after day over the churning gray water while falling more and more deeply in love. Harriet wanted to hear more—she couldn't imagine how the rest had unfolded. She wanted to hear every detail of how they fell in love and what it was like, and hoped to do so in the coming days and weeks. The duchess had requested that she spend extensive time talking to Virginia to find out and memorize the answers to virtually any question she was likely to be asked in polite society. It was going to be a lengthy process, but they had started out slowly the day before, and Virginia was also planning to teach Harriet clever methods to avoid answering impertinent questions.

"Morning, miss," Mandie grunted cheerfully as she burst through the door and threw open the curtains. Harriet shot out of bed and was on her feet in less than a second. Mandie nearly fell over with surprise when she turned away from the window.

"Zooks!" she cried. "What are you doing out of your bed?"

"Well, it's morning, isn't it?"

Mandie shook her head, a hand on her chest. "You may *look* like Virginia, but you an utterly different creature! Virginia sleeps until her stomach demands food."

Harriet smiled. "I've never been allowed to sleep late before."

"Well, you'll need to learn to. Are you at all familiar with *ton* parties?"

Harriet frowned. She'd said she'd be willing to return to the Donahues to help with the children whenever she wasn't engaged by the duchess, but had thought she'd return home by a respectable ten o'clock or so each evening. When she mentioned this, Mandie snorted.

"Yes. Ten o'clock . . . oh, do pray tell that to the duchess while I'm present so I can watch her face!"

"Is it *very* much later?"

Mandie nodded vigorously. "During the season, the duchess isn't home until the wee hours of the morning—nearly dawn. Once she did not come back until past four."

Harriet's head spun. "That cannot be healthy."

Mandie crowed with laughter. "Oh, I like you. You and I are more alike than you think, miss. You a farmer's daughter, and me a steward's daughter. Stewards are like farmers of the city—they're the only ones that make the master's fortune worth anything."

Harriet laughed at the comparison. "I had never thought of it that way before."

After Mandie helped Harriet get dressed, in yet another one of the finest gowns Harriet had ever touched, they headed to the duchess's rooms. The duchess looked up from her dressing table as soon as they arrived. "Excellent. Harriet, I'm going to begin calling you Virginia, to solidify the habit. I do not wish to make a mistake in public, or else this whole charade will fail."

Harriet nodded. The duchess was always so certain of what she wanted that she could not help but feel cowed in her presence. "Of course."

The duchess smiled. "Well, then, *Virginia*, would you like to go shopping with me? It will be excellent practice for the morning calls we shall make together."

The two drove out immediately after breakfast, before Virginia had even awakened. The duchess led the way to a Barouche waiting in front of the house and Harriet paused a moment in silent admiration before mounting the carriage's elegant steps. She marveled at how different the world looked through its gilded windows—as if the streets and everything on them existed for their benefit alone. Harriet wasn't sure how she felt about this distortion of reality. Their first stop was a fine milliner's shop on Bond street.

"Har—Virginia," the duchess quickly corrected herself as the door opened before them, "you'll be needing a more modish bonnet than the one you now wear. You haven't had a new one yet this season."

Harriet was thus far finding it quite easy to pretend to be Virginia. All she needed to do was look bored and comply with her mother's demands with a simple, "Yes, Mother." The more Harriet tried to put herself in Virginia's shoes, the sadder she became. Virginia's portrayal did not suit the glamorous life of a young, fashionable lady that she had always imagined, but at least she felt she was performing her part well.

Harriet strolled about the shop, ignoring the young shop girl fluttering about them offering suggestions. She'd never seen so many hats, and such fine ones. The milliner's in Burnham-on-Sea was far smaller, with never more than a handful of truly modish bonnets. In this shop there were dozens far more elegant and well-made than even the nicest one she'd ever seen in her village. She looked from a navy velvet bonnet adorned with white feathers to a green satin bonnet trimmed with blue flowers. There was a pretty pink and straw bonnet trimmed with creamy lace and the loveliest, softest pink ribbon she'd ever felt.

"What of this one?" she heard herself say, forgetting for a moment to sound bored.

"Hmm?" The duchess looked up and walked over to the bonnet Harriet was eyeing. She looked at it, and back at Harriet. "I do not think it quite suits a lady of your station," she demurred, and went back to the bonnets she had been inspecting.

Harriet flushed and was forcibly reminded of Mrs. Grimsby's remarks. Was she supposed to act and be treated like Virginia in public or was she to be treated like the servant she was? She walked over to the duchess with a gloomy expression and half a mind to ask her about it.

"What do you think of this one?" the duchess asked.

Harriet stared. The bonnet she held up looked far more expensive than the pink straw one she'd admired. It was covered in deep blue taffeta and adorned with beautiful cream and white silk flowers and pearls, an ostrich feather topping off the adornments. She'd never before seen such a beautiful, elegant bonnet.

"Th-that one?" she asked. "For *me*?"

The duchess gave her a sharp warning look, but she softened quickly and when she spoke there was a twinkle in her eye that made Harriet feel better. "Of course, my dear. You need not wear pastels anymore if you do not wish—you are three seasons out, after all."

Harriet smiled. She had clearly been asking about elegance and expense, not appropriateness, but the duchess knew this and covered for her. Harriet determined to fall into character more completely, when she saw how much it pleased the duchess. As the duchess purchased the bonnet and had it wrapped, she gave Harriet a conspiratorial look and suggested they next look for some new gloves.

Palace Court, London

It was far more trouble than it was worth to borrow Frank's phaeton, but Stephan had at long last managed to convince his cousin that he wouldn't overturn it or abuse his horses. For a fleeting moment during this argument, Stephan had wished that he could afford to keep a house and stable of his own in town.

When he stopped at the correct number on Palace Court, he handed the reins to the groom and asked him to keep the horses warm for a few minutes. He stared up at the house, suddenly feeling like an utter fool. He had traveled all the way to London to chase after a young lady who clearly wanted nothing to do with him.

He had tried to dissect what it was he loved so much about Harriet, and although the simple answer was *everything*, there was one memory in particular he'd never forget. He'd been out playing with Harriet past dark one summer, and Stephan knew his mother would be madder than a hornet. He had decided then and there that he would simply have to run away from home and find some gypsies to live with, but Harriet had taken his hand and walked home with him. His mother had met them on the doorstep and he had never seen her so angry before. She began shouting, her face red, and when she raised her hand against him, Harriet swiftly barred the way. "No, you shall not strike him!" she had yelled back in her firm little voice.

His mother had slapped Harriet so hard that her face had a bruise the next day. He'd known since then whom he would choose if forced to make a decision between Harriet and his mother.

Stephan slowly mounted the steps. He had to try.

Would she be there at all? Would she be happy to see him? The steps seemed interminable to Stephan, and he almost began to regret his decision to come to Palace Court as his heart pounded wild rhythms in his chest. Would she be still angry that he had taken the liberty of kissing her? He winced and forced himself to think thoughts that instead gave him courage—visions of Harriet's warm brown eyes glowed in his mind's eye, and he saw her mussed hair lit with a halo of golden sunshine.

Once at the door, he knocked firmly, and a moment later, the housekeeper appeared.

"Yes?" she asked.

Stephan cleared his throat. "I have come to ask after Miss Harriet Shore. If she is in, might I speak with her?"

The servant frowned. "Miss Shore?" she asked. "I do not know if she is here." She hesitated for only a moment in the doorway before he quickly smiled and said, "I shall await her out here."

The servant seemed grateful not to need to invite a servant's caller to come inside, and she bobbed a little curtsy before disappearing behind the door again. The minutes that passed were few, but they felt painfully long to Stephan. He looked up and down the street, trying to occupy his mind while he thought of what he ought to say.

Too soon, before he felt fully prepared, the housekeeper returned, popping her head out the door. "I'm afraid she is not here, sir."

Stephan frowned. "Has she gone out with her pupils?" he asked.

"I do not know where she has gone. She will likely be back tomorrow, sir. Shall I tell her that you came by?"

Stephan quickly reached into his pocket for a calling card, wondering all the while where Harriet could possibly be if not at her place of employment. He had run out of his own cards, so it was one of Frank's with his name blotted out and Stephan's written in its place. He felt embarrassed by the card, by Harriet's absence, and by the housekeeper's demeanor, and said apologetically, "She knows who I am—we are old childhood friends. If you could let her know that I came to see her . . ."

The housekeeper nodded, took the card, and immediately closed the door.

Stephan turned away from the house feeling embarrassed, disappointed, and once more in painful suspense of whether or not Harriet would forgive him and welcome his suit.

Curzon Street, London

The duchess all but commanded Harriet to remain on Curzon Street for supper, even though Harriet was more than ready to escape to the relative calm of the Donahue nursery. No guests were expected, but the duchess wished to discuss supper manners in the safety of her own home, where no one but a footman or two would notice any errors she made.

"I am already so *tired*," she yawned as Mandie helped her into her dinner gown.

Mandie yawned, too. "Stop that—if you yawn, then I yawn."

There was no warning before the duchess burst into the room and closed the door behind her. "The duke is here," she said, her cheeks pale. "And he will be dining with us this evening."

Harriet blinked a couple of times, confused at the duchess's odd reaction to the arrival of her husband. "Does he not normally dine at home?"

The duchess shook her head and paced the room anxiously. "No! He has a private set of apartments in East Finchley. He normally dines there, with his . . ." she trailed off with a little growl.

"With his *what*?" Harriet asked.

"His *mistress*," the duchess whispered loudly. "He thinks I do not know about her."

Harriet's cheeks warmed with embarrassment. My, people behaved differently here than in the country!

"Never mind," the duchess said, "but I had not intended to present you to him so *soon*."

Harriet frowned as realization dawned. "Do you mean . . . is it possible that the duke is not aware of Virginia's true state? Are you trying to include *him* with the rest of the *ton* we would like to deceive?"

"Of course I am," she snapped.

Harriet tried to hide her horror, and chose her words carefully. "Would it not be better for him to be made aware of Virginia's condition sooner than later? He is Virginia's father, after all. Why should you not confide in him?"

It was the duchess's turn to appear confused. "*Confide* in him?"

Harriet shrugged, glancing down at her feet. Her tone grew more subdued. "He is your husband, Your Grace. Are you not partners in life?"

The duchess scoffed and shook her head. "The youth today, with their insufferable notions of *romance*. When I was courted by the duke, I did as all young ladies ought to and married to please my family. I am the duchess of Dorset, not a moon-eyed debutante hanging on the arm of her devoted swain. Of course I am not going to tell him!"

Harriet felt her face flush. Though inexcusable, it was no wonder the duke considered escaping to another pair of arms when this pair was so prickly. But she might be prickly too if her husband had a wandering eye! She cast a searching glance at the duchess and could discern some real fear behind the woman's frustration. What was she so afraid of?

"How can I possibly present you to him?" the duchess moaned to herself. "You are not prepared!"

Harriet swallowed a sigh. "I shall do my best, Your Grace."

The duchess looked at her and blinked a couple of times before wrinkling her nose and then nodding. "It appears we have no other choice. Come quickly, Harriet—I mean Virginia—and I shall help you practice your table manners in my private sitting room before supper."

After several minutes of dining drills, the duchess finally proclaimed Harriet prepared enough for supper, though Harriet could not help but notice that the duchess's stomach let out a small but audible growl just before she announced her decision. As they entered the dining room, Harriet carefully put on the bored, neutral expression she had learned from Virginia. She thought she was getting rather good at it, but was careful not to allow the thought to excite her, lest her expression change.

The duke stood at the window near the head of the table. He turned when the two women entered the room. "At last," he said. "Virginia, it has been quite some time since I have seen you. Have you been keeping well?"

Harriet swallowed and nodded. "Yes. I have, Father." She stubbornly kept the mask on her face, but it was difficult. The Duke of Dorset's eyes had a sharp look to them that reminded Harriet of a military commander. He had ruddy cheeks and thick gray hair near his ears that thinned on the top of his head. He was fairly thin, aside from the rounded belly that was fashionable for men of his age.

The duke cast a searching glance at Harriet before inviting everyone to sit and being seated himself. As servants brought the food around, Harriet was careful to swallow her enthusiasm at the offerings. Her table at home was only ever this rich on holidays. She was grateful she had been instructed to remain silent wherever possible—that meant she might better enjoy the meal. The duchess and duke made light conversation as they ate, and Harriet was asked several questions. She endeavored to answer very carefully, only occasionally shooting glances at the duchess to see if her responses met with approval.

On the whole, the meal was far less frightening than Harriet had imagined it would be. When the meal ended and the duchess was just about to stand, however, the duke asked her to stay and gestured for the servants to leave. The duchess sat stiffly as she watched the door close behind the footmen.

The duke smiled at the duchess. "My dear, when were you going to tell me that you have replaced my daughter with quite a different young lady?"

If Harriet had not been so terrified herself, she would have laughed at the expression on the duchess's face. Her complexion turned an unhealthy red and white and the corners of her open mouth turned down even as her eyes widened in shock.

"I had not . . . that is to say—" the duchess could not regain her bearings.

Harriet looked shyly up at the duke, afraid of what she might see, but he was smiling at her through his confused expression. Harriet stood, heart pounding, and walked toward the duke, giving her best curtsy. "My name is Harriet Shore," she said softly. "Virginia is well, but is not able to be present herself."

The duke smiled at Harriet and nodded before turning to the duchess with a frown. "I understand that Virginia may have any number of reasons to absent herself. That does not explain, however, the attempt to deceive and insult me by presenting me with a young lady that is *not* my daughter."

The duchess stared at the table. "Your *daughter*," she said through tight lips, "is with *child*."

The duke sat back in his chair in surprise. His expression was stern and unreadable for a long moment before he smiled sadly. "But she is well? Where is she?"

The duchess heaved a sigh. "Upstairs, of course. In the guest quarters. I can't have the whole staff knowing—"

"Thank you." The duke gave his wife a brisk nod, rose from his chair, and abruptly left the room.

Chapter Ten

Between Palace Court and Curzon Street, London

Virginia confessed to Harriet later that she had been frightened when her father had shown up in her room unexpectedly. He was not often at home. But they had enjoyed a lovely visit together—the first of many more to come. The duke consistently refused to speak directly about Virginia's delicate state or the man who had put her into it, but he would often shake his head sadly and offer Virginia looks and words of sympathy and support.

After the laborious first few days pretending to be Virginia, the weeks began to pass so quickly that, to Harriet, everything was a blur. She was expected to be present with the duchess for morning calls three days per week, and went to evening parties with her three nights per week, as well. She spent her days away from Curzon street teaching Susan and Katherine music, dancing, history, and drawing, although sometimes she was so tired from staying up late that she fell asleep while assisting the girls with their studies more frequently than she wanted to admit. She loved her time with Susan and Katherine and often wished she could spend more time with them.

The evening parties with Her Grace went well. She managed to feign boredom convincingly enough that she worried she had actually offended a couple of her hostesses. She made polite conversation, and managed to discourage the flirtations of a couple of gentlemen even the inexperienced Harriet could recognize were fortune hunters.

"Oh, that was a capital party, was it not?" the duchess sighed in the carriage ride home from an evening soiree. "It is so wonderful to have you with me. You move about society so *naturally!*"

Harriet shifted in her seat. The duchess had made it clear, though never in so many words, that Harriet was the daughter she'd always wanted to have. It was a horrible, awkward feeling for all parties involved.

"And you are so compliant," the duchess sighed.

The duchess liked to be in control—that much was apparent from the weeks she had known her.

Harriet took in a sharp breath through her nostrils. "Well, yes, Your Grace. I am more or less in your employ," Harriet felt the need to remind her.

The duchess made a somewhat frustrated sound. "That ought not signify. My servants, my friends, all of *society* respects me and yet my own daughter . . ." she shook her head.

Harriet did not know how she found the courage to say what she did next, but it had to be said. "Your daughter is not your servant and cannot be expected to do your bidding without thoughts and feelings of her own. And nor can your husband," she added as an afterthought.

The duchess did not remonstrate Harriet for her impertinence, but instead turned her attention to the city street outside the carriage window. After a long pause she said, "It is true that . . . I had not realized how very bored she generally seems until you began striving to emulate her."

Harriet stared at her hands. "It isn't easy for me to do. I must confess I rather *like* society parties."

"I can tell," The duchess said knowingly. "And you know, it's never been easy for *me*, attempting to coax Virginia into attending parties and balls with me. And into courting! She never would consider the young men I presented to her. And I may not be a romantic, but I did *try* to please her!"

The duchess stared out the window in angry distraction. "I used to know what she wanted. I thought I had an *excellent* life planned for her."

Harriet spoke cautiously. "But perhaps she wanted to plan her *own* life, Your Grace?"

The duchess narrowed her eyes at Harriet. "And her plan turned out *so* well." The duchess swallowed her sarcasm and looked away again. "Virginia never *did* understand that simple truth. If you open your heart, you are likely to find it broken, along with your dignity, confidence, and all else that you've worked hard to achieve. It is far better to guard it, and thus protect yourself from harm."

Harriet frowned. It was clear that, at least part way through that little speech, the duchess had stopped thinking of Virginia and allowed her thoughts to wander elsewhere. She took a deep breath, determined to strike while the iron was hot.

"Your Grace, I cannot help but wonder . . . why is it that you and the duke are near-strangers? He seems like quite a pleasant gentleman, from what little I've seen of him. You could be friends, partners, and confidants, but you seem to avoid even the sight of one another."

The duchess did not look at Harriet, but closed her eyes. Her mouth drew into a stiff line, and she inhaled sharply through flared nostrils. "The duke has not proven himself a trustworthy companion . . . , and she had doubts."

Harriet hesitated. This really was none of her business. But she'd come too far to turn back now. "And are you *certain* he has a mistress?"

The duchess let out an irreverent bark of laughter. "Of course he has! Where else would he disappear to so frequently? Why else would he have a private set of apartments just outside the city? But that is high society for you, my dear. It is a far more common practice for the *haut ton* than you romantic young country folk tend to imagine it is."

Harriet remained silent, her brow knitting together, and the duchess again resumed her study of the city street outside her window, taking a deep breath. It was as she had thought—the duchess did not appear to have any proof.

"Your first ball will be this week," she said. "It is odd that there has been such a dry spell of acceptable social engagements thus far this season, but finally we shall attend Lady Gregor's ball tomorrow evening. I have not seen your new gown since it was fitted to you. May I see it in the morning?"

"Of course. I am not expected at the Donahues' until Sunday. That is . . . tomorrow as it is already Saturday morning now."

"Some might say so, I suppose." The duchess stifled a yawn.

The rest of the carriage ride was silent, but the duchess seemed thoughtful all the way home. Harriet realized it was possible that the duchess, although more difficult to pity, could be as much in need of comfort as her daughter was.

Curzon Street, London

"Are you *never* enthusiastic at parties?" Harriet asked Virginia with a frustrated sigh as she collapsed on the sofa in Virginia's quarters.

Virginia frowned at her and looked away, focusing her attention once more on her sewing project. She was depicting a honeybee on the front of a tiny nightgown. "I have always been more comfortable in intimate settings."

"Aren't we all?" Harriet asked. "All people are most comfortable with their closest friends, of course, but it seems as though you treat others as poisonous snakes rather than as potential friends. I am sure most people do not mean you any harm."

"There *are* snakes among them, Harriet," Virginia said quietly, "and if you have not run into any yet, I am happy for you. I know that there are many decent souls among them, but sorting between the true and the false is exhausting for me."

Harriet bit back her responses at the pain she saw in Virginia's face. She was far more sensitive and reserved than Harriet ever had been, and Harriet wondered if she had always been that way and, if not, what had happened to make her that way.

"It is very hard on your mother, you know." Harriet said. "Your situation is obviously unhappy, but hers is difficult in its own way."

Virginia set down her needlework and fixed Harriet with a cool glare. "Please do not censure me, Harriet. I am certain that it is easy for *you* to be a perfect daughter, but I never could seem to avoid disappointing my mother whatever I did."

Virginia had not needed to shout for her words to pierce Harriet to her core. She didn't get the nerve to speak again until Virginia had finished stitching a wing.

"Tell me," Harriet finally said.

"What?"

"*Tell* me."

"Tell you what?"

"Everything." Harriet's eyes glowed with excitement. "Your story. Tell me what you mean—that you can't help but disappoint. Tell me about Ralph. Tell me what your feelings are. Tell me what it is that makes you so very unhappy all of the time."

Virginia pursed her lips before relaxing with a frustrated sigh. "Oh, Harriet. I do wish I had more friends like you."

"Well, at least you have *one*," Harriet said cheerfully, batting her eyelashes.

Virginia chuckled and leaned back into the sofa, staring at the ceiling. "All right. You know I didn't choose the high-society life—but my mother did. She was born the daughter of a gentleman, of course, but she was not the leader of the *ton* that she is now. She met my father, the duke, and immediately set her sights on him. She worked very hard to turn herself into exactly the sort of woman he wanted to marry, and she succeeded. And you may have noticed already—my father is rarely here. He tends to give my mother free reign. He spends most of his time at White's, or perhaps with the mistress my mother is certain he keeps. . . . But both of them are contented. My father has retained his independence and he has an heir in my younger brother, who is away at Oxford. My mother is one of the leaders of fashionable society with a tidy fortune at her disposal. And so they both have what they want."

Harriet frowned thoughtfully. It did not sound ideal to her, but the duchess did generally seem to enjoy her life.

"So the duchess has always wanted you to be like *her*," Harriet clarified, "but you would choose the opposite life for yourself."

"Exactly," agreed Virginia. "I have always preferred a quiet country life over the busy London season. I quickly tire of the parties, of the drama enacting itself in the higher circles. Of the chase of courtship, and all the engagement announcements that follow."

"I must admit it all sounds rather exciting to me," Harriet mumbled, playing with an escaped tendril of hair at the nape of her neck.

Virginia groaned. "I would infinitely prefer to climb a tree."

"Really?" Harriet giggled. "That's hard to imagine. Although I always *did* enjoy climbing trees."

"You mean you have actually climbed one yourself?" Virginia whispered, leaning forward.

"Of course. Haven't you?"

"Never!"

Harriet's eyes widened. She would have thought Virginia was joking if it weren't for the serious look on her face. "Oh, Virginia, I had no idea! I truly *do* pity you now!"

Virginia laughed and wiped a sudden tear from the corner of her eye. "Tell me *your* story now, Harriet. About your childhood. Your family. What was it like?"

"You hadn't finished telling me about—"

"Shh! Tell me. *Please.*"

Harriet smiled as Virginia echoed her own words and sat forward with a childlike eagerness to listen. "Very well. I was born in a little village called Burnham-on-Sea."

"Oh, it sounds wonderful already." Virginia was in dreamy raptures.

"Do you know, Virginia, this may be the most excited I've ever seen you?"

"Shh! Do go on."

"My father was born the second son of a gentleman, but did not wish to go into the church or study the law, and so he used his portion of the inheritance to lease a farm, which he has run ever since. It is a fairly large farm, on the estate of Squire Grimsby. My mother was a governess, the daughter of a rector on a country estate outside Berrow. They met at a community party, and my father received her employer's permission to court my mother. The rest of their story you can easily guess, and here I am."

"And what did your mother's family think?"

"They were happy she was making such a good match. My father isn't *poor*, you know. He may not be a landed gentleman by the strictest definition, but he is quite respectable. We have always been happy and comfortable."

"And do you have any brothers or sisters?"

Harriet frowned. "No. I ought to have had some, but none survived birth and infancy. So you see, my parents dote on me, and my mother tends to worry about me a little *too* much. There's also an odd sort of pressure to live an unreasonably happy life, to make up for the happiness of their lost children."

Virginia's brow quirked upward. "Do they know what you're doing right now?"

"Not *precisely*." Harriet felt her cheeks warm as she grew sheepish. "They only know that I am governess to Mrs. Donahue's daughters."

Virginia chuckled. "Your parents are the lucky ones, then."

"What do you mean?" asked Harriet. She pulled her knees up beneath her on the sofa so she could continue talking more comfortably.

"My mother wishes she had a different daughter, I wish I had different circumstances, you wish you were a more fit bride for your gentleman, and there your mother and father are, perfectly content with their lot in life, their daughter—to their knowledge, at least—doing precisely as they wish her to."

Harriet laughed. "They *are* happy," she sounded almost grumpy about it, "but my father, at least, does not precisely *wish* for me to be a governess. He wants me to be married. Being a governess was my mother's idea."

"And what was yours?"

Harriet groaned. "Oh, I didn't *have* one. I've already told you I've always felt out of place, like I don't belong anywhere. I think I would like to be respectable enough to *belong* a bit more thoroughly in polite society. I do enjoy a good party, and I love to dance."

"You're a natural performer."

Harriet smiled and took an overly dramatic bow from her seat on the sofa, and Virginia laughed before she sighed and stood up, stretching her sore limbs.

"I wish that you could go out," Harriet suddenly stood as well. "Trapped in this room all day, breathing the same air hour after hour . . . you *ought* to go out, even if only for a little while!"

Virginia's eyes bulged. "What? You cannot be serious!"

The door suddenly opened, and both Harriet and Virginia jumped. "I heard that!" Mandie said cheerfully, "and I think that is an excellent idea. Where shall we go?"

Harriet looped her arm through Virginia's. "There aren't exactly many trees to climb nearby, so we may have to remain indoors. But perhaps not in *these* rooms! And I'm famished."

"Me too," confessed Virginia.

"I could do with some refreshment myself," Mandie added casually.

A few minutes later, the household all in bed, the three of them tiptoed down to the kitchen and sat around the servants' table. Mandie cut some leftover ham and bread and boiled some water for tea. The three of them chatted until late into the night, and this small ounce of freedom seemed exactly the medicine to lift Virginia's spirits.

Chapter Eleven

Grosvenor Hill, London

Harriet gave a small gasp as a servant took her cloak at the door. She had never seen so many elegantly dressed people in one room before. Lady Gregor's ball was her first real London ball as well as the first essential *ton* party of the season, and hundreds were in attendance.

"What a terrible crush," the duchess murmured behind her, not sounding remotely disappointed.

Harriet nodded, since she could not speak past her excitement, but she let out a slight squeak. The duchess noticed and chuckled, taking Harriet's arm authoritatively and resting it over her own as they maneuvered through the crowd.

They passed several exceptionally handsome young men and Harriet, for the first time she could remember, discovered that her heart was beating a little more quickly than before for someone besides Stephan. She couldn't help but regret that Virginia's personality was known for being withdrawn, sullen, and uninterested. Keeping her expression a study in boredom while ogling the crowd was one of the most difficult things she'd ever done.

"Let us go down toward the dance floor, my dear," the duchess gave Harriet a nudge, "no one is going to ask you to dance here on the balcony."

Harriet looked at the duchess, trying to maintain Virginia's reluctant personality through her excitement, but the duchess seemed to understand precisely how Harriet felt.

"Very well, Mother," Harriet's voice shook a little with excitement behind her bored façade.

Harriet was resplendent in the grandest gown she had ever seen. It was cream-colored crepe with a high waist and it had a deep red satin overlay that split at the waist. She wore pearls about her neck and rubies in her ears, and her chestnut hair was piled high on her head in a fashionable knot of little curls. Mandie had spent hours on her hair, and had naturally complained about it the entire time, even though Harriet suspected she had enjoyed it a great deal. A gold comb adorned her curls and her hands and arms were covered by cream-colored gloves that rose past her elbows. She had never felt more elegant or lovely in her life.

They arrived at the ballroom floor as a dance was about to end, and the duchess subtly left her side to go and speak with an old acquaintance, handing her a dance card as she left. Harriet noted with considerable nerves that there were far more young ladies than young men in the room, and pulled out her fan, waving it at her face with enthusiasm to keep her forehead from glistening unattractively as she examined the dance card. There were only a few men's names written on it thus far, and they seemed vaguely familiar. She searched on the card for the dance that was shortly to begin and found the line blank.

The dance broke up and Harriet looked around anxiously for a partner as the next set was being organized. This was the first time she'd had the opportunity to dance in London, and she was even more nervous than she'd thought she would be. Back at home in Burnham-on-Sea, the local assembly dances were filled with a small and odd assortment of young people, and she, being fairly pretty, had never had difficulty finding a partner. Here, however, everyone looked wealthy and glamorous. She'd never seen so much satin, so many beautiful plumes, so many priceless gems. This was no ordinary party—this was the first major ball of the season, and the *ton* had risen to the occasion and were wearing their very finest.

She could feel her hands sweating beneath her gloves and had a fleeting wish that society did not dictate she cover her arms. She changed her mind a moment later when she remembered that a lack of gloves would mean that a man would need to make contact with her clammy, nerve-dampened hands to dance with her.

When the set was already nearly organized and the musicians were starting in, Harriet looked around, attempting as boldly as she dared to make eye contact with a few young men as they milled around looking for partners, but it was very difficult for her to remember if she'd made the acquaintance of any of them yet. A couple of them looked back at her, but inevitably turned and asked another young lady for a dance at the last moment. Harriet felt herself growing increasingly nervous as her options diminished, and when the next dance had begun in earnest and she was left without a partner, she felt deflated. She found herself wishing that she were attempting to impersonate someone who had a more flirtatious reputation. She was embarrassed to feel herself blinking back a tear.

"Let me guess. You wanted to dance," a voice suddenly said at her elbow. She whirled to face the source of the voice and found herself nose-to-nose with a gentleman in a black satin waistcoat and a very fine dark suit that seemed molded to his broad shoulders and trim but muscular legs. He had dark hair and eyes, and a sardonic expression etched onto his face.

"I did," Harriet confessed breathlessly, breaking character for one moment before catching herself. She took a step backward from him. "That is . . . I—"

"You seemed disappointed not to find a partner—pardon my frankness." He took a half-step closer to her, and she could feel her heart thudding in her chest.

She pursed her lips. She'd clearly have to do better at feigning disinterest. The man was very handsome, and his face was so well-formed that it could have been chiseled from stone in Ancient Greece. However, he seemed to be mocking her, and she found that trait most unattractive.

"I'm afraid we haven't been properly introduced." She put her nose back in the air where it belonged.

The man's eyebrow shot up and he smirked at her. "I beg you will forgive me, my lady. We were introduced last season, but I would be surprised for such a grand figure as yourself to remember one such as I."

Harriet felt overwhelmed and she swallowed down her growing panic. She had hardly snubbed any former acquaintances at all,
thanks to the duchess and her vigorous reminders, and not when she
had already been caught breaking character. "I'm terribly sorry," she
managed to say, "but I'm afraid I've forgotten your name, Mr. . . ."

"Desford. Thomas Desford."

He bowed, and she curtsied. Her mind was a blur. She had no
idea what to talk about, or whether she ought to excuse herself entirely
from the conversation.

"I could not help but notice that you have a lovely fan." There was
a twinkle in his deep blue eyes.

Harriet smiled involuntarily. She had selected it herself on an
outing with the duchess and Mrs. Donahue. It suited her dress nearly
perfectly. It was gold, depicting a large ivory-colored bird with sweep-
ing feathers resting on a branch covered in rich red blossoms.

"Thank you, sir."

"But you were waving it rather quickly for one that wishes to be
asked to dance."

Harriet's stomach dropped. Of course. She hadn't been paying
attention at all to what she must have looked like to passing gentlemen. Naturally none of the genteel men *here* would ask her to dance
while she was waving them away with her fan. In Burnham-on-Sea it
was so hot and there had been so few young ladies at the assemblies
that no prospective partner had ever bothered to notice how she had
been waving her fan.

Harriet fiddled with the end of one long glove. Not only had she
failed to mimic Virginia's behavior—she had failed to mimic any sort
of fashionable behavior. And she had been caught doing so by a handsome gentleman, no less. A handsome gentleman whose cravat was
perfectly tied in a fashionable knot. The crush of people put him so
close to her that she noticed that he even *smelled* wonderful—a clean,
manly scent she couldn't quite pin down but that she found quite
exciting. Many gentlemen taking part in the dancing had glistening
foreheads and limp cravats, but Mr. Desford's appearance remained
immaculate. He wore a fashionable Brutus hairstyle, and a single
golden fob hung from his breast pocket. He had truly elegant taste,

and Harriet could not help but feel both intimidated and fascinated by him.

After what felt like an age of hesitation, Harriet finally nodded her gratitude and turned away from Mr. Desford as subtly and politely as she could manage. She folded her fan and hung it from her wrist even though she felt even more warm than she had before.

"Lady Virginia, do me the honor of the next dance," he commanded.

"Pardon?"

He stepped behind her and leaned in so close that she could feel his breath on her cheek. "Dance with me, Lady Virginia," he murmured smoothly, "That is, if you are not already spoken for."

She swallowed, her knees suddenly feeling unsteady and her mouth dry when she turned to reply. "I am not otherwise engaged."

He smiled and nodded, swiveling to better watch the dancers. He did not speak again until they moved to take their place in the line. He took her gloved hand with his and she had the terrifying, fleeting thought that if her hands were damp enough to wet her gloves, he might notice that she was perspiring, but the thought passed, leaving her to enjoy herself.

The dance began and all her attention went to performing the steps with the grace and ease of a fashionable, cultured young lady who felt at home in elegant circles. It was not easy.

"Have you been enjoying the season thus far, Lady Virginia?"

"Indeed." She could not think of a more thorough response while dancing.

"Have you been able to hear Miss Harrington sing yet?

"I'm afraid not," she responded, "where is she performing?"

"Drury lane. They're playing Verdi."

"Oh! I have not yet seen one of his works, but I look forward to doing so. I believe mother and I have planned to attend a performance next week. They certainly seem popular pieces in Italy."

"Indeed. I am sure you will enjoy the opera when you see it," Mr. Desford replied. When the motions became repetitive and Harriet began to relax a little and enjoy the dance, she tried asking him a question.

"How did you pass your summer, Mr. Desford?"

He smiled fleetingly, seeming bored at the question. "At my estate in Kent."

"Oh, Kent," she said awkwardly, "I . . . I hear it is lovely there."

He looked as though he were about to laugh. "You have never visited Kent before?"

Harriet inwardly made a frustrated noise that she hoped was not audible. She found herself growing more uncomfortable and irritated by the second. Here was a man who claimed he knew Lady Virginia, and who had caught her acting out of character. Even worse, she did not have any way of ascertaining that they actually *had* met, or whether he was taking her for a fool. He had caught her warding off potential dance partners—something Virginia would never have done unintentionally—and it seemed that nearly every word that left his mouth was mocking and condescending. Harriet could hardly wait for the dance to be over so that she might dance with more friendly bachelors.

The dance wound to a close and Harriet politely thanked Mr. Desford before moving away quickly to try to find another partner. She walked around for a few minutes, struggling to remember the names of people she had met recently at other evening parties, dinners, and soirees. No names came to her and as she could not approach people whose names she did not recall, she did not speak with anyone. She suddenly wished that the duchess had never left her side.

She finally made eye contact with a young man seeking a partner for the next dance, a country dance. She recalled meeting him at least once before, although she did not remember his name. He seemed to recognize her, however, and began walking in her direction. She stood up a little straighter and gave him an encouraging little smile.

Before the young man could stand before her and bow in greeting, Mr. Desford suddenly appeared next to her.

"Forgive my tardiness. A cup of punch, my lady?"

The other young man seemed embarrassed and veered off to the left to ask another lady to dance.

Harriet scowled and turned to Mr. Desford, accepting the cup of punch with the best approximation of a smile she was able to supply in her annoyance. She whipped out her fan and began fluttering it quickly in his direction as she sipped from the little cup.

"You will forgive me for driving him off," The corners of his mouth twitched up in a smirk. He didn't sound sorry at all, and ignored her fan.

Harriet looked away from him, her nostrils flaring.

"I simply was not ready to stop speaking with you yet." Harriet risked a glance, and Mr. Desford's eyes were on hers, his expression friendly but mischievous. She felt heat rise to her face and felt flattered by his attentions despite herself.

"Tell me about *your* summer." He casually sipped from his own cup of punch as he gently led her away by the elbow to a pair of upholstered chairs not far from the dance floor. The casual touch made her heart pound and her skin crawl.

"I spent the summer at Brighton with my family." She struggled to remain composed.

"I hear it is lovely there."

"Oh, indeed it is."

"Did you go sea-bathing?"

"Of course not."

Mr. Desford did not respond immediately. Harriet was initially glad, but the silence made her uncomfortable, so she risked another glance at him.

"I enjoy spending time with you, Lady Virginia," his eye caught hers with a sidelong smile.

Harriet sat silent, frowning and wishing she might be able to return the sentiment. For once she was annoyed enough that it was easy for her to remain as aloof and reserved as Virginia generally was. He was so charmingly conceited and self-assured that she wanted nothing more than to wipe the smirk from his face. She sat silently as she planned her escape from his side.

Mr. Desford finally spoke. "See there? Mr. Winchester going after Miss Clavendish again."

"What?" she asked, trying unsuccessfully to sound uninterested even as she craned her neck to see who he meant.

"There," he gestured, "that elderly foppish gentleman and plain little Miss Clavendish."

Harriet took offense. "She is not *plain*."

Mr. Desford laughed, "How would *you* describe her?"

"She's . . . wearing a lavender gown."

His eyebrow shot upward. "See? Even *you* can't manage to call her pretty."

Heat rose in her face again. Miss Clavendish *was* a little plain, but it wasn't kind of Mr. Desford to point that out. She wondered how Lady Virginia would've approached the situation.

She sipped at the last bits of punch in her cup as she continued to watch the oddly matched couple and, after a moment, she giggled.

"Why *does* he continue to pursue her?" she asked. "She clearly doesn't like him at all."

Mr. Desford laughed lightly under his breath, and the sound made the hair on Harriet's neck raise in an exciting way, but she was not sure if that were good or bad. "Well, he doesn't seem to notice. He continues to preen and strut about like the greatest fop in England— his fifty years do nothing to stop him."

"*He* is fifty?" Harriet gasped. "Are you quite certain?"

"What? Does he not look it?"

Harriet's eyes were sparkling and she grinned at Mr. Desford. "I would have guessed at *least* sixty."

They both laughed then. They easily whiled away the next half-hour by observing the other guests at the ball and providing commentary for them.

"See that young man, there?" Harriet asked.

"Who, the Earl of Davenport?"

"I can't remember his name for the life of me, but he has the mint green cravat?"

"Yes. What of him?"

"Well, he was at a soiree I attended the other evening and smelled so strongly of cheese that I couldn't help but wonder what on earth could have brought it about."

"Swiss or stilton?"

Harriet giggled guiltily. She found she was having a difficult time *not* giggling as she talked with Mr. Desford. Perhaps it was the several cups of punch she'd had, or perhaps it was the guilty thrill she got from mocking members of fashionable society, but whatever the reason, she was enjoying herself more than she had in weeks.

"Virginia," a stern voice said near her.

She sat bolt upright and looked toward the voice with her cheeks aflush.

"Yes, M-mother."

"Please come with me. There's someone I'd like to introduce you to." She turned toward the now standing Mr. Desford with an appraising glance, "I beg your pardon, Mr. . . ."

"Mr. Desford, Your Grace. A pleasure." He bowed and extended his hand.

She ignored his hand. "Ah, yes. I *thought* you seemed familiar. Good evening, sir."

The duchess turned and quickly led Harriet away, her grasp on Harriet's arm uncomfortably tight.

Chapter Twelve

Grosvenor Hill, London

Harriet looked up at the duchess hesitantly as they left Mr. Desford, wondering what she had done wrong.

"Is something the matter, Mama?" she asked hesitantly.

Her lips pinched as though she tasted something sour. "You were speaking far too long with him." She wrinkled her nose. "And he isn't good *ton*."

Harriet's brow quirked upward. Mr. Desford was one of the handsomest and most fashionable men she had ever met. She couldn't think why he wouldn't be good *ton*, but figured perhaps the duchess or Virginia knew the reason, so she determined to ask about him later.

"The real reason I pulled you away," the duchess continued, "is that I would like to introduce you to *another* young man whose mother has said she would like to have him dance with you."

Harriet bit back a retort. Willingly dancing with a young man whose mother forced him to dance with her seemed like admitting defeat, but she quickly reminded herself that she was representing Lady Virginia and not herself, and set her own dignity aside.

"Lady Margaret?" the duchess said.

"Ah, Your Grace!" the woman replied. She had on a bright purple gown, was wearing a large silk headdress, and carried an enormous, overwrought fan in her gloved hand. "And Lady Virginia."

"Yes, this is Virginia," the duchess said, gesturing. Harriet took the cue and curtsied in greeting.

"I am quite charmed to meet you, my dear." The woman swiveled around. "Andrew!"

A young man turned around and walked over toward them. "Yes, Mother?"

Harriet bit her lip. It was one of the people she and Mr. Desford had been chatting about—the young man whose hands and feet seemed slightly too large for the rest of his body. She forced herself to smile.

Aside from his slightly odd proportions he was a nice-looking young man who seemed perfectly amiable. She was determined to have a nice time making his acquaintance.

"I'd like you to meet Lady Virginia, the daughter of the Duke of Dorset."

His eyebrows shot up. "The Duke of Dorset?"

"Yes." The duchess lifted her chin with a little smile. "Perhaps the two of you might like to dance?"

Harriet could feel her cheeks heat up. "Mother, can you not wait for *him* to ask?" she muttered under her breath.

Lady Margaret's son grinned a pleasant, crooked smile. "It's a pleasure to make your acquaintance. I am Andrew Brougham, and I would love to dance with you, Lady Virginia. If you'll have me for the next?"

Harriet curtsied. Her cheeks were still flushed, but his response made her feel far less embarrassed. "I will, sir."

His mother loudly cleared his throat and Harriet thought she saw her elbow Mr. Brougham in the back.

His smile grew wider, and a trifle forced. "And perhaps the one after that, as well? If you are not engaged?"

Harriet glanced quickly from one smiling, nodding mother to the other and nodded briefly herself. "Yes, thank you."

Mr. Brougham bowed and walked away, and Harriet made her way directly toward the dance floor. She straightened her gloves and glanced into a nearby mirror to see if her hair remained in place. She stood a little taller as she assessed her elegant appearance. She truly did look like the daughter of a duchess, and the thought sent a shiver of excitement down her spine.

Mr. Brougham walked over toward her as one dance was ending and the next beginning, and Harriet nodded at him politely as he arrived. He smiled as he took her hand to lead her to the floor and take his place across from her in the set. She smiled back at him. He was fairly handsome, despite his awkward hands and feet. He had shapely shoulders and a trim waist and wore a very well-cut black suit with a deep green cravat and frosty white linens. His hair was a warm brown color, and it curled softly at its edges. He also looked very young—no older than twenty-three.

They began dancing, and the niceties passed by painlessly. He was doing well, and they had both enjoyed the weather lately, which had been more foggy than rainy.

"Do you enjoy your stay in London during the season?" he asked her.

"I . . ." Harriet paused. "I do not," she forced herself to say. She mentally sighed as she pulled on the cape of Virginia's character, though it felt heavy and unpleasant on her shoulders—even more so that evening than it usually did. Harriet thought it was wonderful to be in society—to be surrounded by fashionable, interesting people and to enjoy all the glamorous surroundings of the London season. But if she needed to pretend to hate it, she would.

"Indeed?" He was surprised by her reaction. "I rather enjoy London during the season—although the variety of birds one can find in Hyde Park is not nearly so good as it is near my estate!"

Harriet smiled weakly. *Birds*?

"But I should be happy to walk with you in the park and point out the different species sometime, if you'd like.

"Thank you, sir."

Harriet did not speak again for a while, but she did enjoy the dance, and found it easy to smile frequently.

"What do you like to do?" Mr. Brougham asked her.

"You mean when I am not at parties?"

"So you *do* enjoy attending parties, then?"

"I . . . not particularly," she confessed slowly, "but perhaps it is simply because I never took the trouble of seeing social occasions as pleasant opportunities," she continued, thinking of Virginia as she spoke.

"Well, I would be happy to help you do so," Mr. Brougham said cheerfully.

Harriet smiled again. "I would be grateful for it, sir."

They lapsed into comfortable silence for the rest of the dance. In between the next dances, Mr. Brougham led her to the side to be seated for a moment.

"Painting," Harriet suddenly said, remembering a couple of the lovely pictures on the wall Virginia said she'd done herself. "When I'm not at society functions, I enjoy painting."

It's not half-untrue for myself, either, she thought.

"What do you like to paint?" he asked, leading her into the next set.

"The sea," she answered truthfully. Both she and Virginia liked painting the sea. Harriet liked to paint it as part of a colorful, sunny landscape, and Virginia liked to paint it during storms with roiling, iron-gray waves. She frowned, thinking of how unhappy Virginia was—not only now that she was in a terrible situation, but how unhappy she always had been in the months and years leading up to her unfortunate decision.

"The sea," echoed Mr. Brougham, "I do like the sea."

"Have you traveled upon it?"

He nodded. "Not as much as I would like to. I did a short tour of the North and returned not too long ago. I enjoyed visiting the Scottish highlands the most, even though I could not understand what they were saying for the life of me. I was able to spot a whole flock of Dotterel there—a rare find, indeed."

Harriet smiled. "It would be wonderful to be able to travel."

"You ought to marry a man who likes to travel so he can take you places," Mr. Brougham said helpfully.

Harriet nodded, but her smile that time was forced. She did not want to marry a man so that he could take her around the world—she only wished to marry Stephan and return home. But there was no guarantee that Stephan would ask her to marry him, and no guarantee that his family would approve the match even with a hearty dowry on her side.

They continued dancing and found another common interest or two. They both enjoyed strawberry tarts and Mr. Wordsworth's poetry—but then, who didn't? Harriet had begun to feel empty inside. It was difficult to remain as stoic as Virginia would have, and she was having a hard time comparing the glamour and excitement of her masquerade with the dull life of a governess that she would need to return to. Not to mention that Mr. Brougham was turning out to be a bit of a bore upon closer acquaintance.

She sighed and continued to fiddle with the lace on the edge of her fan, and Mr. Brougham noticed her glumness and tried to be that much more jovial to lift her spirits. His efforts only made them sink lower, however, and both seemed glad when their last dance was finally over and they parted ways for the evening.

Harriet danced with a few more gentlemen that evening, but as the night wore on and it began to get late, she became less and less thrilled to be there, and it was getting easier and easier to play Virginia's sour part. After another while, when even the duchess seemed ready to leave, the two of them went to gather their cloaks and head for home.

As they made their way toward the door, however, a wave of late-comers washed in and they paused to let them pass. The party had grown less crowded, but this new rush of guests enlivened it a bit more, and suddenly the duchess seemed less ready to depart.

Harriet's heart sank when she saw the light in the duchess's eyes, and she steeled herself to stay even longer, but a glimpse of a familiar face in the crowd made her eyes widen and her heart pound uncontrollably. *Stephan.*

Chapter Thirteen

Grosvenor Hill, London

Stephan blinked but still felt like he was dreaming. His aunt's family did not normally receive invitations to functions quite as grand as Lady Gregor's ball, and he had never felt more intimidated and surrounded by glamour in his life than he had upon entering that grand hall. And yet there, in the middle of all that splendor, was a face that looked like home.

It can't be Harriet, he thought to himself. *She's a governess, not a duchess. But I believe that woman she's standing next to might be a duchess herself! All those ostrich feathers . . .*

They looked absolutely silly, but there was no mistaking the expense.

The young woman turned and looked at him and a flush rose in her cheeks. Stephan's eyes widened as she faced him. It was impossible, but true. He knew her face. And was that a look of recognition? She *was* Harriet. Right down to that solitary freckle above her eyebrow. Her right eyebrow. But it couldn't be.

Stephan's thoughts continued whirring circles around him, and he lost all track of time and space until his aunt rapped his arm with her fan.

"Stephan! Did you not hear me?"

"Ow! Sorry, Aunt Millicent. What is it?"

"I'm going over there to speak with Mrs. Bulward. Unless you would like me to introduce you to some young ladies first?" Stephan swallowed his horrified expression and shook his head.

"I'll take care of that, Mother." Stephan's genial cousin Frank steered him away. "Come along, Stephan. I see a nice young lady over there I met last winter. A Miss Stepney—Frances Stepney, if I remember true. Perhaps she has a friend. Come."

Stephan looked back as Harriet's twin disappeared through the door. She was probably too far above him to be introduced in any case. Seeing her leave brought back the memory of Harriet's sprinting away from him and his mother as quickly as she could, and he shook his head to come back to the present.

Frank clapped the reluctant Stephan on the back and Stephan forced his legs to follow his cousin. He tried to listen to what he said, but his mind was full of Harriet, their ill-fated kiss, and his mother's wretched timing.

He had enjoyed the short time he'd spent with his aunt's family thus far. He suspected his mother's ulterior design in encouraging him to visit his aunt in London for the season was for him to get the unsuitable Harriet out of his mind and stop mourning the void caused by her absence. Little did she know that Harriet had gone to London, and when Stephan had written his aunt it was with the intent to seek out Harriet in London and beg her to marry him.

He shook his head as he thought of his mother's likely reaction. No matter how hard he tried to convince his mother that Harriet was more than worthy of their esteem, Mrs. Grimsby would rail against her and say the nastiest things. If anything, all this only made him love Harriet more, because he knew how undeserving she was of the unkindness. His mother was not yet aware how things were about to change on the estate since Stephan had accepted Mr. Shore's proposition, but it behooved her to see reason sooner rather than later. He was no longer a child and his mother had long ago lost her power to change his mind using fear.

Stephan was not given as long as he would've liked to ruminate in these thoughts. Frank's friend, Miss Stepney, introduced Stephan to several pleasant young ladies and he danced until the early morning when the party thinned and finally wound to a close. All the way home that night, all Stephan could think of was seeing Harriet's face in such an unusually fashionable situation. The elegance suited her, he admitted to himself. For all that his own mother paraded about in far nicer clothes than their neighbors, Harriet—or her double, at least—wore them far better. But Stephan also thought Harriet beautiful in a plain day dress and apron, with mussed curls and berry-stained fingers.

He closed his eyes and tried to think of other things. Even supposing that his mother could be persuaded to gracefully accept Harriet as a daughter-in-law, surely even someone as forgiving as Harriet could not be prevailed upon to accept Caroline Grimsby as a mother.

"What a party!" Harriet was breathless as she entered Virginia's room after the ball.

Virginia snorted as she jolted awake, blinking rapidly.

"Oh!" Harriet said, "I forgot. Virginia, I am so sorry! Were you . . . Did you wish to go to bed already?"

Virginia sat back up on the sofa, plucking the half-read novel from her chest. "I must have fallen asleep while waiting for you," she yawned, "that's a frequent occurrence these days." She smiled and looked up at Harriet. Virginia's belly was growing larger by the day—it was finally visible even beneath her loose-fitting nightgown.

"Have a nice time?" Virginia asked, patting the seat next to her.

Harriet flopped onto the sofa with relief. "Yes, I did, but . . ."

"But what?" Virginia leaned forward with interest.

"*He* was there!"

"Who?"

"Stephan, of course."

Virginia's sleepy grin was so eager that Harriet could not help but laugh. "Your young man from Somerset was there?" Virginia exclaimed.

Mandie burst in then. "What have I missed? Did you have a nice time, Harriet?"

Virginia's eyebrows wiggled suggestively as she leaned back into the sofa with a yawn. "Her young man was there."

"He's not *my* young man," Harriet corrected with a sigh. "Although I do wish he were."

"Stuff and nonsense," Mandie said, "You said that he kissed you!

"Yes, but that was—"

"And he came to visit you at the Donahues', didn't he?"

"Well, yes, I heard that he did from the housekeeper—but I was not there to answer him, and the kiss was a long time ago . . ."

"He's a reputable fellow, Harriet! Not like some rakes as up and leave after they've gotten—" Mandie stopped herself abruptly and glanced at Virginia, whose nostrils were flared. "Dash it, milady, I am *not* talking of Ralph!"

Virginia's eyes closed and she winced as though the words stung. Harriet moved quickly to her side and put a comforting hand on her arm.

Virginia pinched the bridge of her nose. "Let's not talk about me." She looked up and tried to force some cheer. "I want to hear more about Harriet's evening. It's her first *ton* ball, after all! Whom did you dance with, Harriet?"

Harriet felt sick with guilt. She wished she could take away all Virginia's pain. But she couldn't help but want to learn more about what had happened with Ralph. All that Harriet had been told about the affair thus far was all terribly romantic. She did not want to believe he was the sort of man who would abandon his lover and child.

"I . . . I danced with a couple of young men that you might know. One was Thomas Desford."

"Ugh!" said Virginia, "What a dead bore."

"A bore?" Harriet asked, confused. Whatever else Mr. Desford was, he hadn't struck Harriet as boring.

"He's more of a rake than a bore, if you ask me," Mandie gave Harriet a suggestive little nudge.

"Well, no one did," Virginia groaned slightly. "All right, Harriet. I admit that he is *not* a bore. But I do not like him."

Harriet's confusion was plain on her face. "What has he done to vex you, Virginia? And is he really a rake? Is that why your mother says he's not good *ton*?"

Virginia pursed her lips, wrinkling her nose. "He's just always so smug. As if he is certain you admire him regardless of what you say or do."

Harriet smiled to herself. "And . . . did you admire him?"

Virginia's face flushed a brighter pink. "What does it signify?" she snapped. "He . . . oh, I found him mildly interesting last year, but for many months now I've not spared a single thought for him. And as for his being a rake, I could not care less. I try not to pay attention to rumors, let alone the ones I hear from my mother. Do please go on describing your evening, Harriet. I could use some excitement."

At the mention of rumors, Harriet could not help but recall a question she'd been turning over in her mind. "Virginia, speaking of . . . of rakes and such. Do you think your father really has a mistress?"

Virginia rolled her eyes. "You've been talking with my mother again."

Harriet shrugged defensively. "I am with her so often! And it is a question that inspires curiosity."

Virginia sighed and pondered before answering. "I do not know. But I do not believe so. I spoke with him only last week, and he said that he wished his home could be a refuge, and that giving my mother her way was the best method of maintaining peace. Those don't strike me as the words of a man with a mistress."

Harriet nodded, but she was frowning. It was a mystery, indeed. A little voice in her mind seemed to beg her to mind her own business and leave it alone, but yet another curious little voice niggled at her to discover the truth of the matter.

"I am certain it does not matter," she mumbled.

"Tell me more about the ball," Virginia prompted.

Harriet latched onto the distraction. "Well, I danced with Mr. Desford a bit before he drew me off to the side and we chatted for half an hour or so."

"Really? And mother let you?"

Harriet felt rueful at Virginia's surprise. "I don't think she knew at first. But she did pull me away from him after a while and had me meet Mr. Brougham, who was also very nice."

"Andrew Brougham?"

"Yes."

"I've heard of him, but he's never really been to town before this season from what I've heard. My mother would love for me to set my cap at him, though. You know, Harriet, I'll wager that she'd rather you were her daughter than I."

Harriet felt sick to her stomach at the truth in that statement. "I am certain your mother loves you, Virginia," was all she could manage.

Virginia looked at the ceiling and let her eyes flutter closed, as if trying to hold back tears.

There was silence for a moment, and when it grew so heavy that Harriet could feel her shoulders slumping, she stood. "Let's speak of something else if this upsets you, Virginia. I did not mean to irritate you, coming in and speaking of the party."

"You do not upset me, Harriet!" Virginia insisted, flustered. "I . . . I am only frustrated because of my present circumstances. It is so vexing. I no longer feel ill, you know. I haven't for weeks now. The midwife has been by, but she says all is well and that I ought to have felt the child move by now, but I h-haven't. I simply worry for the baby. I know the nausea was tiresome, but I was told it was a sign the baby was healthy. . . . I know the loss of the baby at this point would be considered a blessing by my mother, but I *cannot* feel that way."

"I do not feel that way either," Harriet whispered, her eyes stinging with sudden tears as she clasped Virginia's hand.

"I am frightened," Virginia admitted. "I cannot *see* the baby. How can I know that all is right? It already feels like a child to me. *My* child. But my only signs of it are my growing belly and steadily increasing appetite."

Harriet's stomach twisted. No one—not the duchess, Virginia, or Mandie—had been able to give her a satisfactory answer about what was destined to happen to the child once it was born. And the way the duchess dismissed her questions made her nervous.

"Did Ralph not tell you he would return?" Harriet asked.

"He did." Virginia closed her eyes as though she were basking in a memory. "He promised that he would always come for me."

Harriet brightened. "Then I am sure he *shall*." Harriet took Virginia's hand and squeezed it. "And all this charade, in the end, will be for nothing. For he will take you away and the pair of you shall live happily together for always with your sweet baby."

Virginia chuckled, and Harriet realized that, should what she said really come to pass, she likely would receive no dowry. She shook that selfish thought from her mind, feeling ashamed of herself.

"I'm certain he still thinks of you," Harriet pressed. "From everything you've said, I cannot help but feel that way."

"He told me he loved me, and always would. He could not afford an elopement to Gretna Green—you know that he could barely afford to mar . . . er, to take me away in the first place once I'd begged him to. He truly hasn't a thing in all the world. When I began showing signs of being with child, he took me to his sister's house and urged me to write home for mother and father to send a carriage for me. Then he left. He . . . he simply *left*." She burst into tears and Harriet frantically patted her back.

"But he said he would return for you!" Harriet insisted. "Didn't he?"

"Y-yes," Virginia gulped, still crying.

"So have a little faith!" Harriet lifted Virginia's chin.

Virginia tried, and failed, to smile.

Harriet sighed, and swallowed the tears that threatened to rise. "I have as many doubts about Stephan as you have about Ralph, Virginia, but what choice do we have but to be hopeful?"

Virginia's face was resigned behind her tears. "There is no other choice," she agreed. "He *has* to return for me. I could not bear it if he didn't."

"Yes, he does." Mandie stood sharply. "And he will, too, if he doesn't want to have *me* to deal with!"

They all laughed. "Thank you, Mandie," Virginia said, "and I'm certain you'll find someone too, sooner or later."

"What? Find someone that deserves all *this*?" Mandie stood and rotated, swaying her generous hips. All three of them laughed even harder, and when the laughing quieted, all was still for a moment.

Suddenly Virginia's eyes widened and she placed a hand on her abdomen. A moment later, she smiled and there were tears in her eyes. "I . . . there's something there. I think I felt the baby move."

Harriet grinned so wide she thought her face might split in two. For that one shining moment, in the face of all the doubt they labored against, and the impossible situations they had to surmount, all was right, and nothing could possibly go wrong. If only the feeling could last.

Chapter Fourteen

Curzon Street, London

They had stayed up talking late into the night once again, so Harriet had a trying time keeping her eyes open while she and the duchess were entertaining morning callers.

An old friend of the duchess's had left and Harriet had finally allowed herself an enormous yawn when another caller was announced. When the butler showed in Mr. Thomas Desford, both she and the duchess seemed equally surprised.

"I pray I'm not intruding?" he said upon being announced and allowed entrance.

The duchess looked so annoyed she did not speak, but simply waved a hand at an available sofa.

"I had hoped to visit with Lady Virginia again." He smiled innocently at the duchess, unfazed by her cold greeting. "I enjoyed speaking with her at the ball last night." He smiled his usual sardonic smile at Harriet once again, and as his blue eyes met hers, she felt a slight shiver down her spine.

The duchess stood. She did not seem to want to feign politeness to Mr. Desford any more than necessary. "Hughes!" she called to the footman outside, who popped his head into the room. She gestured to Harriet and Mr. Desford and the man nodded in understanding before taking his place against a wall and acting as chaperone. "Do not be long, Virginia. I shall return shortly."

She flounced out of the room, and Harriet was left alone with Mr. Desford under Hughes' watchful eye. She tried to remember what it was, exactly, about Mr. Desford that Virginia had said she had not liked aside from his general smugness, and couldn't recall. He seemed perfectly amiable and friendly, although at the ball last evening he did tend to stand closer to her than she would wish. Harriet also did not like the conceited look he tended to wear, but she could not deny that he was an extremely handsome gentleman.

"I am sorry for my mother's . . . coldness," Harriet apologized.

"Don't be!" Mr. Desford laughed lightly. "In her eyes, I'm barely respectable enough to acknowledge, let alone encourage."

Harriet smiled, but wasn't sure of what to say. "You aren't respectable?" she asked.

He shook his head with a light laugh. "Not to a worthy duchess with an ancient name, I'm not," he easily deflected the question and returned with one of his own. "Are you engaged this afternoon?" Mr. Desford asked her.

"I must go calling with Mama."

"And then? What next?" he seemed oddly fascinated by her comings and goings.

"Er . . . To be honest, Mr. Desford, I have an, erm . . ." Her mind drew a blank. "A private matter to attend to." She flushed as soon as she'd spoken the words, immediately regretting them. She was going to teach Mrs. Donahue's girls how to mix paint properly, but she couldn't exactly tell him that.

His eyebrow flickered as though he had caught onto something interesting she hadn't said aloud. "Well, if you find time amid caring for your private matters, I would be honored if you would take a turn around the park with me."

"I cannot today."

"Another day, then?" he pressed.

Harriet's heart beat faster as she mentally sought an excuse not to, but short of telling him she did not wish to, could not think of one. She felt herself warm around the edges as she realized that there was a part of her—she wasn't certain how large—that *did* wish to walk with him. He was persistent enough to have left her no honest recourse short of telling him outright that she disliked him. But she could not look into his hard navy eyes without realizing that to do so would hardly convince anyone, least of all herself, that it were true.

"Mr. Desford, I . . . Yes."

His eyes glinted, and he looked thoroughly pleased with himself. "Yes?"

She took a deep breath. "Yes, you may repeat the invitation, provided my mother does not bar your entry, of course. I may have time next week."

He smiled, displaying teeth unusually straight and white. It made Harriet want to run her tongue over her own imperfect front teeth, to compare them to his. "You honor me, Lady Virginia," he murmured.

She gave a curt nod and straightened her skirts, hoping he would take the hint that she wished for him to leave. When she finally looked back up at Mr. Desford, he was smiling knowingly at her.

"Lady Virginia, I am certain you have other visits to make this morning, and I must not detain you. Forgive me if I've taken up too much of your valuable time."

He took her hand in his and pressed it gently before straightening and turning to leave.

Harriet's ungloved hand tingled where he had pressed it even after the door closed behind him. The door opened again only moments later to reveal the duke himself peering inside. He frowned when he saw Harriet, and gestured for the footman to leave the room. As soon as he had gone, the duke entered.

"Harriet, isn't it?" he asked.

Harriet's heart pounded with nerves, but she forced herself to smile. "Yes, Your Grace." The duke had flatly refused the duchess's request to refer to Harriet by Virginia's name, at least at home.

He smiled lightly and nodded, remaining awkwardly near the door. "And, erm . . . how are you holding up? Are you being treated fairly?"

Harriet raised an eyebrow. "I . . . of course, Your Grace. You are likely aware your wife has promised me a considerable sum for er . . . my assistance."

The duke nodded, his brow creasing with worry. "Well, if you ever need anything, don't hesitate to let me know, child. Cannot have anyone treated ill under my roof." His eyes became sad and far away and he turned to leave, only to nearly run into the duchess as she briskly entered the room.

"I hope I'm not interrupting, but we really must be—" the duchess charged into the room but came to a halt when she came nose-to-nose with the duke. "Ah," she said. "How do you do, Charles?"

The duke nodded politely. "Ruth, I am well. I only had a brief question for Harriet. How are you?"

Harriet wished that she could hide from the awkwardness of their exchange. They spoke to one another like strangers! She inwardly shook her head and promised herself she would never allow herself to grow so distant from one she married.

"I am well." The duchess stared, confused, even as the duke gave her a short nod and left the room.

"Well, that was . . ." she shook her head and turned to Harriet. "What did he say to you?"

Harriet could feel her cheeks heat up. "He only wished to know that I am being treated fairly."

"And what did you tell him?"

"I said that I was."

The duchess nodded, seeming mildly relieved. "Oh, but . . . Desford, wasn't it? He is gone. What did *he* want?"

"He asked me to walk in the park with him next week."

"And?"

"And I told him I would likely be at liberty to do so."

The duchess sighed and tutted disapprovingly. "I am certain we can find a good excuse to evade him by then."

"Yes, Mother," but Harriet wasn't paying attention. She was looking out the window, thinking of Desford, the duke, the duchess, and Stephan.

Hyde Park, London

Frank chuckled next to Stephan. "Hello? Where *are* you today, Stephan? Surely not in Hyde Park with me."

Stephan looked up at his cousin, who was dressed in his finest riding clothes astride a chestnut stallion and was preening for all the pretty girls walking along the Serpentine. "I'm sorry, I suppose my thoughts have been elsewhere."

"I saw you danced two sets with that little Miss Lloyd at yesterday's ball. Miss Isabel Lloyd, wasn't it? She's pretty enough."

Stephan didn't respond immediately. He struggled to remember the young lady in question, and finally recalled that there was one girl at the ball who had flirted with him so obscenely it would've been rude not to ask her to dance a second set. He hadn't liked her at all.

"No, I was not thinking of her."

Frank's jovial attitude withered a bit. "Come, man. Why not be open with me?"

Stephan smiled. "Because you hardly ever let me get at word in edgewise," he shot back.

"Straight to the heart!" Frank crowed, clutching his chest irreverently. "Come now. Have I not been a friend to you? You've been one to me, I know—have gotten me out of more trouble than I can ever thank you for. But haven't I been a friend to *you*, as well?"

Stephan chuckled. "Indeed, Frank. And if it means that much to you to know, I will freely tell you that the lady on my thoughts is *not* Miss Lloyd."

"There *is* a lady, then. Who is she?"

"Miss Harriet Shore."

Frank drew up his stallion short. His brows formed a heavy line as he thought. Stephan chuckled to himself. He thought about teasing Frank for how difficult a task thinking appeared to be for him, but held back the remark.

"I've heard her name before," Frank finally said, "She's from Burnham, isn't she? Not far from your estate. Wasn't her father a tenant of yours?"

Stephan was surprised. He hadn't recalled ever mentioning Harriet to Frank before. "Yes, her father was a tenant."

"*Was* a tenant? Is he not anymore?"

Stephan grimaced. "For now, yes. But it does not appear he will be my tenant much longer."

Frank drummed his fingers on his horse's pommel, but Stephan said no more, so Frank returned the subject to Harriet. "But if her father was your tenant, she would hardly make an appropriate bride for you."

Stephan looked away and smoothly quickened his mare's pace. "I don't see why not. Her father is a born gentleman."

"A gentleman-turned-farmer? I've never heard of such a thing," Frank scoffed.

Stephan felt his jaw tighten against his will. There was a reason that he rarely told others about his attachment to Harriet. But he was determined that Frank, his favorite family member, could and would be made to understand that he was in earnest.

"She would be an excellent wife," Stephan said, "if I could only convince her to marry me. A true lady. Beautiful, kind, selfless, refined and she has . . ." Stephan felt idiotic trying to supply the words, but he stubbornly drove on, "Her eyes are full of smiles, secrets, and laughter. I honestly can't think how else to describe her."

Frank appeared to bite back a retort. "And what has brought this *Miss Shore* to the front of your mind, my friend?"

Stephan's gaze was far away for a moment. "She is never far from the front of my mind. But the reason I can't seem to think of anything else today is that I *saw* her at Lady Gregor's ball."

"You saw her there? Impossible," Frank said indignantly, his cheeks turning rosy, "Are you claiming that a country farmer's daughter was at one of the most exclusive, most fashionable *ton* functions in London?"

Stephan smiled to himself and spurred his horse faster. "Yes. That is exactly what I'm saying, Frank."

Chapter Fifteen

Curzon Street, London

Harriet giggled. "Oh, tell me your story again. *Please*, Virginia? And do it properly this time!"

Virginia heaved an almighty sigh and looked up at the ceiling, but she couldn't hold back a smile.

"He took my hand and pressed a kiss on the back of it. A jolt ran from my hand to my heart and from my head to my toes, and I knew I was in love. Ralph could have been a fishmonger for all I cared. He was the most wonderful man I'd ever met, and the only one I ever wanted to marry."

"But you knew you couldn't," Harriet finished the sentence for her, sitting cross-legged on Virginia's bed like an eager schoolgirl. "Your parents would never allow it."

"Right you are!" Virginia was getting into the spirit of it. "And so I knew we'd have to run away together."

"Tell me again!" Harriet was nearly hysterical. Mandie was laughing so hard at Harriet's enthusiasm that she was clutching her sides and tears were streaming silently out of her eyes.

"He came to the house just before dawn, when we were all abed, and threw the tiniest of pebbles at my window. I opened the window, and he climbed up to the balcony from the back of his horse. He lowered me onto his gentle stallion using a rope made of bed linens and away we rode!"

Harriet sighed and splayed herself across the bed, allowing her warm brown curls to tumble all over the crumpled blankets.

Virginia took another sip of water from the glass at her bedside and took a deep breath. "He took me directly to the chur—" Virginia bit her lip and hesitated, thinking a moment, "cottage. He took me to his humble cottage by the seaside, where we could hear the waves splashing against the cliffs outside, and there he made me his."

Mandie interrupted her laughter in order to heave an involuntary sigh. "Such a grand romance. I'm not laughing at *you*, milady, but at this ninny over here."

Harriet stuck out a tongue at Mandie and gave her a gentle whack with a pillow.

"I shall never grow tired of that story," Harriet declared, "And I will never stop saying what I've said before—he *will* come for you. I'm sure of it!"

Virginia smiled, but quietly started examining a stray thread on the cuff of her nightgown.

Mandie sat up taller. "If you do not wish to speak of it, we won't, but I must first say that I agree with Harriet—of *course* he will come for you!"

"You are *both* a pair of romantic ninnies!" she laughed, shaking her head and hitting them both with a pillow, only to have them erupt with giggles.

The door burst open then, terrifying the three of them into silence.

"Ladies!" hissed the duchess, "I cannot believe I am hearing the three of you giggling all the way in my own chambers!"

"But mother, your chambers are next-door to mine. It is hardly surprising," protested Virginia.

Harriet swallowed a giggle with great difficulty and tried to seem penitent.

"Be *quiet*," said the duchess with finality. She gave all three of them a piercing look and flounced out of the room.

The giggles died away and the three young women sat together in silence. After a moment, Harriet sat up and fiddled with the fringe on her shawl before speaking. "Does it bother you if I go out walking with Mr. Desford, Virginia?" she asked. "Because if it does, I'll tell him to leave me alone in no uncertain terms."

Virginia shook her head. "Do as you please, Harriet."

"But if he has a reputation as a rake . . ."

Virginia laughed. "I believe I have a bit more of the rebel spirit in my nature than you have, Harriet. I struggle to see why you hesitate."

Harriet frowned. "But why do people say he is a rake? What has he done?"

Virginia's ears turned red—a sure sign she was about to say something impassioned. "Oh, there are more rumors than I can count. That his mother was promiscuous and that he's not his father's real son, that he's seduced young women—the daughter of one of his servants, for example—and left them with child . . . But the rumors aren't consistent. Some will say the daughters of obscure country gentlemen were ruined, others say his maids have children that look like him . . . either all of the rumors are false, or they're all true—there are simply too many to make sense of."

Harriet chewed on her lower lip. "Perhaps I ought to avoid him, then. It sounds as though his reputation is—"

Virginia's nostrils flared. "Heaven knows how much I care about what you do with my reputation while you wield it. It does not matter what the *ton* thinks of him, Harriet—it is up to you to find out what you believe about him. If you wish to be his friend and if you enjoy time spent in his company, then hang what society says!"

Harriet gave a startled little laugh and sat up stiffly, saluting like a soldier. "Yes, milady!"

Palace Court, London

Knowing how difficult it would be to borrow Frank's phaeton, Stephan decided to take a hackney instead. After a few minutes' ride, the driver left him in front of the narrow but elegant town house where Harriet purportedly worked. Stephan mounted the steps two at a time yet again, hoping against hope to catch Harriet for even a few stolen moments' conversation.

She seemed to be absent far more frequently than other governesses he'd heard of. She had not been there the last time he'd checked. Or the time before. Perhaps he ought to stop coming, but until she asked him herself to stop coming, he could not bear to give up his last shred of hope.

Once at the door, he knocked firmly, and a moment later, the housekeeper appeared.

"Oh, it's you again," she said.

Stephan cleared his throat. "I have come to ask after Miss Harriet Shore. Is she in? If so, might I speak with her?"

The servant frowned and gave a little sigh. "I shall see if she is in."

"Thank you. I shall wait here."

The servant nodded and disappeared behind the door again. He looked up and down the street, trying to occupy his mind while he thought of what he ought to say.

Only a minute or two later, the servant's face reappeared in the doorway. "I'm afraid she is not here, sir."

Stephan frowned. *Again?*

"I shall tell her that you came by, sir."

Stephan reached into his pocket for another hastily edited calling card. He checked the card again to be sure the direction was correct—not that he had any hope that a young lady as respectable as Harriet would ever flout society's rules by writing to him directly.

The housekeeper hesitated in the doorway with a sympathetic look before taking the card, bobbing a polite nod, and closing the door.

Stephan turned away from the house feeling downtrodden, wondering for the first time if he ought to abandon his pursuit entirely, and once more in painful suspense of whether or not Harriet would ever forgive him or speak with him again.

Few carriages passed by this way, but westward, at the end of the street, he could see the fence surrounding Kensington Gardens. He was as likely to find a hackney near the park as anywhere else. He walked up the road, crossed the street, and continued walking along it outside Kensington Gardens. At the entrance to the park, an elegant phaeton pulled up bearing a fashionable gentleman and a beautiful young woman.

Stephan stopped, not wishing to pass too near the handsome couple lest he disturb them. As he watched, however, the young woman turned so that Stephan could see her face, and his eyes grew wide.

Harriet.

Chapter Sixteen

Kensington Gardens, London

Mandie was decidedly not a conscientious chaperone. From the instant Harriet, Mr. Desford, and she had entered the park, Mandie had hung back, settled onto a bench, pulled a small book out of her bag, and started to read it. She had long been out of sight. Harriet had been initially pleased at the privacy, but the further from Mandie they became, the more uncomfortable she felt alone with Mr. Desford.

It was a bright and lovely day in late autumn, and Harriet's cheeks were rosy from the cold. Her purple velvet spencer provided the perfect amount of warmth against the chill and her hands clutched a small, elegant ermine muff. Although her bonnet pinched a bit, it protected her against the cool breeze. What few leaves left on the trees were shades of orange and brown, and the sky was almost white with bright clouds completely obscuring the sun. It made all the world look soft and romantic, and set her skin off to best advantage.

"Lady Virginia," Mr. Desford's tone was innocent, "I can't help but feel that there is something . . . different about you this season."

Harriet's heart began to pound rapidly, and suddenly she wished that rain would cut their walk short.

"Something different?" she managed to say, struggling to keep her tone indifferent.

His navy eyes bored into hers, and she noticed as he stepped a little closer that his dark hair curled a bit at his sideburns. She felt the sudden irrational urge to touch them, but merely lifted her chin and stared back at him, even though she could feel her cheeks warming.

He smiled at her, and she took an involuntary step backward.

He laughed. "You used to be so very solemn—the great Lady Virginia Sackville! Always saying exactly what you meant, no more and no less. You used to practically scowl from the edges of a ballroom, frightening away any that might dare ask you to dance."

Harriet frowned. "And I no longer do so?"

Mr. Desford met her eyes with his usual smirk. He shook his head slowly.

Harriet tried to disguise her nerves behind a light laugh. "You're right," she conceded ruefully. "I suppose I am rather . . . different than I was last May."

"Well, I like you this way."

Harriet sneaked a shy glance his way before continuing down the path, looking forward. She did not reply.

"Won't you call me Thomas?" he asked suddenly.

Harriet's heart skipped a beat. "You know my mother would not approve."

"And you do everything your mother tells you, do you?"

Harriet only shook her head. "No, but you've met Her Grace—are *you* willing to cross her?"

"We needn't tell her," he coaxed, stepping so close to her that she could feel his warmth.

Her heart was pounding in her chest. She shook her head. "We are not on familiar enough terms, sir."

"And what terms would those need to be?" Mr. Desford asked playfully.

"Do you *never* relent?" Harriet asked, exasperated.

Thomas leaned in so close that she could feel his breath on her cheek, and his grin was a mischievous one. "No."

Harriet smiled in spite of herself, although she took another step away from him. She sighed again. "Why do you flirt with me so, sir? What am I to you?"

"Oh, and there it is. *There* is the Virginia I remember—diving straight to the point of things. None of these society games. I always did like that about you."

Harriet inhaled sharply. Mr. Desford was so observant that he caught her off-guard time and again. She continued walking along the path, ignoring him. She stopped in front of the pond, staring at the water rippling before her, shimmering like tarnished silver under the bright cloudy sky. Mr. Desford was infuriating and he made her nervous, but he also made her heart throb in the most embarrassing way, and she had to admit to herself that spending time with him was exciting and she couldn't seem to stop.

"I can see what you are thinking," Thomas interrupted her reverie.

She turned to him with a pert little scowl on her rosy lips. *Entirely too observant.* "And what am I thinking?"

His eyes caught hers in a trap, holding her immobile as he neared her. "You are thinking . . . that I am far too handsome to ignore, as you know you ought to."

Harriet gasped. "Of all the arrogant, conceited . . . " she fumed, unsure of how to finish the sentence. He waited patiently for her to continue, the inevitable smirk in his navy eyes as innocent as ever. She would not have been surprised if smoke had issued from her nostrils.

"Surely I'm not so *very* bad?" He gave her a pleading look that did nothing to make him seem more humble.

She pursed her lips, but a moment later she shook her head in disbelief and a laugh slipped out in spite of herself. Mr. Desford laughed, too, and Harriet couldn't help but admire the sound of it. It was robust, and seemed to bubble up from deep within him.

"My mother does not approve of you, Mr. Desford."

"Yes, that was fairly obvious. Though I do not consider that problem insurmountable."

Harriet shook her head. "Displeasing my mother is never pleasant for me. I always need to be prepared to sustain a long, hard fight if I ever hope to win."

"And would you fight for *me*?" he batted his eyelashes at her.

She glanced heavenward, changing the subject. "Tell me, Mr. Desford . . . Why *should* my mother disapprove of you?"

Mr. Desford froze for an instant, relaxed. He chuckled lightly. "Well, my dear Lady Virginia, I *am* a notorious rake."

Harriet's heart began to pound faster, and she stumbled slightly as she took a hasty step away from him, looking about for Mandie. They should never have left her sight. Where was she?

"Come now!" Mr. Desford smiled. "You've nothing to fear from me, my lady. I assure you my intentions toward you are strictly honorable."

Harriet frowned at him as they continued walking together.

"And . . . how does one become a notorious rake, exactly?" she asked innocently.

Mr. Desford sighed. "Why, by setting my sights on ladies that outrank me and by flirting outrageously with them all."

"I do not see how that is so very disreputable," Harriet wondered if he could possibly be telling her the truth. She could not exactly ask him outright if he had ruined innocent young ladies from the country or taken advantage of his female servants.

Mr. Desford smiled. "Nor do I, but it is decidedly unfashionable."

Harriet sighed. "I am growing tired of that word."

Mr. Desford laughed again and the gathering tension dissipated. "Again, something I've always liked about you."

"I suppose that is something that has not changed?"

"Indeed." He smiled at her, and their conversation moved down more innocent avenues. They talked about the Verdi opera that Harriet had finally seen. They had both enjoyed it, and talked animatedly about the various performers.

Once Harriet had grown comfortable again, the time sped by, and before she knew it, Mandie was walking up to her. Harriet's smile slipped instantly from her face. "We've been walking too long, Mr. Desford. I am expected at home."

"A shame, my lady."

The carriage ride home was just as pleasant as the rest of the walk before it. When they pulled up in Curzon Street she nodded to him in farewell and began to walk away, but Mr. Desford took her hand in his, stopping her. He raised her hand to his mouth and kissed the air above it. A shiver of pleasure ran up her arm and she pulled her hand away as quickly as she could politely do so, clearing her throat lightly.

"I hope to see you again soon, Lady Virginia."

She gave a quick curtsy. "Farewell, Mr. Desford."

He smiled and tipped his hat as she turned and sped up the steps to the house with Mandie at her side.

"My goodness, he's absolutely smitten!" Mandie exclaimed. "What on earth did you do to the poor man?"

"I have no idea," Harriet said faintly.

"It doesn't sound like you're complaining," Mandie pointed out.

Harriet didn't say anything, but barely resisted the urge to turn back and look at Mr. Desford once more. She was already excited to see him again, even though she knew she should not be.

Palace Court, London

As soon as Harriet had returned to the Donahues' that afternoon, her finery left behind at the grand house on Curzon Street, Mrs. Green came to speak with her, frowning. "Your young man called on you again today. Mr. Grimsby. Are you ever going to return his visits, miss?" She held out a calling card to Harriet.

Harriet took the card, turning it over in her hands and admiring Stephan's hurried penmanship, ink blots and all. "Yes, I am."

"Hmm," the housekeeper said. "Mrs. Donahue is not fond of those in her employ taking social calls whilst they are working."

"Of course not," Harriet said quickly. "I would never wish to over-step my bounds."

With a brisk nod, Mrs. Green left her alone with her thoughts. As Harriet walked slowly up the steps with the card, her mind was whiz-zing. Stephan was in town, as his card clearly indicated. She really could have seen him at Lady Gregor's ball not a fortnight before. Why was he in London? The hopeful thought that he had come all the way to London just to visit *her* was checked by recalling the original name on the card that had been blotted out. "That's right," she murmured to herself, "his cousin lives in town. He has come to visit *him*."

But knowing that Stephan was only a few blocks away from her made her heart pound. She hesitated outside the door to the nursery, thinking. One part of her—the larger part—had a hard time remembering why she left Burnham-on-Sea in the first place, and wanted to see Stephan again as soon as possible. Another part of her held her back. She had never sent a letter to an unrelated gentleman before. Her mother had always told her that sending private letters to a gentleman was inappropriate unless she was engaged to him. Her respectability had always been paramount to her because, without it, any hope of marrying Stephan, however small, would immediately vanish.

But there was another reason stopping her, and with a sinking feeling, she realized it was pride. Cinderella had run away from her prince instead of toward him when her ball gown had disappeared and she was dressed once more as a servant. Sitting there in her plain, ink-smeared day dress, Harriet suddenly understood how Cinderella must have felt as the clock struck twelve.

Chapter Seventeen

Westbourne Terrace, London

Frank groaned again. "Stephan, *really*. He is a dreadful bore."

Stephan sighed in near surrender. "I beg you, Frank."

Frank's face became resigned, if still skeptical. "You want to meet the man that much? I *cannot* believe it. Andrew Brougham never speaks of anything but birds and is dull enough to make our rector fall asleep—I don't stand a chance. Tell me. What is your real intention? Why are you so determined to meet him?"

Stephan sat down on the sofa next to Frank, but failed to meet eyes with him. He cleared his throat, fiddling with his pocket watch. "It is for a lady," he admitted.

Frank grinned and cupped his cheek in his hand, his elbow leaning on the back of the sofa. "You're charming, Stephan. Truly charming. You thought that would be enough for me? You are very funny, Stephan."

Stephan laughed. "Fine. If you absolutely *must* know, it is so I can make the acquaintance of the Duke of Dorset's daughter, Lady Virginia."

To say Frank looked surprised was an understatement. "You must be joking. Or mad. Are you mad? Even I would never *dream* of pursuing the Duke of Dorset's daughter, and my father's fairly well set up. Our estates are *nothing* to His Grace's! They'd as soon spit in my face as encourage my suit! You've far more courage than I do, Stephan."

Stephan's heart thudded in his chest and he glared at Frank. "Thank you for the vote of confidence." He spoke with biting sarcasm.

Frank narrowed his eyes and shook his head. "This . . . this seems unlike you, Stephan. One moment you're pining for a commoner back home, and the next you're throwing a line out to the biggest fish in the London marriage mart? Her fortune has to be at least fifty thousand pounds! You've clearly never been taught the value of a happy medium."

"It isn't for her fortune," Stephan quickly said. "If you must know . . . she very strongly resembles my good friend Miss Shore."

Frank seemed skeptical. "She looks like . . . your farmer's daughter?"

Stephan finally looked Frank in the eyes. "Exactly the same."

Frank shook his head, his mouth gaping slightly. "I must say . . ."

"Call it what you will, Frank—courage, desperation, morbid curiosity—but I *must* try it."

Frank laughed. "And Brougham is the way to get to her?"

Stephan nodded. "When last we went to White's, I saw their names together in the betting book. Most of the money says they will be married by the end of the season. I assume that means they are at least acquainted already."

"You must be joking. It says that about *Brougham*?"

"Yes. So, you see, I have to make his acquaintance."

"To attempt to steal his fiance."

"Yes," Stephan shook his head. "I mean, no. They aren't even engaged yet! It would have been in the society papers."

Frank laughed again, so hard that Stephan frowned at him impatiently and crossed his arms until he'd finished.

"There. I've thoroughly explained myself," Stephan said. "Now will you *please* make the introduction?"

Frank leaned back into the sofa cushions with one of the biggest smirks Stephan had ever seen. "You are so desperate for this woman that you're willing to befriend one of the biggest bores in London in order to meet someone who *looks* like her? You're hopeless, man!"

"Don't speak to me of hopeless, Frank. You've been unable to think or speak of anything but your darling Miss Stepney for well over a week. Come! Introduce me to this Brougham fellow and let's have a game of piquet while we are at it. He frequents White's, does he not?"

Frank wrinkled his nose. "Piquet? With Brougham?" He said nothing further, though, and proceeded to ready himself for the club.

Stephan stood and straightened his suit coat in preparation to leave his aunt's house. He was not exactly happy to befriend someone who was supposedly the biggest bore in London, and he was even less thrilled that he needed Frank's begrudging help to do it, but he was determined to unravel this mystery.

After a few minutes being prepared by his valet, and another good laugh or two at Stephan's expense, Frank was ready to leave and the two of them climbed into Frank's phaeton. Stephan sighed as he once more admired the beautifully matched pair of bays that Frank would never let him drive. Even when he'd borrowed the phaeton, he'd needed to use their common carriage-horses. As they both perched on the high seat, Frank handed the reins to Stephan.

"I'll let you drive if we can put off meeting Brougham for another time."

Stephan was not tempted. He refused the reins with a shake of his head, and Frank let out a small sigh. "It was worth a try, wasn't it?"

They arrived at the club in record time, thanks to Frank's hapless, speedy driving.

Frank immediately started drifting toward the faro tables as soon as they had entered. "Should you not like a game of faro first, Stephan?"

Stephan shook his head with a frown. "I am not interested in cards right now. Perhaps we could practice fencing, instead?"

The casual threat worked marvels. Frank knew he hadn't a prayer of beating Stephan in the practice ring. "Ah, look. It's my old friend Andrew Brougham. Have the two of you already been introduced?"

"Why no, we have not. Will you do me the honor?"

"Andrew!" Frank called, sounding a little hurried. The two of them walked over to Mr. Brougham.

"Frank! It's been ages. How have you been? Might I interest you in a game of piquet?"

Frank's frown slowly melted into a smile, as if an idea had suddenly occurred to him. "Indeed! Let's have a game, shall we?"

Stephan swallowed his laughter. It was clear that Frank had just recalled that Mr. Brougham was terrible at piquet and his own pockets were empty for the quarter. Before they could have a seat at a table, Stephan cleared his throat.

"Ah, and have you met my cousin Stephan?" Frank asked quickly.

Mr. Brougham shook his head and Stephan stepped forward, taking the man's proffered hand. "Stephan Grimsby of Somerset."

"I'm Andrew Brougham, of Suffolk. Pleasure to meet any friend of Frank's."

Stephan smiled. "Shall we have a game of piquet, then? You two play, and I shall distract you both."

The three young men spent the better part of the next two hours playing at cards. Frank was pleased because he managed to win a generous wad of cash from Andrew. Andrew was pleased because he seemed to like being considered a friend of Frank and Stephan's, and Stephan was pleased because Andrew had cheerfully agreed to introduce him to Lady Virginia at the next ball they all attended.

Westbourne Terrace, London

"What think you of this neckcloth?" Frank was staring at himself in the mirror as he spoke, poking and prodding an elaborately tied cravat.

Stephan glanced over. "You look ridiculous."

Frank glared back. "Well, *your* tired old knot is a full season out of fashion."

Stephan nodded. "It likely is. I am less experimental than you are."

Frank frowned and turned his attention to the rest of Stephan's clothes. "Is *that* what you are wearing to this evening's ball?"

Stephan laughed. "Of course not. 'Tis barely three o'clock! Why should I be already preparing for an engagement six hours away?"

"Your brown suit fits you ill, you know."

Stephan folded his arms. "Then I shall wear the gray."

"Would you like me to loan you a fob or two?"

Stephan pursed his lips in thought. "Perhaps one," he relented.

Frank nodded, looking triumphant.

A light knock at the door signaled the arrival of a servant, who entered silently, approaching Stephan with a letter on a small silver tray.

His eyebrows flicked upward as he broke the seal on the missive and pored over its contents. It did not take long for some of the color to drain from his cheeks.

"I shall not require the loan of a fob this evening." He was already at the door as he spoke. "For I have urgent business at my estate to attend to."

"You'll not be at the ball this evening? But what of your introduction to Lady Virginia?"

Stephan grimaced. "As much as it pains me, it will have to wait."

Less than an hour later, Stephan's valise was packed and hired a post chaise to convey him back home. But before he could leave London, there was one more thing he needed to do. He took a hackney directly to Palace Court.

The Donahue's housekeeper sighed when she saw who was at the door. "You again?"

"Yes. Me." Stephan said apologetically.

"You ever think it's possible she does not *wish* to see you, sir?"

Stephan frowned. "I worry about that every day, but I care too much for her to surrender so easily."

The housekeeper's face softened. "I am sorry that she is not here."

Stephan's forehead knit in thought before he spoke. "I don't suppose you could take a message for me?"

The housekeeper frowned. "For a governess?"

Stephan nodded eagerly.

The housekeeper sighed and relented with a small smile. "What would you have me tell her?"

Stephan thought for a moment before starting in. "Tell her that I am sorry I was not able to see her before I had to leave London to conduct a few affairs of my estate. I do not quite know when I will return, but it will likely not be until the new year."

The housekeeper blinked several times. "Your estate, eh?" She cleared her throat and suddenly became much more polite. "I shall be sure she receives the message."

"I would indeed be grateful." He tipped his hat to the housekeeper, who flushed a little and dropped a quick curtsy to him.

Curzon Street, London

"You're certain my passing time with Mr. Desford does not bother you?" Harriet asked for what seemed the hundredth time.

Virginia sighed. "It *doesn't*, Harriet, I promise you!" She was growing exasperated.

Harriet chewed on her lower lip, and Virginia narrowed her eyes. "For the sake of my wounded pride, if nothing else, go ahead and make that proud, rakish dandy grovel at your feet!"

Harriet laughed in spite of herself. "I do enjoy spending time with him, but I also . . . cannot help but compare him to Stephan."

Virginia smiled. "And how does he fare next to your childhood sweetheart?"

Harriet sighed. "Very poorly, I'm afraid. You know Stephan came by the Donahues' to ask after me? And not just once, either."

"And what did he say?"

Harriet looked down at the ground. "I was not there when he came by."

"Did you not write him a note?"

Harriet's cheeks flushed. "My mother has always told me that it is not respectable for a lady to write notes to a gentleman she is not courting."

"So court him! Didn't he offer it? Why are you being so missish about this?" Mandie's brow wrinkled as she spoke.

"I . . . it's hard to explain. His mother disapproves, of course, and—"

Virginia gave a little snort. "What can *she* do?"

Harriet shrugged. She did not know if Virginia would understand her Cinderella-like feelings. "She called me a fortune-hunter. And a hussy. Between that and the feelings of inferiority I already have about our difference in stations . . ."

"She *said* that?" Mandie was shocked. "What a pig!"

"She wishes him to marry a young lady of fortune. Because their estate is troubled." Harriet could not meet their eyes.

Virginia growled. "Yes, you've told me this. And it's no less hypocritical now than it was the last time."

Harriet felt her face flushing. She pulled her knees up in front of her and buried her face behind them. "Aside from this little . . . venture, I have always been so careful to be respectable and obedient. Always! And it has never been enough." She sighed and there was a heavy pause before she continued. "But Stephan really *ought* to marry a young lady of fortune—their estate is in debt, and I would not have him lose it for my sake."

Both Mandie and Virginia fell silent. After a moment, Harriet felt Virginia's hand in her long, curly hair, smoothing out some of the tangles. "All will be well, Harriet. You'll see. Stephan is a fool if he can't see past his mother's disapproval of you to the wonderful person that you are."

"But I could not ask him to sacrifice both his mother's approval *and* the welfare of his estate for me."

Mandie chuckled. "You're far less selfish than I am, Harriet! No one can say you are without scruples."

Virginia frowned at Harriet. "All the same, though, you ought to let the man decide for himself. He's a grown man."

Harriet looked up at Virginia with hesitation and reached for her hand. "Thank you, Virginia. I will . . . think about it. But I cannot promise to become as brave as you are overnight."

Virginia laughed and settled into a smiled. "You flatter me, Harriet. You are far braver than I in many ways."

Palace Court, London

"You had a visitor yesterday, Miss Shore," Mrs. Green told her as soon as she'd returned to the Donahues' the next day.

"Oh?"

"A Mr. Stephan Grimsby of Somerset again. That makes the fourth time the poor man's come by, miss, and you not being here or seeing him."

Harriet nodded. "I . . . yes. I am sorry to inconvenience you." She turned to walk back up the stairs to the nursery.

"It's not my inconvenience, miss, so much as his."

"Did he leave a message for me by chance?"

Mrs. Green stood up straight. "Aye. That he was sorry he'd not been able to see you while in London. He's gone back to conduct affairs of his estate."

"For the rest of the season?"

"He did not say, but he said he wouldn't return until sometime in the new year."

Harriet took a deep breath to try to slow her pounding heart. "Thank you for letting me know."

As she slowly climbed the stairs, she allowed her waiting tears to fall. He had come and gone, and she had not written. What had she done? Was it too late? What would've happened if Cinderella had run too far and too fast for her prince to catch her? Or perhaps he did not *wish* to catch her. Little thoughts, all beginning with "what if" haunted her throughout the girls' lessons, through mealtime, and late into the night.

Chapter Eighteen

Burnham-on-Sea, Somerset

Time passed. For Stephan it intermittently dragged and raced by. When he was spending time with his mother, time was impossibly sluggish. She inevitably found an excuse to speak disparagingly of Harriet and talk instead about all the different young ladies of her acquaintance that she wanted Stephan to consider.

When he was working to arrange Harriet's father's acquisition, however—speaking with tenants, drafting contracts with his attorney, and seeing to the affairs of his estate—the time sped by. It always seemed that there was too much to do and too little time with which to do it. But he always called Harriet's face to mind, and reminded himself that the greatest prize he hoped to win by the sacrifice of his family lands was that of being able to look into her lovely golden brown eyes every day and call her his.

His mother had wheedled for him to stay at home and pass Christmas and the New Year with his neighbors and family, but the celebrations were hollow. The annual village Christmas party was lacking the one familiar face he'd always looked forward to seeing in the past. He did not spend much time at idle social gatherings, however. There was so much to do before he could pronounce the whole business finished that, even working as hard as he could, more than six weeks passed before he found a chance to return to London.

A week into the new year, Stephan was finally ready to return to town.

"Do promise me you'll visit those young ladies I told you about, Stephan!"

"I shall earnestly try *not* to, though I cannot promise to succeed in my attempt."

His mother smiled and nodded, but paused as the true meaning of his words began to register, and her expression became sour as he leaned forward to kiss her cheek.

"Farewell, Mother! Take care not to spend too much money while I am away."

Mrs. Grimsby was still glaring at him as he climbed into the carriage and drove off.

Curzon Street to Harley Street, London

"Virginia?" the duchess called. "We are going to be late. Come down at once."

Harriet continued to stare out the window while Mandie hurried to finish the last details of her coiffure. Virginia gave a little sigh and continued working on the tiny baby bonnet she had been sewing as the duchess swept into the room, a vision in deep red satin.

"What is taking so long?" she snapped.

"Finished! And look how lovely her hair turned out this evening." Mandie was panting slightly as she gestured.

The duchess's mood immediately brightened as she took in Harriet's elegant appearance in powder blue silk, her chestnut hair piled high on her head in perfect little ringlets, baby's breath tucked here and there. "My dear, you *do* look very nice. Only your neck wants pearls. Come, and I will loan you some of mine."

The duchess's attention swiveled back to Virginia and she wrinkled her nose in disgust. "You are positively *enormous*, Virginia."

Virginia's cheeks turned a humiliated crimson and Harriet felt a pang of sympathy for her. She followed the duchess out of the room with considerably less enthusiasm than she'd had before.

It had been a long couple of months for Harriet. Never had she been away from her parents for such a long time, let alone for the holiday season, and it had been a melancholy one for her. She was far from her family and dear friends, and her hopes were gloomier than ever. The pervasive gray skies of London seemed to seep deeper into her heart the longer Stephan was away. A cowardly part of her wished to resign herself to his loss, and to a long life as a governess, but another part of her continued to hope for a distant future with Stephan. And as long as there was hope, the edge of the pain remained sharp.

The duchess chose a necklace and clasped it around Harriet's neck for her. During the carriage ride to the ball, Harriet tried to respond normally as the duchess hypocritically prattled on about Mrs. So-and-So's scandalous daughter with relish.

Her eyes found the window again and stared out into the night. The duchess had been less and less kind to her daughter the larger she grew. Harriet didn't approve of her poor treatment, but what could she do? If the duchess had always possessed this smothering, controlling personality, it was little wonder that Virginia had been miserable in her old life and had sought a change. Harriet admitted to herself that she had judged her far too quickly—she hadn't said anything, but had found Virginia's behavior scandalous when she'd first heard of it. The longer she wore her identity, however, the more she realized that she had no idea what she may have done had her situation and Virginia's been reversed.

"Virginia?" the duchess asked, prompting a response from a distracted Harriet.

"Yes, indeed, Mama." She had lost the thread of the conversation and hoped that was an appropriate response.

The duchess seemed satisfied and continued gossiping cheerfully for the duration of the ride.

Harriet's mind turned to the duke. It was little wonder that she and the duke had become so distanced. From her few meetings with His Grace, she had noticed a similar personality to Virginia's. He would frequently withdraw when he became overwhelmed at social gatherings, ignoring proper social graces in order to do so. Perhaps the duchess's overbearing personality had affected *him*, as well. Harriet frowned, and did not speak another word until they pulled up to the curb and the footman helped them down.

As they mounted the steps to the elegant mansion on Harley Street where Mrs. Grantham's ball that evening was held, the duchess said, "Now, Virginia, my dear, be sure to dance at *least* two with Mr. Brougham this evening."

Harriet agreed that she would dance with him. Mr. Brougham had the happy fortune of being the Duchess of Dorset's preferred choice for her daughter, Virginia. His behavior was thoroughly respectable, he came from a thoroughly respectable family, and he had a thoroughly respectable fortune to inherit. He was young, moderately handsome, and polite. The duchess had admitted to thinking him rather dull company, but considered this a point in his favor, as she had always found Virginia rather dull company, as well.

Harriet had passed plenty of time with both Mr. Desford and Mr. Brougham over the last several weeks, including the absurd crush of parties and visits that accompanied the Christmas season. Mr. Brougham *did* seem to enjoy passing time with her, but she had to be very careful not to yawn when he began discussing wildlife.

As they walked into the ballroom, Harriet immediately began scouting the room for people she knew. If she had been honest with herself, she might have admitted that she was looking for Stephan. Ever since the new year, she had anxiously scanned each face in every crowd in the hopes of seeing him.

"Lady Virginia," a voice said behind her.

She turned around, thinking it was Mr. Desford, but it was only Mr. Brougham. She tried to mask her disappointment. "Oh. Good evening, Mr. Brougham."

"Lovely to see you again. May I have the honor of the next dance?"

Harriet managed a cheerful smile and accepted, thanking him graciously. They chatted for a few minutes, mostly about how moderate a winter it had been thus far. Harriet, in seeking a clock, caught a glimpse of the duchess, who made eye contact and smiled approvingly. Harriet forced a smile in return and turned her attention back to Mr. Brougham. She still tried to please the duchess, but could not stop thinking about how unkindly the duchess had been treating Virginia lately. Christmas had come and gone—Harriet had been masquerading for over three months—and Virginia's spirits had steadily fallen as her belly had grown.

If she was honest with herself, however, it wasn't just the duchess's behavior that disgusted her, but the attitude of the general *ton*. The more time she spent in society, the more she began to recognize the insincerity of those about her. She had heard society matrons compliment a young lady to her face and then immediately turn to one another and spread vicious rumors about her. She had seen young men act the part of devoted swain to multiple young ladies at once, and had overheard them saying vulgar things about the young ladies in private. She recognized she was not the only one who was playing a part, and she began to wonder if she would ever find a place where she—*Harriet*—could truly belong, and drop all of these pretenses.

Harriet was so distracted by this reverie that she missed a step or two as they danced, and even the oblivious Mr. Brougham began to notice how distant she seemed. The moment the dance ended he offered to fetch her a glass of punch.

"Yes, thank you." She closed her eyes and vigorously fanned herself. She needed to return to the present. She tried forcing Virginia out of her mind, but the only other face she could conjure was Stephan's. And that did nothing to calm her.

"You must be thinking something fascinating, my lady," a voice said at her elbow. "I do wish I knew what it was."

Harriet blinked and opened her eyes. "Mr. Desford." She did not bother to hide the fact that she was pleased to see him.

"What a warm welcome." He slid onto the chair next to hers. "Are you already engaged for the next dance?"

"Not yet, Mr. Desford, although I probably ought to dance it with Mr. Brougham."

His nose wrinkled with distaste. "So, is there *any* room left on that dance card of yours for this evening?"

She scowled. Was he mocking her? It was always so difficult to tell. "Of course there is. I've only just arrived."

"And can you spare a single dance for your humble servant?" he asked, fluttering his eyelashes innocently.

She rolled her eyes. "As I have for every ball we've both attended this season, yes."

He took her hand. "Excellent. Because you are by far the loveliest woman in attendance—at this ball as well as at all the others." He kissed the back of her hand—barely grazing her glove with his lips.

She could feel her cheeks flush, but she smiled in spite of herself. "I certainly shan't dance with you if you insist on flattering me so!"

Mr. Desford smiled, and Harriet felt a little twinge of guilt rise up—not only because she was enjoying herself while Virginia remained caged and lonely, but because Stephan was never far from her thoughts. She wondered what he was doing at that moment.

"Er, hello again," Mr. Brougham stopped in front of Harriet and Mr. Desford. He looked back and forth between them. Mr. Desford looked up at Mr. Brougham with something of a challenge in his eyes.

Mr. Brougham thrust the little cup of punch he had gotten for Harriet into her hands with almost enough force to splash her immaculate white gloves with the red liquid. "I hope I'm not intruding," he said awkwardly. "If I am, I can return later . . ."

A throat cleared meaningfully behind Mr. Brougham, and Mr. Brougham seemed to find his determination at the sound of it. "Ah, right. I'd nearly forgotten. Lady Virginia, if I may be so bold, I wanted to introduce you to my new friend: Mr. Stephan Grimsby."

Chapter Nineteen

Harley Street, London

Stephan stepped forward and took Harriet's hand in one smooth, fluid motion. Harriet could not speak, and could not stop a shocked smile from spreading across her face. Her eyes were riveted to the most lovely, familiar sight she could imagine, and for a second she wondered if she were dreaming. The emotion surging in her chest caught her off guard. She knew she should be as cool and uninterested as Lady Virginia would be, yet seeing Stephan once more, so close to her, looking right into her eyes, she was overwhelmed by a wave of homesickness and longing.

"I am honored to meet you, Lady Virginia." He bowed over her hand and she swallowed hard. Her heart was pounding, her mouth dry, and she could not speak.

Mr. Desford looked back and forth between Harriet and Stephan with a frown, but he said nothing.

"I had hoped to be so bold as to ask a dance of you during the course of the evening, Lady Virginia," Stephan said softly, his gaze slowly lifting until it met hers.

Her breath caught, and she suddenly returned to the present, just in time to remain silent and hold back the squeak of delight she would have uttered had she been less guarded. She managed a cool smile and reined back her racing heart. "I would be happy to oblige you," she gave a dignified nod.

The current dance was coming to a close. Harriet took a sip of punch as Mr. Desford stood up next to her and held out a hand to escort her to the floor. "Lady Virginia, if you would honor me with this next dance?"

She frowned at his persistence and glanced over at Mr. Brougham, but he was not looking back at her. Her heart still pounding, she took a hurried sip of punch before she allowed Mr. Desford to lead her to the floor.

She resisted the urge—she wasn't quite certain how—to look back at Stephan as she walked away from him, and focused instead on the smooth shave next to Mr. Desford's dark, perfectly trimmed sideburns. She frowned slightly as she realized that, in the *ton*'s eyes, at least, Mr. Desford was clearly the superior specimen of the three—Mr. Brougham was awkward and reserved, and when compared to the two London gentlemen Stephan looked sadly shabby and out of fashion.

She still felt the same attraction to Mr. Desford that she had whenever they were together. How could she not? He was handsome, charming, and paid her far too much attention. But the knowledge that Stephan was there, in the same room as she, and treating her like the daughter of a duchess . . . it was utterly overwhelming.

She mentally gave herself a little shake. Although her pounding heart may argue otherwise, she knew that Stephan's presence here was not a good one. As a country squire's son he was barely worthy of Virginia's notice, let alone a dance with her. And he was one of the only people in the world who knew Harriet well enough to guess her secret.

Perhaps Harriet could find an excuse not to dance with him. As she swirled about the floor, her hand clasped in Mr. Desford's, she caught a glimpse of Stephan at the edge of the floor and the knowledge that she ought to refuse him melted away as ice would in the hot sun. Other thoughts at the back of her mind were also held at bay—that she ought to spend her evening with Mr. Brougham instead of chatting with Mr. Desford. That she ought not to dance with Stephan at all, or pass time in conversation with him. But she was tired of acting against her own will, and surely giving in to her heart's desires for *one* night would not hurt.

"Tell me what you are thinking," Mr. Desford commanded, his deep blue eyes beckoning for her to sink into them once more.

Harriet smiled at Mr. Desford, too exhilarated to be anything but honest. "I am thinking that this ball is lovely. I am happy to make Stephan's acquaintance, and I am happy that I am dancing with you, too."

Mr. Desford seemed surprised. "Stephan? An intimate address for a first meeting." A muscle twitched in his jaw, the only sign that he was displeased.

Harriet's cheeks burned at her error and she said nothing.

"It seems the two of you have met before."

"I've a young cousin named Stephan he vaguely resembles," Harriet lied coolly. "It was an honest mistake. Pray do not mention it again."

Mr. Desford obediently remained silent, and Harriet looked about anxiously for something to distract him. When she caught a glimpse of the Earl of Davenport, her eye sparkled. "Did you notice, Mr. Desford, that this evening the Earl of Davenport appears to be making a most impressive conquest?"

Mr. Desford craned his neck to look at the Earl's lovely young partner and barked out a laugh. "There she is—you are one of a kind, Lady Virginia. I'm glad they haven't found anyone else to replace you."

Harriet's eyes widened at Mr. Desford's accidental stumbling onto the truth, and she was grateful the dance dictated she turn from him for a moment. Perhaps giving in to her own desires *was* dangerous. She determined not to break character for the rest of the evening.

She quashed the optimism rising within herself and pulled Virginia's usual stoic cynicism about her like a cloak. Whenever she was not being sarcastic, she only spoke in monosyllables.

As the dance wound to a close, she curtsied to Mr. Desford and left his side.

"Only one dance, Lady Virginia? Come now, let us dance another."

Harriet shook her head as she left the dance floor. "You know very well my mother does not want me to fall—to pass too much time with you."

The corner of his lip twitched. "To fall? What were you going to say, dearest Lady Virginia?" his voice managed to stay just shy of mocking.

Harriet could feel her cheeks warming, but she did not respond.

"To fall in love with me?" he asked, leaning closer.

Harriet ignored her blushes and lifted her chin in defiance. "Naturally she would not desire that."

He took a step even closer to her, so close that she caught the scent of him—a clean, masculine smell of snuff and soap. Her heart beat rapidly as he murmured in her ear. "And are you in any danger of falling in love with me, Lady Virginia?"

A throat was cleared next to them. "Lady Virginia, is Mr. Desford irritating you? Because it seems as though he is standing unusually close to you." Mr. Brougham looked concerned and Stephan, standing next to him, had an unreadable expression on his face.

Harriet stepped away, but could only manage to say, "I am quite well, Mr. Brougham. Mr. Desford was just leaving." She looked at him pointedly until he obeyed.

Before she could so much as think of what Lady Virginia *ought* to have done next, Stephan walked up and held out a hand to her. "May I claim you for this next dance, Lady Virginia? If you are not engaged?"

Harriet placed her hand in his without thinking and nodded silently, enjoying the pleasant little shiver that passed through her at his touch.

They did not speak as the dance began. Harriet did not know how she would keep her wits about her while she could feel Stephan's strong, familiar hand through her satin glove.

Looking at him now, through the newly acquired lens of the Duke of Dorset's daughter, Harriet was surprised at what she saw.

She had always considered him elegant, glamorous, and miles above her back in Somerset, but compared to those of the other London bachelors, his suit was shabby and ill-fitted. His cravat was plain, not tied into one of the fashionable, starched knots of the season, and his thin, dust-colored hair was trimmed very close instead of emulating the latest full-headed hairstyles. His nose was on the larger side, and his lips were thin, so different from the full, pink lips of Lord Byron that the ladies exclaimed over.

So why was it, then, that Harriet's heart swelled in size and warmed at the very sight of him? Could it be the familiar twinkle in his bright blue eyes? The noble profile? The strong chin? She would look at him one moment and need to catch her breath, and look at him the next, comparing him directly with Mr. Desford or any other of the more dashing young men of fashion and realize she ought to feel embarrassed to be seen with someone dressed so shabbily.

The realization that Stephan was so far below Virginia brought on a wave of sadness. Even living a fantasy, they could never be together. She was tired of playing this part that was so very different from her own. She was tired of gossiping and saying rude things about other people, tired of listening to the duchess's endless monologue about the imperfections of the *ton*'s members, and tired of allowing her own desires and opinions to be swallowed up into her role. She only held this high position because she was masquerading as another woman. Of herself, she was nothing—far below Stephan in rank.

She had a very real idea now of what it could feel like to lower oneself for a loved one, and was hit by a fresh wave of disappointment. She was far too low to be courted by Stephan. But he *had* mentioned courtship, had he not? Could he truly be willing to consider making such an inferior connection even now? And could she possibly permit him to sink so low?

"Tell me what you are thinking, Har—er, Lady Virginia," he murmured, stumbling over her pretended name.

Harriet's stomach nearly leapt to her throat. She looked around to see if anyone had heard his near-mistake. She couldn't resist probing, even though she knew she oughtn't.

"What was that?"

"I, er . . . forgive me, but you look quite a bit like a friend of mine. A Miss Shore of Burnham-on-Sea."

Harriet simultaneously felt excited and terrified at his frankness. The terror won out and in response she heightened the haughtiness of her portrayal of Lady Virginia. "I've never heard of that place. How quaint-sounding. Where is it located?"

Stephan flushed. "It is in Somerset. Between Bristol and Exeter."

Harriet nodded. She felt guilty for making Stephan feel uncomfortable, but she also felt safer keeping him at a distance. "Tell me more of your friend Harriet."

Stephan frowned, and stared at her. The dance forced them to turn away from one another for a few seconds, but his eyes followed her nonetheless.

She swallowed so hard she could have sworn the entire room heard it. "What is it?"

"I never mentioned the name Harriet," he said.

Harriet laughed in what she hoped was a confident manner. "Oh, silly me! I only thought you mentioned it. Only did you not say something like 'Hair'? What other feminine name begins that way, pray?"

Stephan continued to look at her curiously. "Indeed." He was silent, focused on the dance, but the kind of thoughts likely to be in his head at that moment made Harriet nervous.

"And have you been amused in town since you arrived?" she tried to keep her air as bored and disinterested as she thought Virginia's would have been. It proved difficult.

"I am certain my comings and goings would not interest you, my lady. I am only in town visiting a sister of my mother's. Most of my time has been spent with my aunt and her family. I have a cousin of my age with whom I spend most leisure time."

Harriet nodded, and could think of nothing more to say. Fortunately, Stephan spoke again before long.

"Do you not tire of the smoky city streets, Lady Virginia? I own that although I occasionally crave the excitement of Town, when I am here, I find myself yearning for the quiet, green landscape of home."

"The streets *are* smoky," she agreed, her mind already walking the paths of Burnham-on-Sea on Stephan's arm. She recalled their kiss that fateful day she decided to leave and looked away from Stephan. Perhaps she should not have left in the first place. She had never considered herself a coward, but her avoidance of him before leaving Burnham-on-Sea was not exactly courageous. She could remember feeling trapped, and having a desperate need to be free—to escape her surroundings. But her attempt at escape had left her no more free than before.

As realization struck her, she recalled her regrets after Stephan's last visit to the Donahues'. She could not escape her circumstances. She knew that now. No matter how far away she ran, where she went, or what she did, she could never escape them. She had two choices. She could resign herself to her circumstances, or try to change them.

The dance began winding to a close, and Harriet was torn between intense relief and anguish that Stephan would leave her side once more. But she was not herself, and could not act as she wished while wearing Lady Virginia's identity. Knowing this, she steeled herself to bid him farewell.

"I thank you for the dance, sir." She only held his hand as long as strictly necessary before pulling out her fan and fluttering it quickly before her face as she hurried from the dance floor. She caught a glimpse of the duchess out of the corner of her eye and made her way directly toward her without a backward glance. It took all of her will-power to do so.

Chapter Twenty

The Fencing Academy, Bond Street, London

Stephan parried Frank's advance and thrust his foil into Frank's chest, the tip of the practice blade bending as contact was made.

"Ah! You have bested me again!" Frank's cheeks were red. "Come, another match!" He swished his sword in invitation.

Stephan was only slightly out of breath, but noted with some annoyance that the vigorous exercise did nothing to distract his mind from thoughts of Harriet and Lady Virginia.

The more he thought of the two, the more the resemblances struck him. Harriet had a small freckle over her right eyebrow, although the rest of her face was mostly free of them. Lady Virginia looked identical to Harriet right down to that small freckle and the little dimple that appeared in her left cheek when she smiled. He knew his suspicion that Harriet and Lady Virginia were one and the same was outlandish, but he could think of no other explanation for such a perfect resemblance. And how had she guessed the name Harriet?

Frank grew tired of waiting for Stephan's response and thrust forward with his foil, only to have Stephan snap from his reverie and hastily block him, slapping his foil against Frank's exposed fingers. Frank cried out, and Stephan groaned in frustration.

"Have a care, Frank!" he cried.

Frank scowled at Stephan as he nursed his red fingers. "What is it, Stephan? Do not tell me that you are still thinking of your little governess friend from home. While in London, you ought to think of courting an elegant young lady of fashion!"

"Such as Lady Virginia?"

"Yes! Such as—no," Frank caught himself quickly, "*not* Lady Virginia. What about Frances's friend, Miss Giles? You said you thought she was charming."

"And so she is," Stephan sighed, walking over to a nearby bench to sit down. "But I seem to have trouble remaining conscious while she is speaking to me."

"Yes, I suppose she is a bit of a bore," Frank muttered, "but that is no matter! There are plenty of other young ladies of quality you could—and should—instead be focusing your attentions upon. You know it is your mother's desire that you marry a young lady of fortune. Why should you not enjoy your search for an appropriate woman?"

"The beautiful daughter of the Duke of Dorset does not qualify as a young lady of fortune?" Stephan asked innocently.

Frank sighed, now exasperated. "She isn't your precious Harriet!" he snapped, "She's the daughter of a duchess!"

Stephan hushed his cousin and looked around anxiously, nodding at the gentleman or two who had seemed distracted by their exchange until they again looked away. Stephan stood and moved to change back into his riding clothes.

"Stephan," Frank said. When Stephan did not stop walking, Frank quickly jogged to meet his stride. "I am sorry. But truly, why do you persist?"

Stephan's mouth was a hard line, and he did not immediately answer. When he did begin to speak, he prefaced his words with a small sigh. "I know her face, Frank. Truly. I may be mad to think they look so much alike, but I vow they are identical."

Frank's expression remained disbelieving, and Stephan grasped Frank by the shoulder, repeating, "*Identical.*"

Frank's disbelieving expression finally gave way to a skeptical surrender. "If your Harriet really is as beautiful as the Duke of Dorset's daughter, I think you far less addled for setting your sights on a farmer's daughter. That Lady Virginia is . . . lovely, beyond a doubt. You haven't a chance with her, of course, but she's a goddess."

Stephan raised an eyebrow. "Nearly as lovely as Miss Frances Stepney?"

Frank gave Stephan a friendly shove. "I may be courting the *beautiful* Miss Stepney, but I am not blind! Lady Virginia is as well-known for her looks as for her rank."

Stephan laughed. "She is. But as much as it pains me, Frank, I must correct you on one point. Earlier you said, '*my* Harriet.' She is unfortunately not *my* Harriet. Not yet."

"Then I suppose you had better change that," Frank said with his usual disarming grin. Stephan could not help but smile in return. They were both quiet as they changed their clothing in preparation to leave the fencing hall.

"Stephan, I cannot pretend to envy you or to understand your motives, despite the loveliness of these two—dare I say—nearly equally unattainable women, but I do wish you luck."

Stephan clapped Frank on the shoulder. No further words were necessary.

Curzon Street, London

"My lady, where is your little purse with your pin-money? I need to send a letter," Mandie asked casually.

Virginia looked up with a little laugh. "I've not left the house in over four months, Mandie. Why should I have pin-money?"

"Of course, Miss," she replied, her cheeks glowing. "I feel silly to have forgotten."

Virginia shot Mandie a suspicious glance. "Whomever are you writing, Mandie? And why do you need me to send your letter?"

Mandie pursed her lips. "The recipient, miss, is my business. I need to send a letter, but I haven't enough for the postage."

Virginia returned to her lacework and Mandie bit her lip before turning on her heel and leaving. Harriet pulled out her reticule, checked inside it, and followed Mandie out of the room.

"Here, Mandie. How much do you need?"

She handed Mandie the requested coins and narrowly resisted the temptation to pry into her letter's intended recipient. It was clear this was a secret Mandie intended to keep, at least from Virginia. Coins safe in hand, Mandie glanced at Virginia through the open door, who was sketching the image of a ship out at sea. "I'll tell you later," she whispered conspiratorially, and squeezed Harriet's hand before disappearing down the stairs.

Kensington Gardens, London

Harriet left for a walk on a fine Tuesday morning, before the duchess even had time to ask who would accompany her. The cool air stung her cheeks as she rode through the London streets on Mr. Desford's phaeton toward the park, Mandie in tow as chaperone.

When the three of them entered the gardens, there were several people that Harriet recognized from some of her previous visits with the duchess. She nodded politely to them, and bit her lip when she noticed that their eyes raked over Mr. Desford's presence next to her. They seemed to be gossiping before they even left her sight.

Harriet narrowly resisted the urge to grumble aloud and instead focused on admiring the twisted branches of the leafless trees. It was a cold day, but she was warm enough in her spencer, muff, and bonnet. The park was somewhat dour and gray in its wintry state, but Harriet was still grateful to be out of doors.

"I would say it is a beautiful day, but I consider myself an honest gentleman," Mr. Desford remarked.

Harriet laughed. The park was as gray and leafless as she'd ever seen it. "I don't know if I'll agree with *that*, but I'll admit it's not the most flattering season for the park."

"She is in a shocking state of undress."

Harriet overheard Mandie chuckle a little as she followed behind about twenty paces, walking while reading her book. It was too cold for her to take up residence on a park bench, and Harriet had asked her to remain near. As much as she liked spending time with Mr. Desford, she did not want to be left alone with him.

Nevertheless, time passed quickly, and Harriet's cheeks were flushed with a combination of the cool breeze and her enjoyment of Mr. Desford's presence. He was a very fine-looking man, and he was also elegant, ever sporting the highest fashions without quite being a dandy. He was the sort of man who would never look twice at her if she were only a governess and a farmer's daughter from Burnham-on-Sea, and to her surprise, the thought made her smile.

She would only be "Virginia" for the next few months, until after the baby was born. Her smile fading, Harriet looked off into the distance. The child. The closer they drew to the inevitable day, the more anxious Virginia became. She felt the baby move each day, and the child was vigorous enough that even Harriet had been able to feel its pert little kicks on Virginia's burgeoning belly. She did not want to think about what might become of the child. The duchess had told Virginia that she'd decided on a specific course of action, but had refused to elaborate.

"You are far away again, Lady Virginia," Mr. Desford said.

Harriet realized that Mr. Desford had been quietly watching her. She blinked and turned to him. "So I was. Forgive me."

"I wish you would tell me what you are thinking of."

Harriet shook her head. "I do not wish to."

Mr. Desford looked disappointed for a moment. "Lady Virginia, I wanted to ask you something. You see, I've had the oddest thought . . ."

He glanced up at her, and a shiver ran down Harriet's spine at the look in Mr. Desford's eyes, but it wasn't from the cold. "What is it, Mr. Desford?"

"Lady Virginia!" A male voice called from some fifteen paces away as they neared an intersecting path.

She blinked a couple of times, turning toward the voice. It was Stephan. She stopped walking. The usual emotions bubbled up inside her as he approached: pleasure at the sight of him accompanied by the growing apprehension that she would be found out.

"Mr. Grimsby, was it?" She forced herself to address him coolly.

He stopped short, his smile fading. The disappointment in his eyes stung her as a slap on her cheek would. He bowed formally, removing his hat and exposing the patch of thin, mousy hair on top of his head. "Forgive me for intruding, my lady. I hope that you are well."

Harriet felt as though a knife were twisting in a wound somewhere near her heart. She felt sick causing Stephan so much disappointment. She could not help but give him a small, encouraging little smile. "It is good to see you again, Mr. Grimsby,"

His face immediately brightened and Harriet was again struck by how very genuine and expressive he was. He had never been able to hide secrets from her for very long while they were growing up. She could always sense when he was trying to keep something from her, and she had inevitably discovered what it was. It was one of her favorite things about him.

Stephan took her hand and bowed over it, so close that she could feel the warmth of his breath through her thin gloves.

Mr. Desford seemed mildly irritated, but he held out an amicable hand to Stephan. The two men shook hands with what appeared to be slightly more vigor than necessary. She could sense that Mr. Desford did not like Stephan very much.

Harriet had no idea how she ought to act. Her mind fluttered with confusion, nerves, a desire to make everyone around her happy, and determination to maintain Virginia's character accurately. She had no idea what she ought to say, so she remained silent and continued walking down the wide path as the two men fell into step next to her.

The tension in the air between Mr. Desford and Stephan was thick enough Harriet felt she could cut it with a knife and served it with tea. She craned her neck around to see if she could catch Mandie's eye to subtly beg for assistance, but as she did she saw something that made her face turn white as a sheet.

"Miss Shore!" a little girl with blonde curls cried.

How could she have forgotten that Susan and Katherine took their early afternoon walks in this area? She had not been watching the time at all.

"What are you doing walking the park, Miss Shore?" Susan asked.

Katherine ran to catch up with her younger sister, angry that she had run off. "Susan!"

Harriet froze. She could think of nothing to say as the two girls approached. Her mouth dried and her heart was racing as she tried to think of a response that would simultaneously appease Susan and convince her to leave them alone.

After first glancing at Harriet, Mr. Desford turned to the little girl. "I'm afraid you have mistaken Lady Virginia for someone else. I do not know your Miss Shore, but this young lady is not she."

Susan looked confused, and Katherine seemed humiliated. "Yes, of course." She was clearly trying to sound very grown-up. Katherine put a firm arm around Susan's shoulders and tried to start leading her away, but Stephan stopped her. Harriet's heart was in her throat as he watched Stephan pull out a pair of small, wrapped candies from his overcoat pocket and hand them to the girls.

"I am sorry for the confusion, Miss . . . ?" he raised an eyebrow, asking for their names.

Katherine seemed awestruck by his kindness. "I . . . I am miss Donahue." She presented a clumsy little curtsy. "My sister is called Susan." Harriet could not help frowning. She would need to have the girls practice their curtsies and addresses more.

Stephan stood once more and stepped back to rejoin the walking party. "I am sorry this young woman is not who you thought she was."

Harriet fiddled with her glove, determined not to look the children in the eye lest they guess the truth for themselves.

Once Katherine had successfully pulled Susan back to the walking companion they'd left behind—the nursemaid, Mrs. Piers—Harriet tried to relax and think of a way to rejoin the conversation.

"How very awkward," she finally said after several moments of silence. Mr. Desford had not looked at her, but had instead stared after the two young girls as they departed. She didn't dare look at Stephan.

"Indeed!" Mr. Desford chuckled lightly. "Poor little things. Mistaken identities can be so embarrassing."

His wording of the commiserative phrase did nothing to calm her raging heartbeat. When she finally did meet eyes with Stephan, his expression was as readable as ever: shock, confusion, and excitement. He knew who she was—she was certain of it.

Harriet caught Mandie's eye and shot her a desperate expression. "My lady," Mandie immediately jogged to catch up to them—dear Mandie! "Milady, we had better go to luncheon with your mother. She will be upset if you are not present."

"How right you are, Mandie," Harriet turned to the gentlemen and stopped walking. "I had better return. Thank you for the charming walk, Mr. Desford. Stephan, it was nice to meet you again." She gave him a curtsy, and turned to walk back the way they had come.

"When shall I see you again, my lady?" Stephan asked. She reluctantly turned to answer, but Mr. Desford responded before she could.

"Lady Virginia has an address," Mr. Desford said condescendingly, "perhaps you could come by and leave your card."

Stephan did not respond to Mr. Desford, instead looking right at Harriet.

"I shall be at Lord and Lady Pinkerton's ball on the sixteenth." She gave him a shy smile.

Stephan grinned back. "Then I shall strive to secure an invitation. Goodbye . . . Lady Virginia." Stephan tipped his hat at her as he walked away.

As Mr. Desford was handing her up into his phaeton, she recalled that he had been about to say something when Stephan had interrupted.

"What was it you were going to say earlier, Mr. Desford? I beg pardon for the interruption."

He hesitated. "Perhaps I shall tell you another time, on another walk. For now, I do not wish to disappoint your mama any further." The look in his eyes was hard and unreadable, and Harriet was all too willing to let the thought fade from her mind as they drove over the dirty cobblestone streets.

Chapter Twenty-One

Curzon Street, London

Harriet practically tumbled through the doorway in a wave of nerves. "He *knows*!" she exclaimed as she collapsed onto the sofa next to Virginia, who was knitting a tiny white stocking with a frilly edge. It was so adorable that Harriet needed to stifle a little squeal of admiration when she looked at it.

"Who knows what?" Virginia looked up from her work. For her, that was a sign of definite interest.

"Stephan knows I am Harriet! Susan and Katherine saw me and called me *Miss Shore*!"

Mandie joined them in the room then.

"Mandie, does he *really* know or is she just being theatrical again?"

Mandie asked, "Did your Stephan fellow know you were to be governess to the Donahues?"

"Yes. He has tried to visit me there before, remember?"

Mandie laughed. "Then he definitely knows!"

Harriet groaned and buried her face in a cushion.

"Do you think Desford knows, too?" Virginia asked.

"Of that I'm not sure," Mandie replied, "But it was so sweet, Virginia. I saw the look he gave her—that Stephan fellow's clearly besotted with her, whether she's Harriet *or* Virginia."

Virginia couldn't hold back a smile. "Your false version of my life is far more exciting than my own ever was, Harriet. Three suitors all vying for your attention at once? My, my."

Harriet stared at the ceiling, melting into the couch with a gusty sigh until her stays cut into her sides. Her brow was still knit in concern, but she could not keep a smile off her face. "'Tis only Stephan I think of," she mumbled.

Mandie laughed. "'Tis a pity we're your only audience, miss. Your performance right now is fit for Drury Lane."

Harriet sat up with an affronted little scoff. "You two do not seem at all concerned about this!"

"Well, naturally, no." Virginia returned to her knitting. "If the entire scheme falls apart, I will not have to return to society. In fact, I have considered ruining the whole charade myself by running away, only . . . I have been so very tired lately. And moving about hurts my feet."

Harriet laughed, finally relaxing, as Mandie chimed, "Why should he *not* know?"

Virginia nodded. "Indeed. Harriet, if your Stephan *didn't* recognize you immediately, I should have been ashamed of him. You claim that he loves you, and knows you, but if that is true and he didn't recognize you whilst you stood before him, he would be far too dense to merit falling in love with."

"Surely I do a better job than *that* acting your part," Harriet mumbled.

Mandie gave a little snort. "Harriet, you are a charismatic flirt and cannot help yourself."

Harriet felt both flattered and insulted.

Virginia laughed. "Perhaps if Miss Harriet has half the eligible beau in town dangling after me, returning to my place in society would not be so bad as I'd feared."

Harriet giggled against her will. Unable to keep a scowl on her face, she gave a great sigh. "Perhaps it is *not* so bad if Stephan knows. I feel a sort of . . . relief now that I cannot describe."

Harriet had to get back to the Donahues', but even before she left, she started to notice that Mandie was not quite her usual, jovial self. As soon as she left Virginia's guest chambers, she waited for Mandie to join her in the hallway.

"All right, Mandie," she said quietly. "Out with it. What's weighing on you?"

"Harriet, I've written to Ralph," Mandie blurted.

Harriet blinked a couple of times before the words had meaning to her. *Ralph?* Not even Virginia had written to Ralph in the months they had been separated. "You did?"

Mandie nodded. "It was the letter you sent for me not a week past. I also wrote to inquire after him months ago, as soon as Virginia arrived here."

"And has he ever responded? Tell me more," Harriet breathed.

"He had gone off—that was all Virginia knew. I figured he'd be difficult to find. I didn't want milady to worry, or to wonder why he didn't respond, so I never told her I wrote him. But I had to know if he'd be coming back."

"And is he?" Harriet asked, hope rising in her chest.

Mandie sighed. "I am not sure. I managed to track him to Spain— he's likely been working out of a port there, from what I've heard from his comrades. But I don't know if he will respond in a timely manner, and Virginia only has a few more months left before the baby comes."

"What did the midwife say?"

"Could be born as soon as mid-April."

Harriet sucked in a breath. Only three months away. And letters to sailors could take even longer than that to get to them, let alone to allow for a response.

Harriet released a shaky breath. "Thank you for telling me, Mandie. Is there anything I can do?"

Mandie shook her head. "But I didn't want to be the only one worried about it, Miss. You understand why I couldn't tell Virginia, or anyone else, either."

Harriet nodded. "Of course. I only wish I'd thought to do something of the kind, Mandie. You are a true friend."

Mandie grunted modestly as she bustled about putting Harriet's gown away, but she seemed absurdly pleased.

Palace Court, London

Stephan pulled at his neckcloth as he bounced along in Frank's well-sprung phaeton. It was abominably tight that day—Frank had tied it into a large, stylish knot, against his protestations. Stephan had ultimately allowed it, but also determined that he'd never again let Frank force him into fashionable discomfort.

"All will go well," Frank assured him.

When Stephan hesitated for a moment before stepping down to the pavement, Frank loudly cleared his throat. "Are you going, or not?"

Stephan snapped back to the present with a chuckle. "Yes, I am." He stepped down from the coach. "Now you may go and visit your precious Miss Stepney, Frank, and good luck to you!"

Frank grinned in response. "Thank you, Stephan. If I don't come back with the phaeton to get you before you're through here . . . be a dear and hire a hackney, would you?"

Stephan assured him he would. It wasn't every day that his cousin and best friend offered to formally court a lady. He supposed hiring a hackney was the least he could do to support him in this endeavor.

Frank tossed his cousin a salute as he closed the door to the carriage behind Stephan and drove off. Stephan looked up at the red brick home and took a deep breath. He had been nearly ready to give up after his last visit, but his mission this time was different. He had to see her again. Had to confirm his suspicion.

He climbed the steps and knocked at the door. He wasn't certain what to do with his hands, so he clasped them behind his back as he waited for a response.

The housekeeper answered the door and after a second, a spark of recognition lit in her eyes.

"Mr. . . . was it Grinnell?"

"Grimsby."

"Yes, yes. Pardon me. You'll be here to see Miss Shore, then? Do come in."

Stephan wondered at her change in behavior toward him. The last time he had come, she had still hesitated to invite him inside. He also wondered why Harriet had never responded to his call with a note or a call of her own. Surely even governesses had a *little* spare time to themselves to make social calls?

The housekeeper skipped up the steps of the staircase in the main hall and turned a corner. He heard a door open. Stephan almost wished he might not hear everything so clearly, but could not resist training his ear on the conversation up the stairs.

"Miss Shore?" The housekeeper knocked softly on a door that Stephan heard open a moment later.

"Yes, George?"

"A young man is here to see you. A Mr. Grimsby."

There was a pause. Silence. She was *here*. He heard her voice. A single syllable was all it took for him to recognize her.

"Stephan? Here? Now?" She sounded concerned. Stephan frowned.

"Yes, Miss. And he said—"

"Oh, dear. I really ought to stay with the girls."

"You needn't stay with us," a lilting young voice replied.

Stephan stiffened and did not hear more. Harriet did not wish to see him. Was all hope lost? Would she never forgive him for that impertinent kiss? Did she no longer . . . was it possible that she had *never* been interested in him, despite what her father said?

But as his mind whirred, he heard someone on the stairs and eagerly looked up. There was Harriet, descending the stairs in a simple blue dress, her hair in an ordinary chignon at the nape of her neck. "Stephan," she used his Christian name, but her expression was shy. "I am sorry I did not . . . that I was not here to greet you when you visited before."

He shook his head. "Harriet, I am so happy to see you." He took a step toward her, holding out his hands for hers.

She gave her hands to him, and he kissed the back of each. She closed her eyes, and when they fluttered back open, her cheeks were flushed.

"I've missed you," he whispered.

She smiled, and her eyes filled with tears. "And I have missed you."

He did not speak for a moment. Would she invite him to a parlor, where they could talk? How long did she have? Would her employer be angry?

After a moment, she finally answered the questions on his mind. "I cannot talk for long—I am not supposed to receive social calls while I am working."

"I was worried that was the case, but I had to see you."

She smiled. Just then, a small crash was heard from the direction of the nursery and Harriet's face went pale. She started inching toward the stairs. "Oh, dear. I really must—" she began.

"I shan't keep you, Harriet. Only please tell me that I might see you again."

Her face softened as she looked into his eyes. "Of course you shall." She turned and headed up the stairs, but stopped when she was nearly at the top of them and fixed him with a look he could not quite read. "At twenty-five Grosvenor's Square, on the sixteenth."

His eyes widened, but she disappeared up the stairs before he could say another word.

He left the house in a daze, his mind crammed to bursting with confused thoughts. How was it possible that the Lady Virginia and Harriet Shore were one and the same? They clearly were—he had known this, but the confirmation invited a myriad of unanswered questions into his head. As he skipped down the steps, he was surprised to see a well-dressed gentleman exit a patch of shadow to the left of the stairs. Stephan nearly fell over in surprise when he recognized him.

"Hello there," he said. The dark-haired man only glanced at him, an odd smile at the corner of his mouth and something approaching madness in his eyes. Desford turned and walked swiftly away from Stephan without so much as a nod.

Stephan frowned after him. Mr. Desford made the hair on the back of his neck stand on end. He did not trust him. But Lady Virginia had been walking at the park with him, and had danced with at the last ball. *Harriet* had danced with him. Stephan sucked in a breath as the implications hit him like a wall of brick. If that fashionable gentleman was seeking her out *here* . . . He shook his head. He did not know what exactly what Harriet was doing impersonating nobility, but it was dangerous, and he was clearly not the only one to recognize her double-life.

Chapter Twenty-Two

Grosvenor Square, London

It was easy enough to laugh and refuse to worry about Stephan recognizing her in the safety of Virginia's private quarters. It was quite a bit harder once she was on her way to her next ball with the duchess. She fretted the entire way there, questions running through her mind. Will Mr. Desford be there? Does he also suspect her true identity? Will Stephan be there? Stephan . . . her mind tried to pull her off into a happy daydream with him, but she berated herself and managed to remain in the present.

Harriet already had a headache by the time she arrived at the ball. She considered mentioning this to the duchess, but the duchess was already miffed with her for walking in the park with Mr. Desford without her permission, especially since she'd had to learn about the jaunt from a gossiping society lady rather than from Harriet herself.

"Be sure to show every attention to Mr. Brougham this evening," the duchess said coldly, not meeting Harriet's eyes, "I don't want to hear about any more flirtations with that Desford rake."

Harriet pursed her lips. The duchess had ways of punishing those who did not do as she wished. She ignored them, imbued each of her words with frost, made them feel as though they were unworthy, or spoke through them as though they didn't exist. Harriet was feeling less and less charitable toward her by the day.

"I shall, Mother." She allowed the footman to hand her down from the carriage. That evening she wore a coral pink high-waisted gown with a sheer ivory-colored lace overlay. Little pink hothouse roses were nestled amongst her brown curls, along with a single large cream-colored feather. Her earrings were garnet and although she had thought the duchess's pearls would have complemented the outfit very becomingly, the duchess had not offered to loan them, so Harriet instead wore a thin gold chain with a small garnet pendant. Her gloves were ivory and rose past her elbows. Her fan was a cream-colored lace affair, and, despite her agitated nerves, her cheeks still glowed pink and she looked even more fetching than usual.

It snowed lightly outside, but she simply clutched her fur-lined satin cape about her shoulders and walked up the steps to the house, waiting for the duchess on the top step so that they could both be announced at once.

Once inside the party, they quickly took one another's leave, although the duchess emphasized once more, "Mr. *Brougham*, my dear," before going to meet her friend Lady Marsh.

A servant took Harriet's cloak and she was able to wander around and greet those at the party she knew. She recognized more and more faces at each party they attended, and more people recognized her in return. It continually amazed Harriet how varied society was here in the heart of London. In Burnham-on-Sea, there were only the land-owners, a few of the more important farmers, the clergy, and a handful of others considered worthy to attend the small local assemblies. Everyone knew everyone else, and any new faces at an event prompted gossip for days and sometimes weeks afterward.

Here in London, it was a wonder when you saw the same person at two parties in a row, and was generally a sign that the universe was thrusting the two of you together.

"Lady Virginia," a voice at her elbow said. She turned to see Mr. Desford, and she smiled. As much as he made her nervous, she at least found him more interesting than Mr. Brougham. He was more a friend to her than any other member of the *ton*.

"I hope I may be permitted to dance with you this evening."

She saw Mr. Brougham over her shoulder. He had looked to be coming her way, but at the sight of Mr. Desford, he had stopped and begun to turn away with a discouraged little frown.

"Oh, Mr. Brougham!" she called over Mr. Desford's shoulder, "I do hope that *you* shall ask me to dance this evening."

Mr. Desford frowned and looked over his shoulder at Mr. Brougham, who appeared to have taken heart at Harriet's invitation. He swiftly walked over and took her hand, pressing it gently. "I should very much like to, Lady Virginia. Would you do me the honor of the first two, if you are not otherwise engaged?"

"I shall indeed." She gave him a warm smile. He smiled back, nodded politely, and walked over to speak to another friend for a moment.

Harriet turned back to Mr. Desford. "I need to show him every attention to avoid the wrath of my mother, so don't you dare tease me." Mr. Desford chuckled at that remark. "You know how she dislikes you. But if I dance with *him*, she will not be quite so bothered by the time that I spend with *you*." She gave him a friendly smile and Mr. Desford responded with one of his own.

"You are so clever, my lady, that it is no wonder you have so many gentlemen wrapped about your little finger."

Harriet blushed prettily as the previous dance ended, and Mr. Brougham came to lead her onto the floor.

She enjoyed her dances with Mr. Brougham. He was not quite so much a bore that evening as he often seemed. He did enjoy discussing birds a trifle more than the usual young society buck, but he was pleasant enough, attentive, and fairly handsome. Harriet enjoyed his company far more than the duchess's, and was pleased to note that when the duchess saw her dancing with Mr. Brougham from across the room, she smiled approvingly.

The two dances wound to a close even sooner than Harriet wanted them to and she cheerfully allowed herself to be led to the dance floor by Mr. Desford.

"You are unusually charming this evening."

"Am I?" Harriet was suddenly a little nervous. She mentally cursed—she had been getting worse and worse at playing Virginia's part over time as she grew more comfortable moving about in society. She knew she had already made the mistake of being friendly and polite that evening instead of quiet and withdrawn, as Virginia was inclined to be.

"Indeed," Mr. Desford murmured, "It makes me suspect that you are up to something terribly devious."

Harriet laughed lightly, but she could not help but think of Stephan. She had asked him to meet her here—not just Lady Virginia, but *Harriet*. She needed to think of a clever response for Mr. Desford. She quickly tainted her voice with sarcasm. "I am the soul of innocence, sir. I do not know of what you speak."

Mr. Desford threw back his head and laughed, and Harriet joined in with a little giggle of her own. She was hopeful that the sarcasm was reminiscent of Virginia's usual personality, but she felt as though the longer she spent in society, the more she developed her own version of "Virginia's" personality.

Mr. Desford pulled her into yet another one of their good-natured, enjoyable conversations about the entertaining persons surrounding them, but Harriet's heart was only half in it. She allowed herself to laugh, however, and relegated her vague, bothersome concerns to the back of her mind.

The dance came to a close, and Mr. Desford escorted her toward a seat at the edge of the dance floor.

"I shall fetch you a cup of punch."

Harriet smiled and nodded, and Mr. Desford walked off.

Before she could so much as sit down in the proffered chair, however, someone came up behind her and slipped a hand around her waist, another hand firmly clutching her upper arm. Suddenly, she was gently but forcefully escorted out of the ballroom.

"I do beg your pardon!" she cried, craning her neck to see who it was that held her fast and propelled her down the hall.

She was surprised to meet Stephan's eyes, and she ceased struggling at once. She felt ice slip down her spine at the look in his eye and meekly allowed him to lead her away, her lower lip clamped between her teeth, simultaneously dreading and eagerly anticipating what would come next.

They walked past a door, which he opened, and popped his head inside. It was an empty room—a small study crammed to bursting with books. Once they were both inside, he lit a gas lamp on the desk and firmly closed the door behind them. Harriet's heart started pounding so loudly she was certain Stephan could hear it.

Stephan turned toward her, closed the distance between them, and rested a gentle hand on the side of her face. Harriet looked up and met his gaze—anger, confusion, and happy incredulity.

"*Harriet*," he said.

Chapter Twenty-Three

Grosvenor's Square, London

Harriet's lip quivered. She could neither speak nor hide behind Virginia's identity—he already knew who she was.

"Harriet, it *is* you, isn't it?" he took one of her hands in his.

"Yes," she finally answered, "I *am* Harriet."

She was surprised at how marvelous it felt to say her own name aloud. Almost as good as it felt to see Stephan looking at her and to hear him calling her by her name—her *real* name.

"Harriet," he whispered again, "It is so good to see you."

"Yes," she said. She could not keep a broad smile off her face. Her eyes were filled with tears.

Stephan bit his lip and glanced at her mouth. She felt herself blush, but she did not turn away from him. After a questioning glance, Stephan leaned forward to press a soft kiss onto her waiting mouth. She relaxed into his embrace.

All too soon they parted, and Stephan gave her a warm smile that crumbled all too soon into a worried frown. "Harriet, why are you doing this? It's *dangerous*! How did you get mixed up in all this nonsense?"

She blinked back tears and tried to regain her confidence. "I happen to look *exactly* like the daughter of the Duke of Dorset."

"Apparently so! You do not appear to have caused any ripples in society by your deception. But, how *could* you? How could you engage in such a dangerous venture? Surely you must realize the disaster it would be for you to be found out! Why on earth would you take such a risk?"

Because I love you. The thought bounced around inside her mind, firmly locked behind her lips. Her cheeks burned and she could feel tears falling down her face. Stephan was *here*. His hands on her shoulders, his gaze burning into hers. She had daydreamed similar moments for months since their last encounter, but had not dared try make them a reality. Now that the moment had arrived, all her carefully rehearsed lines disappeared and she found she had nothing to say.

How could she possibly tell him that she had entered the entire charade and risked everything for *him*? In order to secure a dowry that might allow her to marry him one day? The very thought was humiliating. But, important though it had once seemed, the dowry was no longer the primary reason for her involvement, and it felt good to confide in someone besides Virginia and Mandie for once.

"The daughter of the duchess—the real Lady Virginia—is in confinement right now. My role is to prevent others from discovering the truth of her condition."

Stephan's eyebrows shot upward. "Ah. Hence the er . . . deception," he finished lamely.

Harriet nodded. "And she and I have become friends and companions, and I care very much about her. I cannot leave her now."

"What of the . . . father?" Stephan asked, his face burning as much as any sheltered country boy's would, given the subject.

"No one is certain where he is," she said after a pause, "but she and I hope very much that he will return for her." She remembered the letter Mandie had sent, and took a moment to hope desperately that Ralph would answer it and arrive in time to save their child from an unknown fate.

"I see," Stephan finally released Harriet's shoulders and turned away. She felt her heart break a little as he let her go, and took an involuntary step toward him.

"And here I thought you came to London to be a governess."

At the sound of the word governess, Harriet frowned. She thought of Stephan's unbending mother and her determination that Stephan marry well, not dangle after a farmer's daughter. At the end of all her efforts, no matter how grand her dowry, she was still only a governess, and he a landed gentleman. But she could not stop herself from saying, "I never *wanted* to be a governess, Stephan."

He turned back to her, agony in his eyes. "Then why did you do it? Why did you leave? Did I offend you that day? Was it my mother?"

Harriet carelessly wiped one of her tears away. "I . . . I . . ."

Stephan took one of her hands in his. "You *must* know how I feel about you, Harriet."

Her fingers gripped his compulsively, intoxicated by the heat issuing from him. "How *do* you feel about me, Stephan?" she could not stop herself from asking.

He opened his mouth to speak, but his ears turned red and he closed his eyes in thought. "To me, you are like the sun." His eyes were on hers now. "Where you are, there is light. When I am near you, I never wish to leave. When you are away, I think only of the time left until I can see you again. If I could orient my entire life around you, I would do it in a heartbeat."

Tears were coursing down her cheeks. She had to be dreaming. He *did* care for her. Standing here, listening to him now, the obstacles that had seemed so insurmountable as she'd fled Burnham all those months ago diminished to nothing. Thoughts of abandoning this scheme, running away from London, and marrying Stephan rose up before her. After basking in the light of these reflections for a few seconds, she reluctantly pushed them away.

She could not marry Stephan, no matter how they both felt. Not yet. Virginia still needed her. The child still needed her. And the thought that Stephan should debase himself to be with her, with hardly a dowry to speak of, was unbearable. He deserved more.

She turned from him and walked a couple steps away, finding her bearings again.

"I," Stephan said after a moment. When she still did not turn and face him, he sighed. "I love you, Harriet." The silent pause after these words was delicious. Harriet's eyes fluttered closed to savor it.

"I love you, too," she whispered before she could stop herself.

"What?" Stephan covered the distance between them in an instant and met her eyes with his gray-blue ones. "You *love* me?"

Harriet nodded, blinking back more tears. "Of course I do!"

Stephan pulled her into an embrace, her head tucked securely against his chest, his face in her hair. He sighed, and it sounded as though he were about to burst from happiness. "I truly thought you might despise me, Harriet. I thought you fled to London to . . . to leave me far behind."

"I could never despise you," she murmured, pulling him tighter.

"I am so relieved. I could not give up. Although you were not exactly encouraging! Your father told me where I might find you, and I came to London as soon as I was able to secure an invitation from my aunt's family."

"You came all the way to London for *me*?" she asked.

He scoffed. "What—you thought I would come for the *ton* parties, did you?"

She giggled. Once the laughter burbled out of her, her nerves wouldn't allow her to stop, and she giggled helplessly. Stephan joined her, but after a few moments, he pulled away from her, looking her in the eyes. As soon as she had forced herself to be calm again, he said, "Marry me, Harriet. Please."

She closed her eyes and let the words wash over her, but the concerns she had shunted to the side earlier came forward, shoving aside her happiness and pressing down on her like a cart full of cobblestones. She shook her head.

"I can't," she whispered.

The pain in Stephan's expression was impossible to bear, and Harriet turned from him again. If this were the best way she should show her love for him, she would do it. But that didn't mean she had to like it.

"You need to marry a lady, Stephan. And if the rumors are true, it ought to be a lady of . . . fortune."

"What do you mean by *rumors*?" his voice was hard.

Her heart skipped a beat. "Your estate is said to be in debt."

"I can manage my own affairs, Harriet."

She continued, before she could lose her nerve. "But you *ought* to marry a young lady of means—with a sizable dowry. One large enough to help you maintain your lands and . . . and . . ." She trailed off.

"You think me a fortune hunter, Harriet?" His hurt was palpable.

"No, of course not! You can't be—you want to . . . to marry *me*. But I haven't a thing, Stephan! Not compared to all the other young ladies out in that ballroom now." She hazarded a glance at him, and for the first time she could recall, his expression was inscrutable.

"You do not wish to marry me?" he asked.

"That is not what I said."

Stephan took a step toward her, his gray-blue eyes alight with confusion as he took one of her hands in his. "What is it, then? What is troubling you, Harriet?" he asked. "I wish you would confide in me as you used to."

She looked away. If he pressed her, she knew she would not be able to resist.

He reached up to place a gentle hand beneath her chin, lifting her face to meet his eyes. When she saw the sweet expression in them, she burst into tears.

He pulled her, sobbing, into his chest and held her there. She did not know how long she cried, but all the burdens that she carried, one by one, seemed to drop away from her with each tear. The duchess's demands. Trying to lead two separate lives. How much she missed her parents and home. Her concerns about Virginia and her baby. How powerless she felt through all of this.

"I wish everything were different," Harriet mumbled after a few minutes. "That you could take me away from all of this."

"So do I," Stephan murmured in return, his arms tight around her. He pressed a kiss into her hair. "May I take you away, then?"

Harriet shook her head. "No. I *know* that this scheme is utter lunacy, Stephan. But I cannot abandon it. Not yet."

He pulled away from her to look into her eyes. "Are you being forced into it? If so, I won't stand by and—"

She shook her head. "No, that isn't it. Virginia—the real Virginia—is my friend. And she needs my help. I cannot leave her, and I made an agreement with her mother to do this."

"The duchess?" Stephan frowned. "What sort of agreement?"

Harriet's could feel herself blushing. She couldn't bring herself to describe the dowry—not when she may not receive it after all. "Never mind that. But I have to see this through. I promised." She patched together enough of Virginia's noble bearing that she was able to dry her tears, lift her chin, and pull her shoulders back.

"Will you please escort me back to the ballroom?" she asked formally.

Stephan shook his head, and held her tighter. "Oh, no. I'm not going to let you go again so easily. You've admitted that you love me. How long are you going to make me wait and worry about you before you come back home?"

Harriet softened. After a brief moment of hesitation and a conspiratorial look around for nonexistent eavesdroppers, she said, "The midwife expects the baby to arrive in April. If Ralph—Virginia's lover—arrives before then, all will be well. The duchess will not be pleased, but Virginia and her child will be safe, and that is all I care about."

Stephan's brow furrowed slightly. "The duchess would not harm you, would she?"

Harriet twisted her fan between her fingers. "No. She had promised to do something for me in exchange for helping her, that is all. If I don't fulfill my end, she won't fulfill hers."

Stephan was still for a moment. His thumbs traced reassuring patterns on her arms as he thought. Finally, he said, "So you will not leave until this Ralph comes to claim Virginia."

"Yes," Harriet confirmed.

Stephan sighed. "Then I shall have to bring him to her. Where can I find him?"

Harriet gasped. She could not very well go out and look for Ralph herself, but Stephan was a man, free to move about the world as he would. "Oh, Stephan, *would* you?"

Stephan smiled. "If that is what it takes."

Harriet reached up to wrap her arms around her neck and stood on tiptoe to press a kiss onto his waiting lips. His arms reached around her, pulling her closer. After a long moment, she reluctantly pulled away.

"I shall never be deserving of you, Stephan," she whispered, "but I love you so *very* dearly."

Stephan chuckled. "Tell me all you know about this Ralph, er—"

"Clifton."

"Clifton," he repeated, "and I shall do all I can to find him and make him come to Lady Virginia."

Stephan opened a desk against the wall and found a piece of paper, a pen, and an ink well. Harriet quickly recited all she had ever heard about Ralph—his former company in the Navy, his surname, his sister's name, their hometown, and all of the friends of his Virginia had ever mentioned in passing, as well as Mandie's information about Spain. Stephan scrambled to write it all down.

As soon as she had finished, Stephan tossed a handful of powder onto his hastily scribbled note, dusted it off, and folded it into his breeches pocket.

"Thank you, darling. You had best get back to the ball before anyone suspects your absence." He pressed a swift kiss onto her forehead.

She allowed him to lead her into the ballroom, back to Mr. Brougham's side. "Ah, there you are," he said with a smile. "Would you like to dance the next with me, My Lady?"

Harriet nodded and smiled before turning back to Stephan.

"Good evening . . . Lady Virginia," Stephan said softly.

"Do take care, Mr. Grimsby," she breathed.

With a quick, formal kiss on the back of her glove, he was gone.

Chapter Twenty-Four

Grosvenor Square, London

Mr. Desford cornered her after another two dances with Mr. Brougham. "My dear Lady Virginia, are you all right?"

She snapped to attention.

"You look dreadfully flushed."

Harriet felt her cheeks grow even warmer with his notice. "I am well," she insisted.

"In truth, although quite as lovely as ever, you do look ill. May I walk with you to the conservatory to take some air?"

"Yes, please."

As they walked, Harriet's mind calmed enough to realize that Mr. Desford had hardly said a thing, which was unlike him. When they entered the conservatory, Mr. Desford led them to a bench at the edge of the room.

"Are you certain you are quite well, Mr. Desford?"

Mr. Desford smiled, but there was something behind his smile that made Harriet's heart beat a little faster. "I cannot keep secrets from you, Lady Virginia. I admit I am not feeling quite myself."

"Oh? What is the matter?"

"Lady Virginia, I—" he cut himself off then, looking around for potential eavesdroppers. There were few others in the room, and they were having their own private conversations. No one was listening to them.

"Lady Virginia," he resumed, "I have enjoyed the time we've spent together lately."

"As have I," she said warily.

He grasped one of her hands in his. "You must know . . . surely you cannot be ignorant of the feelings I have held for you for so long."

"What? What feelings? How long?" Harriet babbled nervously.

"I love you." His dark blue eyes fixed on hers in a way that ought to have made her heart pound, but didn't. She was left confused by the discomfort she felt at his words.

Harriet smiled, but her smile faded when she realized Mr. Desford was looking at her expectantly, waiting for her response.

"I . . . I like you, as well," she finally answered. When Virginia had playfully encouraged her to flirt with Mr. Desford, neither of them had considered what she would do if her flirting actually moved him to a declaration. She squirmed in her seat, unsure how to proceed.

Mr. Desford smiled confidently, his usual smirk forming again, "I have long felt that you are not entirely indifferent to me, either. My dear Lady Virginia, I would like to seek permission to court you."

She did not know what to say, for whatever she said the real Lady Virginia would need to reckon with one day. She felt dizzy at the responsibility. "I do not know if that is a good idea."

Mr. Desford frowned and removed his hand from hers. Harriet regained enough composure to continue. "My mother is unlikely to give you the permission you seek," she hedged.

The noise he made was somewhere between a groan and a sigh. He looked away from her for a moment. After regaining his composure, he turned back and spoke carefully.

"She thinks me an unworthy rake."

Harriet sighed. "I was not thinking of that, but you may be right. It might cause a bit of a scandal."

Mr. Desford's frown remained, but he looked thoughtful at her remark.

"A scandal," he repeated, the glimmer of a smile playing about his lips.

Harriet smiled back, but there was something about Mr. Desford's smile that made her avert her eyes.

"Let us pretend, for a moment, that the duchess were *not* your mother," Mr. Desford began.

Harriet's heart was pounding. "What do you mean?"

Mr. Desford's triumphant little smile seemed to hold a secret. Harriet swallowed. He could not know. It was not possible that he had guessed the truth . . . was it?

"Lady Virginia . . . if you would still like me to continue to call you that?"

Harriet stumbled to recover before he could continue, though she glanced about her for anyone who might have overheard. "O-of course. That is my name, Mr. Desford. My proper address. To use my Christian name alone at this stage would naturally be inappropriate."

There was a wicked flicker to Mr. Desford's smile that made Harriet feel like ice was flowing through her veins. "Of course. But if you no longer needed to be Lady Virginia, would you be at liberty to love me?"

Harriet did not dare speak. What did he know? What would he— or *could* he—do with the information he had?

She swallowed her fear and stood tall. "I am very sorry if my behavior to this point has led you to believe that I have warmer feelings than those of friendship toward you, Mr. Desford. I consider you, and shall continue to consider you, a friendly acquaintance. I pray this information does not displease you."

Mr. Desford's expression did not change, but there was a sudden hardness to his eyes, and his nostrils flared slightly. "Not at all. I hope my presence does not cause you distress." Mr. Desford rose from the bench. "If you are well now, I shall escort you once more to the ballroom."

Harriet nodded, filled with mingled relief and terror. She was eager for the brief exchange to end, but worried about what Mr. Desford could be thinking.

"Of course. Thank you, Mr. Desford." She accepted his proffered hand.

Back in the ballroom, Harriet forced a bright smile. "Are you going to ask me to dance again, Mr. Desford? I believe the next is the Scotch reel."

"No, I will take my leave of you, Lady Virginia. Perhaps I shall call on you some morning later this week."

"Oh. Well, I hope everything is all right. And that I haven't offended you, Mr. Desford." Harriet said anxiously.

Mr. Desford's smile had a glint in it that made her nervous. "All is quite well, Lady Virginia. I just remembered a prior engagement. I shall bid you farewell now." He took her hand and pressed a kiss on the back of it, making her skin crawl.

He did not wait for her response before turning and walking away.

Harriet pulled out her fan, waved it in her face, and sat down in one of the soft chairs on the edge of the room. First Stephan and now Mr. Desford. She felt dizzy and overwhelmed. Her heart fluttered at the memory of her encounter with Stephan, but her conversation with Mr. Desford had left her unsettled. For a respectable gentleman in fashionable society, offering to court a young lady was almost tantamount to a marriage proposal. It would seem that Mr. Desford had real feelings for her. But there were many that said that Mr. Desford *wasn't* respectable. And that knowing smirk, and the glint in his eye . . . they did not seem so harmless as they once had.

A large part of her felt ready to be finished with the whole charade and accept Stephan's proposal, unworthy though she was. But as she had told Stephan, she could not abandon Lady Virginia now. Any real hope she'd entertained for a dowry had fallen by the wayside the moment she determined to side with Virginia over the duchess, and it had happened so gradually she had hardly recognized it. Virginia was now so dear to her that her safety, happiness, and friendship mattered far more to Harriet than any dowry ever could.

Suddenly Mr. Brougham appeared out of the corner of her eye, and she nearly sighed with relief.

"Lady Virginia! Why are you not dancing?"

She stopped fanning her face. "Mr. Brougham, I've just returned to the ballroom."

"I had not seen you and wondered where it was you had gone to. Would you like to dance the next with me, Lady Virginia?"

For whatever reason, being called Lady Virginia for what seemed the thousandth time that evening was making the hair on the back of her neck prickle. But she stood and took Mr. Brougham's hand, relieved that her encounter with him, at least, was unlikely to be emotionally taxing. "I would like that very much, Mr. Brougham."

Curzon Street, London

"Someone looks exhausted," Mandie sang lightly as soon as Harriet had stumbled into the room. Virginia snorted herself awake at the sudden disturbance.

"I? Or Virginia?" Harriet managed to quip, but only halfheartedly. She made her way to the sofa, where Virginia had clearly just awakened from a nap. Her belly grew noticeably larger by the day. Harriet took the liberty of sitting close to Virginia and pressing a hand against her growing abdomen.

"Oh, hello there, Harriet," Virginia yawned. "Saying hello to the little one?"

Harriet felt a little nudge against her hand and she closed her eyes to savor it. There were characters, props, and endless lines to be had in her life on Curzon Street, but here there was an entirely new character preparing to join the scene. It felt like magic. She smiled, and finally moved her hand away.

"What's the matter, Harriet? Tell me."

"I . . ." She could not think where to begin. Stephan? Mr. Desford? She gave a shuddering breath and began to cry. Mandie rushed to fetch a handkerchief for her. After a few moments Harriet was recovered enough to finally say, "Why does everything have to be so complicated?"

Virginia looked as though she were trying not to smile. "Well, you are acting like you are somebody else entirely, Harriet. It's bound to occur. Now tell me what's happened," she coaxed.

So, Harriet described what happened. She explained how Stephan had whisked her away to speak to her at the ball and had kissed her, and she nearly mentioned that he was going to seek out Ralph but stopped herself. She would need to tell Mandie about that in private to avoid distressing Virginia.

Then she described Mr. Desford's conversation and his sudden declaration of affection and offer to court her.

Virginia laughed. "Two in one evening! My goodness, Harriet."

Harriet's forehead creased. "It isn't something to crow over. The way he spoke to me . . . you were not there. He spoke as though he were threatening me."

Virginia sobered. "You think he knows?" she asked.

Harriet nodded, chaffing her arms to stave off a sudden chill. "It shouldn't be so surprising, I suppose. I've been told I don't portray you accurately at all."

Virginia smiled. "No one asked you to stop being Harriet completely in order to pretend to be Virginia."

"At least this little adventure has entirely quenched any foolish desire I had to be an actress."

Mandie wore a look of horror. "Acting? A sweet little thing like you? That sounds like a terrible idea!"

Harriet groaned ruefully. "It was a childish ambition, and one I haven't given serious thought to since I was about twelve years old. I like performing well enough, but my mother's attempts to dissuade me eventually worked."

Virginia grimaced. "It is fortunate for your mother that she does not have such a disappointing daughter as mine has."

Harriet shook her head. "If my mother knew what I was up to now, she would be furious! And I know your mother has been disappointed in you, but her expectations of you have always been unreasonable. Perhaps one day she'll realize that. You are my dear friend, Virginia, and my loyalties are first to *you*, not your mother—whatever agreements I've made with her. And I do not approve of the way she treats you."

"Nor do I," Virginia admitted with a sad smile, "but I *did* run off with a sailor who left me with child and thrust me back into my mother's hands. Perhaps I deserve it."

Harriet couldn't quite manage a smile at that remark. "That's not exactly how it happened, Virginia. Is it?"

Virginia looked away. "I . . . it is and it isn't. I *did* leave against my parents' wishes, and it *was* with Ralph."

Harriet frowned. "It's hard for me to imagine that a man as nice as the Ralph you've described would run off with you without a word about marriage. One would think he would at least try to elope with you to Gretna Green and—"

Virginia groaned. "Of course he did, but we had no money to speak of, Harriet. Have you any idea of the cost of an elopement over the border?"

Harriet frowned as she began to mentally calculate the cost. Before she could respond, Virginia yawned again.

"It is late. Why don't we continue this tomorrow?"

"All right. But Virginia, I cannot sleep until you tell me. Should I accept the suit of Brougham or of Desford? You may need to sort out the aftermath of anything I decide."

Virginia sighed. "It does not matter in the slightest, Harriet. For I do *not* plan to return to being Lady Virginia Sackville after the baby is born."

Harriet sat back and blinked stupidly. "You . . . don't?" Virginia had always expressed distaste at the idea of returning to her former life, but Harriet had still thought she intended to return to it if Ralph did not come in time.

Virginia shook her head adamantly. "Ralph will return for me in time. He simply *has* to."

"But what if he *doesn't?*" Mandie interjected. "What then?"

Virginia swallowed, and glared at Mandie. "He *will*."

Harriet guiltily realized that neither she nor Mandie shared the same faith in Ralph that Virginia continued to have. But she prayed that Virginia was in the right and they were in the wrong.

She leaned forward and kissed Virginia on the forehead.

"I think I shall go to bed now, if Mandie will be so kind as to help me out of my gown. I shall try not to get you engaged to anyone at all, Virginia."

Virginia smiled, and looked heavenward. "Oh, to be you, Harriet, and need to *avoid* engagements like the plague. If I were more like you, my mother and I would *both* be happier, I think. But alas, I am not, and it does no good to dwell on it. So, Harriet, don't bother yourself about portraying me accurately and do whatever makes you happy."

When Harriet was not able to return a convincing smile, Virginia insisted, "I know I seem miserable trapped in these quarters all day, but it is not so bad for me, being kept out of society. I like being alone, and I like being with Mandie. It's everyone *else* that I do not like."

Harriet frowned. "Do you dislike me, too?"

Virginia took up a cushion and swatted Harriet's arm with it. "Harriet, you silly girl, of course I don't—you're one of the only *real* friends I've ever had."

Harriet glowed at the compliment.

"You must not feel too sorry for me," she insisted, "I have complained a great deal—and I likely will continue to do so—but the only thing that truly makes me miserable is the absence of Ralph, and the . . . the thought of what could happen to me and our child if he does not come for us. But I cannot think of this. I cannot abide the thought of being separated from this child. I cannot bear the thought of being apart from Ralph. He *will* come for us. I know that he will."

She looked away, blinking furiously. Neither Mandie nor Harriet dared say anything further. Harriet could only inwardly vow that if Ralph did *not* come back for Virginia, she would still find a way to make things right.

Chapter Twenty-Five

Westbourne Terrace, London

You have been staring out that window ignoring everything I've said for twenty minutes at least. What are you thinking of?"

Stephan smiled vaguely, his eyes still trained on the horizon. "Your courtship, of course." He turned and clapped a weary hand on Frank's shoulder. "With Miss Frances Stepney of Cheltenham, whose name I now know nearly as well as my own. I congratulate you. When am I to wish you happy?"

Frank raised a quizzical brow. "No."

"What?"

"That is *not* what you were thinking of, Stephan. I'll thank you to tell me what it *was.*"

"Affairs of my estate."

Frank looked about to respond, but then gave Stephan a suspicious look. "You weren't really thinking of your estate just now either, were you?"

Stephan frowned. "It doesn't matter."

"Of course it does. You look as though you're carrying a thousand pounds on your shoulders. What *is* it? Is it that Miss Shore again?" Frank shook a finger at Stephan. "Your mother will make both of your lives a living hell if you marry her, you know."

Stephan smiled and sighed. "I'm certain she'd try her best."

Frank chuckled. "Look, man. If you cannot bear to be apart from Miss Shore, go after her! Hang what your mother says, and hang what society thinks! Why should it signify if being apart from her makes you this unhappy?"

"There are still a few obstacles left to clear before I can do that."

Frank's brow wrinkled into an expression of confusion and he scratched the back of his neck. "Miss Stepney only made me recite a poem for her before she accepted my suit." His ears turned red. "What on earth does this Miss Shore expect from you?"

Stephan burst out laughing. Frank did not join him, but instead pulled up a chair near him and waited. "I need to find a naval officer who's sold out and turned sailor of some kind, and bring him to her."

Frank's nostrils flared angrily. "She's asking you to fetch your *competition*?"

Stephan shook his head, laughing again. *Leave it to Frank,* he thought, *to show me the humor in a bleak situation.* "No, she has a dear friend who's been . . . erm . . . left with child. I'm to retrieve the father for her friend."

"A dear *friend*, eh?"

Stephan frowned at the insinuation. "*Yes,*" he emphasized.

Frank shrugged and then scratched his chin. "How are you supposed to find one sailor at sea among thousands?"

Stephan raised his hands palm-up in helplessness.

"And even if you found him, how would you convince him to return? Surely it's no mistake that he's left."

"I am hoping that won't be a problem."

"But what if he's jilted her?"

Stephan heaved a sigh. "Well, then, I suppose I'll need to call him out."

Frank's mouth dropped open and it looked as though he wanted to argue, but he stopped and thought for a moment. "You know, Stephan, I would say you're absolutely mad to go calling out a man you don't know from Adam, but if it's with the sword, I think you could call anyone out and win. If you're waiting for my permission, go ahead. I'll even be your second!"

Stephan chuckled. "Thank you for the encouragement, Frank."

Palace Court, London

"When shall you be back to stay with us again *all* the time, Miss Shore?" Susan asked. Katherine did not show her affection as willingly as Susan did, but she was clearly listening eagerly for the response.

"To stay with you every day? Not until the season ends, girls." She felt a twinge of guilt knowing that she hoped that an engagement would pull her away from them yet again.

Susan pouted. "Only a few days per week?"

Harriet nodded and finished packing the last few things into her bag to return to the duke's house. "Of course! I shall be back on Tuesday, and shall expect to see some progress on that piano piece we have been working on."

"Yes, Miss Shore," Susan said obediently.

"And your painting, Katherine. It's coming along nicely. I would like to see a finished work when I return next."

Katherine nodded. "You shall, Miss Shore."

Harriet waved a final goodbye to the girls and steeled herself to meet the duchess as the heavy door closed behind her. As she climbed into the waiting carriage with a little sigh, she suddenly felt very uncomfortable, as though she were being watched. She looked up and down the street before settling uneasily into her seat. As the carriage pulled away from the curb and she glanced out the window, she saw a man slip out of the shadows behind a set of stairs and smile directly at her.

Mr. Desford.

Harriet's gut wrenched and her heart began pounding. Then it was certain. He was looking her in the eye—he *knew*. Mr. Desford *knew*. What was he going to do to her? His grin had been the same teasing, sardonic smile he usually wore, but never before had she felt so threatened by it.

Mr. Desford's offer of courtship left a bitter taste in her mouth. Handsome though he was, why could they not simply have remained friends? Harriet regretted allowing herself to flirt so freely with him as she had. She felt a headache coming on as the carriage rolled down the bumpy road, and she tried to banish the image of Mr. Desford's triumphant smile from her mind as they drove.

Curzon Street, London

That evening she was to attend a small evening party with the duchess, and Harriet was dreading it. What if she saw Mr. Desford there? Suddenly she was none too excited to leave behind her safe, dull life as a governess in exchange for Virginia's.

"Ah, Virginia. I am glad you are here." The duchess smiled at her through the mirror of her dressing table. "Here—you are looking a bit pale. Put on some of this rouge."

Harriet stared at the little pot of red cream.

When the duchess turned around to examine her reticule, Harriet pinched her cheeks a few times to turn them red and set the little pot of rouge back on the table. Concealing from her mother that she was going to masquerade as the daughter of a duchess was one thing. Applying rouge—something her mother had made her swear *never* to do—was another thing entirely.

"Your Grace," Harriet said before the duchess could hurry her out the door. "I must tell you something."

The duchess frowned impatiently, but waited for Harriet to speak.

"Mr. Desford knows my true identity."

The lady's nostrils flared and her eyes narrowed. "*How?*" she asked.

Harriet's heart thudded in her chest as she vainly wished herself elsewhere. "He saw me leaving the Donahues to come here. I don't know why he was there, or how he found out that I work there, but it seems that he knows."

The duchess's mouth was set in a hard line and she sat back at her dressing table, lightly fanning herself with a heavy red fan. The silence made Harriet squirm, but at long last, the duchess spoke. "Mr. Desford is unlikely to be believed on his own, and with but a word to a few of my friends, he will have even *less* credit to his name. There is nothing he can do to us."

"Nothing?" Harriet asked skeptically.

"Nothing!" snapped the duchess. Her tone banished arguments, and only a few minutes later, she appeared to have entirely recovered from the shock and disappointment of being discovered. As they set off for the party that evening, the duchess seemed in very high spirits—she was talking ceaselessly in order to catch Harriet up on all the latest town gossip. Harriet stared at her, pretending to absorb all the information while really only marveling that the duchess could continue to care about all these trivialities when she regularly claimed to be above all the petty melodrama of the rest of the *ton*.

When they arrived, Harriet found it easier than she had only the week before to step into Virginia's shoes. She sat in a chair and recited the few Shakespearean sonnets she had memorized over and over in her head until someone came and sat next to her and struck up a conversation. Harriet responded politely but coolly, and the conversation did not last very long.

When they were about to leave for the evening, Harriet recognized Lady Margaret enter the room. She knew that the duchess would desire to speak with her—the two of them were thick as thieves these days—and so Harriet once more found a comfortable place on the sofa. The pair of them chattered eagerly until their conversation died down to muted voices barely louder than whispers. Harriet could not hear their conversation, but due to the glances both of them continually tossed her way, she could only imagine it was about herself and Mr. Brougham.

A few minutes later, the duchess managed to join Harriet in her quiet corner, still apparently in raptures.

"I should very much like to see you married to Andrew Brougham, my dear."

"Oh." Harriet took a sip of her lemonade.

"Do you think he is close to offering courtship, Virginia?"

Harriet's eyes bulged and she nearly choked on her drink. "Are you certain my courting him is a good idea, Mother?"

"Of course it is," the duchess snapped, stiffening.

Harriet looked left and right to be sure no one could hear them before whispering. "I do not feel quite comfortable putting Virginia into situations about which she has no say," she whispered.

The duchess gave a laugh. "But that is one of the primary attractions of the scheme!"

Harriet said nothing. She did not trust herself to speak without losing her temper.

The duchess's lips spread into a self-satisfied smile. "I trust you to properly encourage him, my dear. After the mess you created with Mr. Desford," she simpered, "it is the *least* you can do."

On the road to Curzon Street, London

Harriet glanced at the duke sitting across from her in the carriage on the way home from the party. She had claimed a headache to leave the party early, but the duchess had insisted on staying. It was rare that she saw the duke at all these days, and she had only been left alone with him once before. She awkwardly stared out the window, studiously avoiding him until she heard him clear his throat.

"Harriet, I am sorry you are feeling unwell this evening," he said. "I hope that . . . you continue to be properly cared for while in my wife's employ. I would never wish harm to come to you."

His concern was touching. And he always acted the perfect, formal picture of a duke whenever she had seen him. He was certainly no flirt. Even now, he sat as far from her in the carriage as he could and was looking out the window instead of at her. The more she thought about the duchess's assumption he kept a mistress, the more she doubted it. She glanced curiously at him.

"Your Grace . . . Virginia and your wife have told me that you keep a private set of apartments here in town."

The duke looked at her curiously. "I do."

"Why is that?"

The duke sighed, and seemed to age several years. "Sometimes I simply wish to be alone."

Harriet knew it was impertinent, but she had to know. "Then you don't keep . . . *any* company while you are there?"

The duke frowned at her curiously. "No, I go there to *avoid* company, as I just said. Why do you ask?"

Harriet's cheeks were flushed, and she hoped it was dim enough in the carriage that he could not tell. "Because your wife told me you keep a mistress there."

The duke stared at her for a minute before returning his attention to the window. He said no more and Harriet could not be sure, but it seemed like he was shaking his head sadly as he later exited the carriage.

Madam Salford's gaming hell, Piccadilly, London

Stephan kept his ears trained on the table next to his. He wore a shabby coat and had not shaved in a few days. He aimed to blend in with the middle class and tradesmen that frequented Madam Salford's less-than-respectable gaming house. It appeared to be working, too, as he had not yet been recognized.

He sat at a table by himself not far from the high-stakes hazard table, sipping at port and playing a solitary game of cards as he listened.

"And what new mischief have you been getting up to, then?" the young lady working the game asked Desford.

Mr. Desford laughed. "What mischief, Meg? Here, our fair hostess thinks me a rake!" he winked at her and took another swig of his drink as his friends filled the air with bawdy laughter.

Meg smiled, but Stephan had to hold back a laugh as he recognized that she had clearly rolled in the house's favor.

"Oh, more's the pity—you've lost again, sir," she simpered.

Anger flashed across Mr. Desford's brow, but he calmed quickly. "Tis no matter. Seeing your lovely face is always well worth any amount I lose here."

Meg smiled and nodded as she collected the stakes and prepared the game anew. "You're a handsome one, sir. Seems you ought to have chosen a mistress for that fortune of yours by now."

"I think perhaps I have," Mr. Desford said thoughtfully.

"Out with it, then," a rougher acquaintance told him with a laugh. "Who is she? Ought we to feel sorry for the girl?"

Mr. Desford smiled. "A young lady in a *very* precarious situation indeed."

Meg made a barely concealed noise of disgust as she set up the game. Mr. Desford's gaze flickered up to her and back to his glass of wine. "She is a governess, if you are interested to know."

The lady of the house frowned. "A governess? She's not one of your common girls, then."

"Oh, she's common enough. The daughter of a farmer."

Stephan's right hand formed a white-knuckled fist and his eyes narrowed.

"And you intend to make this farmer's daughter mistress over all you own?"

Mr. Desford laughed. "Mistress over all I own? Of course not! I can't very well *marry* the girl, can I? She's a nobody! Look where that got my father!"

Desford's friends gave a laugh, but Stephan felt his blood boil.

"But she'd make a fine mistress over a beautiful set of apartments near the Thames." He shot a wink at Meg.

Stephan stood suddenly, knocking over his glass in the process, and turned his back on the gaming hell and all its patrons. Even if he could have stomached listening to more, it was time for him to leave. The stagecoach for Brighton was about to leave, and Stephan had planned to seek out Ralph's sister before the week was out. He only hoped that he would not be gone from London long enough for Mr. Desford to make any more mischief for Harriet.

Chapter Twenty-Six

Burnham-on-Sea, Somerset

Stephan had not wanted to stop looking for Ralph Clifton once he had started, but business affairs pulled him home once again. However, he was less irritated than he would have been had he not just learned new information about Ralph that led him to Portsmouth—not half a day's journey from Burnham-on-Sea. He would not need to pause his quest for long.

When he arrived at Harriet's home in Burnham-on-Sea, he sighed. He still pictured her as he had last seen her—wearing a magnificent ball gown, glittering jewels in her ears and around her neck, so beautiful and regal it was almost painful to look at her. He would see that she had at least a few gowns like that one when they married. *If* they married. He had work to do. He took a deep breath before knocking on the door of the house.

The housekeeper answered and led Stephan into Mr. Shore's study, where Mr. Shore sat at his desk in his shirtsleeves, a roaring fire in the grate to chase away the January chill. Another man was already seated on the other side of the desk, who must have been Mr. Shore's solicitor.

"Mr. Grimsby!" The solicitor stood and clasped Stephan's hand in one of his own. "Wonderful to see you, sir. How have you been?"

Harriet's father awaited the answer to the question with unusual eagerness.

Stephan attempted a casual smile. "I have been well. I was visiting my aunt's family in London for the season but was told there was a bit more to do to finalize our agreement."

The solicitor nodded, gesturing toward a few papers already laid out on the desk. "This ought to be the last of them, Mr. Grimsby."

Stephan leaned forward to inspect the papers before him and sign each one in turn. As soon as he had finished, the solicitor dried his ink with powder and collected the papers. "Everything is now in order. Final title documents will be prepared and brought to you soon, sir," he told Mr. Shore. With a polite nod to Stephan, the solicitor left the room.

Mr. Shore smiled. "Now that you've signed everything, all that's left is for me to make a final payment and take ownership."

Stephan nodded. He felt he was making the correct decision for his estate and his tenants by selling nearly a quarter of his lands to Mr. Shore, but it was a bittersweet event. He was grateful the properties would stay with the people who worked and loved them, and that precious little would change in their small community. He also felt slightly defeated by the sale and could not think of its necessity without feeling annoyed with his mother and father.

"If I can do more to assist you with the transition, please let me know," Stephan said quietly.

Mr. Shore fell silent and sat back in his chair, his chin resting thoughtfully in his hand, appraising Stephan's tired countenance.

"How is my Harriet doing all the way in London, Mr. Grimsby?"

Stephan looked up at the other gentleman, his face flushed. "She is . . . keeping very well, it would seem."

"You were able to visit her, were you not?" Mr. Shore asked.

Stephan nodded. "I saw her briefly. She has been thoroughly occupied with her various duties and responsibilities."

Mr. Shore frowned. "Tell me, Mr. Grimsby. Does she seem happy there?"

"Happy?" Stephan asked, thinking to himself. *Happy* was not the first word that came to mind when he thought of his visit with Harriet. Harriet seemed to feel as heavy a weight on his shoulders as he did.

"She did not seem nearly so happy as she did here," Stephan admitted.

Mr. Shore smiled and nodded. "Good."

Stephan blinked in surprise at the man's reaction.

"The sooner she finds herself unhappy in her current situation, the sooner she can return here, where she belongs," her father clarified. "With us."

Us. Stephan knew the "us" Mr. Shore mentioned was likely referring to himself and his wife, but Stephan still could not hold back a bit of excitement at the prospect of one day being included in Harriet's life. However, things were different now. Stephan was indebted to her family. He was by no means certain that his suit would even be accepted once she knew the whole.

"Of course," Stephan said. "She belongs here. With you."

Mr. Shore gave Stephan a hard, appraising look. However, after a moment, Mr. Shore stood. "I would offer you to take some port with me, but it is still too early in the day. So, I hope that you will join me another time. Next week, perhaps?"

Stephan stood and shook Mr. Shore's proffered hand. "Honored, sir. But perhaps tomorrow? I have business in Portsmouth I must attend to before next week."

Mr. Shore's smile was curious. "Until tomorrow, then."

Curzon Street, London

"Your mother wishes me to enter a courtship with Mr. Brougham as soon as possible."

Virginia did not look up from her work. "That's hardly surprising."

"I think he's nice enough," Harriet said hesitantly.

"Oh, I am sure he is." Virginia continued knitting a minuscule pair of white baby stockings. "He would likely make a fine husband for me. He'd never make a fuss at all. Gentle, friendly, impeccably respectable . . . his only irredeemable flaw is that he is not Ralph."

Harriet smothered a grimace, and mentally prayed that Ralph really *would* return. She was not at all certain he would, but she continued to hope for Virginia's sake.

Virginia looked up from her knitting. "I suppose you think I ought to simply marry him," she told Harriet.

Harriet shook her head. "No. While there is still a chance Ralph could return, we must be hopeful. Besides, I would never wish to make this decision for you."

"And yet, you're the only one who *can*." Virginia smiled. "I suppose, in spite of my awkward situation, that makes me lucky."

Harriet couldn't help glancing at Virginia's growing abdomen. It had grown even since the week before when she had thought it couldn't possibly get larger.

"How much longer now?" she asked, nodding toward Virginia's belly.

Virginia patted her midsection. "The midwife says about two months, more or less. It's difficult to say, exactly."

"I imagine it is," Harriet said, her eyes lingering on Virginia's bump.

"Oh, go on. The baby is awake."

Harriet eagerly moved forward and placed a hand on Virginia's swollen midsection, feeling for the telltale nudge of the unborn child. Once she felt it, she smiled. Virginia smiled too.

"You must be excited," Harriet said.

The smile on Virginia's face extinguished. "I am too worried to be *really* excited. I still believe Ralph will come, but . . . what if he is late? What if the baby comes, and my mother . . ."

Harriet tried to hush Virginia, pulling her into a comforting embrace. "It does not do to dwell on it," she said. "Ralph knows your direction here, does he not?"

Virginia nodded, rubbing away a tear.

"He will come," Harriet insisted, as much to convince herself as Virginia. "And if he is delayed," Harriet continued, "I will personally see that your child remains unharmed and by your side. I'm not yet certain *how*, but I will."

Virginia's watery expression became grateful. "Thank you, Harriet."

"Don't thank me yet—I might not be able to avoid your becoming engaged to that gangly, awkward fellow your mother is fixated on."

Virginia giggled. "Whatever makes my mother happy creates the fewest ripples. Go ahead and please her now, while we still have the chance to do so."

"You are certain?" Harriet asked.

Virginia nodded, and gave a little sigh. "I know that Ralph will come . . . but I also trust *you* to do all you can to keep me and the baby together in the event he does not arrive punctually. That does make me feel better."

Harriet froze as the weight of this responsibility settled upon her shoulders, but she also stood a bit taller. "You can depend on me."

Berkeley Square, London

Harriet did not feel at ease at the next ball she attended, even though the duchess and Lady Margaret had arranged for Mr. Brougham to remain close to her throughout the evening. He had been present at their last few social gatherings and she had encouraged his attentions to the point that other young men had all but ceased to speak with her. Even this promise of protection did not make her feel entirely at ease about Mr. Desford, however.

After all, he would almost certainly be there as well. Would he attempt to blackmail her again? After thinking carefully about their strained encounter, although he had spoken romantically, Harriet had left feeling threatened. His veiled threat, underscored by his unwelcome visit to Palace Court, had stolen hours of sleep from Harriet. She supposed there was always the *chance* he had not secured an invitation, but this was so unlikely that it was not worth hoping for.

And Stephan? It had been nearly a month, and seemed longer, since she had last seen or spoken to Stephan. She did not know what to do or say. She did not even know if he was still in town. Every time she sat down to write a letter to him, she had held her pen above paper, immobile, for what felt like hours. There were too many reasons not to write, it seemed. She worried the message could somehow be intercepted. That it would be presumed that Lady Virginia had sent it and unravel the entire charade. That she would be considered loose for sending private correspondence to a gentleman she was not engaged to. But were they courting? It seemed so, but she was not sure. No, it was safest not to write. But, where was he? Was he safe? Had he gone off in search of Ralph? Perhaps she ought not to have enlisted his aid.

Harriet had been so worried while preparing for the ball that she was shaking in her satin slippers, even though her gown was one of her favorites. It was deep blue taffeta, with white embroidery and lace trim, and she wore borrowed pearls from the duchess, Virginia's best diamond earrings, and a perfectly curled coiffure. Nevertheless, she could not manage to feel at ease.

Upon her entering the room, the accommodating Mr. Brougham rushed to her side.

"Hello, Lady Virginia. I hope you have been keeping well since our last meeting?"

She smiled but wondered if he had intended the joke or not. They had last spoken only the night before at Mrs. Marksby's card party. "I have been," she assured him. She allowed him to lead her into the supper room and take his place next to hers at the table. They chatted as easily as usual, but Harriet was continually looking over her shoulder and practically jumping whenever anyone entered the room.

And she had good cause to be nervous. After they had finished supper and begun to walk to the music room, she saw Stephan entering the ballroom. He made eye contact with her and she could not keep from smiling. He winked at her and tried not to smile. It was all she could do to refrain from rushing across the room and leaping into his arms, but it did not seem quite like something Virginia would have done.

They had been seated for a few minutes in the music room and Harriet still felt flushed and exhilarated. She flapped her fan energetically before her face.

"Are you quite well, Lady Virginia?" Mr. Brougham asked next to her.

"Quite," and a hasty smile was all she could manage.

Only a few more minutes passed before her worst fears came true. She had been chatting easily with Mr. Brougham, listening to the excellent performer when everything fell apart. Mr. Brougham suddenly noticed an old friend of his from Oxford and excused himself to go and speak with him. The moment he was gone, a familiar voice spoke at her elbow and set her heart to pounding.

"Lady Virginia," it said innocently, "would you do me the honor of taking a turn with me into the next room?"

She shifted. "I had much rather stay here."

"Ah, but the next room has raspberry punch," Mr. Desford purred, "Your favorite. You will not want to miss it."

He held out his arm, and the look in his eye said that he would not relent easily. She took his arm and allowed herself to be led, not into the next room, but into what appeared to be a library, and quite a private one. The moment the door was closed, Harriet regretted allowing herself to be led so easily. Mr. Desford turned to her and his eyes were even darker than usual, his usually charming smirk replaced with a dangerous leer.

"So, my dear. Are you going to *tell* me who you really are, or shall I be forced to unmask you myself?"

Chapter Twenty-Seven

Berkeley Square, London

"I am Lady Virginia Sackville," Harriet said. She held her head high, but her voice shook. Mr. Desford only chuckled, his smirk widening.

"No, you are not," he sang, his tone mocking. "I repeat. Are you going to tell me the truth yourself, or shall I do so for you?"

Harriet's heart was pounding so loudly in her ears that she wondered why all in attendance at the ball did not hear it. She forced herself to think rationally in spite of her terror. "I cannot."

He seemed exasperated, but his countenance softened slightly and he took a step toward her, only for her to wince. "You are as skittish as a rabbit, my dear. I am sorry to frighten you. I only wanted you to *trust* me with your secret. I have no desire to injure either you or Lady Virginia. I am, as ever, your *friend*."

His eyes glowed the familiar navy she knew and the dangerous glint in his eye disappeared for a moment. Her heart slowed a bit and she once more felt able to breathe more normally.

"I . . . do not know where to begin," she said in a small voice.

Mr. Desford caught her hand and led her to a soft chair next to a bookcase. He sat in the chair next to hers. "Take all the time you need."

"My name is Harriet Shore," she whispered. "I am a governess from Somerset. Lady Virginia is . . . indisposed to be in society herself right now, and her mother desired that I take her place."

"It's been several months," Mr. Desford pressed. "What is the matter with Lady Virginia?"

"It is not my secret to tell."

A self-satisfied, knowing smile slid onto Mr. Desford's face. "I understand completely. She must be in an indelicate state. Is that so? Never fear—the secret is safe with me."

Harriet frowned at him. Nothing seemed "safe" right now. "Why are you doing this?"

Mr. Desford stared off into the distance. "I knew there had to be *something* different about you. Not only is your face very slightly different—a little more narrow and symmetrical, the complexion smoother . . . your personality was different. Instead of resisting my charms and ignoring my attempts to flirt with you, you were receptive. Charming. A veritable country schoolgirl."

Harriet could feel herself flushing in humiliation.

"I must confess, I liked the change. I was flattered and pleased by the success of my attempts to charm you. I was initially disappointed when my suspicions that you are *not*, in fact, Lady Virginia were confirmed, but I quickly realized that I like you even better. And my offer of courtship of a month past applies to *you*, Harriet."

Harriet swallowed hard. She didn't want him to talk about his feelings for her. Her stomach felt like it was trying to climb out through her chest.

"I did have some feelings for Virginia once," he admitted, "but I also have feelings for you now, Harriet. Different feelings. *Stronger* feelings."

Her gaze flickered to the door. She wondered if she could cross the room quickly enough to leave before he could stop her.

His hand rested on hers and he leaned toward her. "After all, you are *very* charming."

Her eyes were still on the door. She tried to subtly slip her hand out from under his. "Charming?"

He leaned closer. "Yes." She felt his warm, clean breath on her cheek.

She leaned away. "Mr. Des—" and his lips covered hers in a kiss.

Harriet jerked away from him as though she'd been shocked and shot out of her chair, wiping away the taste of him.

"How *dare* you!" she cried.

He stood and moved toward her, his movements as lithe as a cat's. "I thought you enjoyed it, *Harriet*."

Harriet felt sick to her stomach, and extremely unsafe. The dangerous gleam in Mr. Desford's eyes was back. She backed away from Mr. Desford and into the door as he inched toward her. Suddenly, she heard Mr. Brougham outside the door, calling for her.

"I am here!" she cried in relief, and she opened and slipped out the door before Mr. Desford could stop her. Mr. Brougham was right on the other side.

"There you are, Lady Virginia! I am sorry to have left you earlier to speak to my schoolmate. Are you quite all right? You appear to be in some distress." He noticed Mr. Desford then, and without waiting for Harriet's response, nodded politely toward him with a concerned smile. "Mr. Desford, isn't it? A pleasure."

"I am quite well," Harriet hastily took Mr. Brougham's arm and stood by his side, grateful that he was ignoring the implications of finding her in a private room with another man. "I am sorry to have ever left your side, Mr. Brougham."

"No harm done," Mr. Brougham said, squeezing the hand she rested on his arm. "Only the quartet's about to begin their set! If you'll excuse us, Mr. Desford?"

Mr. Desford's eyes had darkened again. Harriet barely resisted the urge to shudder. Mr. Brougham whisked Harriet away then, to her extreme relief. It was only once they had settled in to listen to the quartet that she allowed herself the luxury of fretting endlessly about what she could possibly do about Mr. Desford.

Curzon Street, London

"He *kissed* you?" Virginia's voice was shrill.

"Sounds like her social life is a tad more interesting than *yours* used to be, Virginia," Mandie chuckled.

Harriet frowned at the pair of them. "You do not seem quite pre-occupied enough about this—the man is *dangerous!*" she insisted.

Virginia waved a hand carelessly. "Yes, yes. It's all very distress-ing—he knows everything. But let us think of that later—he really kissed you? At a ball? What was it like?"

Harriet folded her arms and frowned, but her cheeks flamed as she responded. "I should imagine you ought to know what it is like to have a gentleman kiss you."

Virginia laughed at Harriet's embarrassment, but looked right-fully ashamed. "I do know what you mean, Harriet, and yet . . . I do not. For Ralph was no gentleman. He did not engage in the farce that the *ton* seems to enjoy. He was simply a man. Not a gentleman, not a scoundrel . . . but a man. And a good one. But to be pulled aside at a well-attended ball and be kissed by a handsome rake! It is too exciting, really, especially for one whose primary amusement these days lies in sewing baby clothes."

Harriet could not help smiling. "So, you admit that he's a rake?"

Virginia laughed. "I do *now!*"

Harriet sighed. "Virginia, when I first met you, I thought your view of the world was sad and strange. I thought the elegant parties and the fine manners and the beautiful gowns left little to be desired. I only wished the character I played were less morose."

Virginia looked down at her lap with a rueful smile before looking back at Harriet.

"But now I *see* what you dislike about it," Harriet continued, "It is all an elaborate farce. I enjoy the performance—but I am not the only one playing a part, and I can know that now. However, to live each day this way . . . pretending and aspiring rather than being who you really are is exhausting. Truly."

Virginia smiled, looking thoughtful. "But although you've been playing a part . . . *you* are the one playing the part. *You* are still Harriet, underneath all those layers of Virginia. Isn't it possible that Mr. Desford saw the true Harriet and fell in love with her?"

Harriet shuddered and shook her head. "Whatever that was, it was not love. And it was far from welcome."

Virginia frowned, and her expression immediately turned serious. "I . . . Harriet, you *are* worried. I thought you might have been joking. I am sorry for making light of all this."

Harriet squeezed Virginia's hand gratefully. "Do not be sorry, Virginia. There was a time, a few months ago, when I was fond of Mr. Desford. He was so very handsome and charming and interesting, and Stephan felt so out of my reach . . . I did like him then. A little. But I do not feel so now. The way he looked at me when we were alone in the library—I've never been more terrified!"

Virginia smirked. "Hmm. And yet . . . you were alone in a library with Stephan, and never felt a bit frightened."

Harriet nodded, and let loose a little sigh. "It is incredible, is it not, how one's feelings for someone can so completely decide a situation? With Stephan, I have never felt anything but safe. When he kissed me, I could have lived forever in that moment."

Mandie sighed audibly and both Harriet and Virginia giggled at her reaction before Harriet continued.

"But with Mr. Desford? I thought I liked Mr. Desford, but I think I was merely taken in by his glamour. He is handsome and charming and fashionable, and I'd simply never met anyone like that before! But I do not feel safe in his presence now. Come to think of it, I'm not certain I ever have."

Virginia nodded, appearing very much the sage. "He is a scoundrel, then. Every bit as bad as others say he is. I trust your intuition more than the *ton*'s general opinion, mind, but it seems they're right about him."

Harriet nodded. "The more he tries to woo me, the easier it is for me to imagine that those stories are true."

"But Harriet, even if Mr. Desford does threaten to reveal your identity, he's unlikely to be believed. The *ton* large considers him an attention-seeking rake, so the scandal if he attempted to unmask you would be almost entirely on his side. He has not the years of respectability in fashionable society that my mother has, nor the clout. Please do not fear overmuch."

Harriet took a deep breath and nodded as she listened to Virginia, forcing herself to relax. "It's hard to believe now that I ever thought him charming. Whenever he's come near me lately I've felt an over-powering urge to run far away."

Virginia wrinkled her nose. "*Run*, you say? That is very dire indeed. I can no longer imagine anything frightening enough to make me run."

Harriet and Mandie both laughed, and as they did so, Harriet's concerns melted into the back of her mind, saved for another day.

The Fencing Academy, Bond Street, London

"You there, Mr. Grendel?"

Stephan continued cleaning his fencing foil and did not look up until Mr. Desford was nearly upon him.

Mr. Desford nudged Stephan's foot with his own foil. "Was it Grendel? Or Grimmly?"

"Oh, were you talking to me?" Stephan finally looked up at Mr. Desford. "It's Mr. Grimsby. And you are . . . Mr. Desperate—No, *Desford*, are you not?"

Mr. Desford's nostrils flared, but he flashed a quick glance about him at the other gentlemen in the large room and forced a polite smile.

"Grimsby, of course. How stupid of me. Would you care to spar with me?"

Stephan smiled and slowly stood. "I would be honored, Mr. Desford."

"Indeed, I suspected you might be. I seem to have seen you every-where of late. It is almost . . . as though you were following me." Mr. Desford chuckled, but his jaw was tight.

Stephan laughed, and there was a sporting gleam in his eye as he bent his knees and raised his blade in invitation. "So glad you've finally noticed."

"I did not realize you were such a great admirer." Mr. Desford glared at Stephan. "En garde!" He dove forward with his sword, but Stephan easily parried the blow and shifted to the side.

"I must confess," he murmured so that only Desford could hear, "I do not like the way you look at Miss Harriet Shore."

Mr. Desford's face flushed. His careful composure slipped and his foil flashed toward Stephan again, only for Stephan to dodge it without looking away from Desford's face.

"Is she under your protection?"

Stephan feinted to the right and dodged Desford's parry before tapping the other man's chest guard with the tip of his blade. He leaped backward to avoid his retaliation.

"She is a very dear friend." Stephan easily parried another attack.

Mr. Desford's scoff was loud enough to redirect half the academy's attention to their match. "And if she desires my company? Who am I to deny it of her?"

"I am not certain she does." Stephan lunged forward in a false attack, smiling at Mr. Desford's reaction.

Mr. Desford's counterattack was so quick that it narrowly missed Stephan, who leapt backwards. Desford sneered. "She'd never turn me down."

"You don't think so? Terribly sorry." Stephan's tone was cheerful and only served to infuriate Mr. Desford more. "Because I think she might prefer to be my wife."

"You'd *marry* her? She's only a governess."

Stephan swallowed his anger and channeled it into a quick flurry of attacks that left Mr. Desford breathless after an ungraceful defense. "Yes, she is. And a farmer's daughter!" Stephan said proudly.

Their blades clashed several more times, and a small crowd of resting gentleman gathered to watch the rest of their exchange.

Mr. Desford's attacks were growing more clumsy, and even Stephan was beginning to grow tired. He allowed Mr. Desford to lunge forward a time or two, neatly parrying his advances. A second later, his foil shot out and slapped the back of Mr. Desford's hand, leaving a painful welt. He finally finished with a combined attack, leaving Mr. Desford disarmed, with Stephan's sword at his throat.

Mr. Desford nursed his injured hand with murder in his eyes.

"You'd do well to mind your own business," he spat.

Stephan dropped his borrowed foil to the floor, panting. "As would you. She is not your property, whatever you may think. Consider that a warning." He turned his back toward Mr. Desford. "For the next time we meet, I shan't go easy on you." With that, he left the hall to change his clothes without a backward glance, ignoring the effusive praises of the spectating gentlemen.

Chapter Twenty-Eight

Hyde Park, London

"Thank you for taking me out for a ride." Harriet gratefully inhaled the brisk early spring air of Hyde Park as Mr. Brougham spurred his phaeton forward down the pathway.

"My pleasure, Lady Virginia."

It was an ugly day—the sky was cloudy and gray, the trees were still bare of leaves, and the grass was an unattractive yellow-brown color. And yet, a few birds had begun to return to the park. February had rushed by in practically a blur, and March had arrived. Harriet hadn't so much as seen Stephan since their very short brush at the ball three weeks before, and missed him more than ever.

Perhaps it was in her mind, but whenever she had seen Mr. Desford of late, his smirk had been wider than usual, as though he knew he held her in the hollow of his hand.

Harriet was still lost in thought and had no warning before Mr. Brougham's phaeton pulled up alongside a certain Mr. Desford.

Harriet mentally swore. "Mr. Desford," she greeted stiffly, her salutation significantly less warm than Mr. Brougham's.

"Desford! Wonderful to see you. How are you?"

"Brougham!" Mr. Desford tipped his hat to Mr. Brougham. "It has been entirely too long since I've had a game of piquet with you, my dear fellow."

"Erm . . . I suppose it has," Mr. Brougham said. "Since Lady Virginia and I began courting, I've been quite occupied of late."

Mr. Desford's eyes shifted to Harriet, and she tried to ignore the way it made her heart pound as she gave him a polite nod and even managed a weak smile.

"That is understandable," Mr. Desford's eyes did not leave Harriet's face. "If I could have secured Lady Virginia's interest, I should never have wished to be apart from her."

Harriet was vaguely aware that next to her Mr. Brougham had flushed as he gave a humble response, but she still could not take her eyes off Mr. Desford's. What was he planning? Could it possibly be honorable? Could he intend to do her ill simply because she was of a lower rank than he?

Mr. Desford brought up his horse as close to the phaeton as possible and reached his hand toward Harriet. She reluctantly gave him hers. He pressed a kiss on the back of her hand and a shiver passed from her hand to her heart. There was a lump in her throat and in that moment, she wished Mr. Desford were as far away as could be.

He let go after what seemed an eternity and Mr. Brougham excused himself and Harriet with a promise that he would play a game of piquet with Mr. Desford soon. Harriet could not resist the urge to look back at Mr. Desford for a moment as they rode away. She met his waiting gaze, and the slight smile playing at the corners of his mouth did nothing to ease her concerns. He faded quickly into the distance, but Harriet's nerves remained on edge for some time afterward.

The Bear and Candle Tavern, Portsmouth, Hampshire

"All the sailors come through here, sir, yes."

Stephan nodded. "But do you particularly remember the one I described?" He hesitated, pulling out the physical description of him that Harriet had gotten from Virginia. "He ought to be tall and dark-haired . . . and very handsome?" Stephan could feel his cheeks flush as the barkeeper gave him an odd look.

"And you said he goes by Ralph Clifton?" The man scratched his chin as he thought. "Aye. I remember him. He come through here several months ago—signed on as a privateer under Captain Avery's letter of Marque. Avery's made port here every six months or so for several years, sir."

Stephan immediately brightened. "Excellent!" he exclaimed. "Please, sir, might I ask you to send Clifton to Number Twelve, Curzon Street in London the instant his ship makes berth?"

The barkeep nodded, still giving Stephan a strange look. "Might I ask what interest you have in the lad?"

"Well, truth be told, his lady is a friend of my lady's. And she is most anxious to see him again."

The barkeep's eyebrows shot up. "His lady is? Or *your* lady is?"

Stephan laughed. "Both of them, I suppose! But it is *his* lady that expects the birth of their child very soon."

The barkeep chuckled. "Aye, I'd be happy to help you."

"Excellent. Here is my direction as well. I will happily repay anything you spend to help Mr. Clifton on his way to London, and here is a guinea or two for taking the trouble."

Stephan eagerly settled into a writing desk in the parlor of the man's establishment to leave directions and a letter. He'd done nothing but search for Ralph and keep an eye on Mr. Desford for weeks, and he'd needed this small victory.

Curzon Street, London

"Things are going perfectly, my dear," the duchess rubbed her hands together. "You could be betrothed any day now. Simply *perfect*! And there is enough time for the banns to be read to allow for . . . well, it will be late April, my dear. And would not a spring wedding at the country estate be divine?"

Harriet swallowed. "The baby may not have even arrived by then. How is Virginia to marry him?"

The duchess pursed her lips as though a fly had landed in her pudding. "Hmph," she grunted. "Well, I suppose we'll have to make it early May, then. That ought to leave enough time. And with a heavy-enough veil, he'd never . . ."

"Regardless, it is Mr. Brougham's decision, is it not? You must be patient, Your Grace . . . and so must I."

It took a few minutes after this outburst for the duchess to regain her cheerful composure, but she did surprisingly quickly. They finished their morning visits that day sooner than usual. Harriet wondered why until they returned to the house and they saw Mr. Brougham as he exited the duke's study, looking somewhat pale, but smiling.

Harriet's heart fluttered—not to see Mr. Brougham, for nothing seemed more dull and calming to her than he, but to see his expression, and his presence outside the duke's study. What had he been discussing with the duke?

Mr. Brougham straightened his shoulders and offered his arm to lead her to the parlor. "Lady Virginia, might I have the honor of a private word with you?"

Harriet swallowed hard. The duchess was halfway up the steps by the time Harriet noticed she was gone. She smiled awkwardly at Mr. Brougham and allowed him to lead her into the parlor. She had known this moment was eventually going to come since the first time she had sought Mr. Brougham out to the exclusion of Mr. Desford . . . and Stephan. She felt simultaneously gratified and terrified. But what was it about young men declaring their devotion that made her wish to break into a run?

She sat with trepidation on the pink sofa and looked up at Mr. Brougham. "Lady Virginia, I . . ." he cleared his throat and looked down at her. He had remained on his feet. "You can be in no doubt of my intentions toward you," he said, a little more quickly than was natural, "I have found you a most interesting and lovely young lady since the moment that my mother introduced you to me. Remember? At Lady Gregor's ball, at the start of the season."

"Yes, I remember," Harriet smiled through her nerves. She hoped she seemed more encouraging than she felt.

"I have wished to court you ever since that first day."

Harriet swallowed, making sure a pleasant smile remained on her face.

"Lady Virginia . . . might I simply call you Virginia?"

Harriet felt a little ripple of distress shudder down her shoulders at hearing Virginia's name without a title.

She paused too long. Mr. Brougham was still waiting for a response and was beginning to look concerned. "Yes, of course!" she said quickly, "I should like that very much. And might I call you . . ." her eyes widened in panic as she realized that she had forgotten his first name.

"Andrew? Of course." He smiled, not seeming fazed in the least. "Virginia, you are the soul of propriety! You hesitate to call me by my Christian name even when appropriate to do so. That is one thing that I do admire about you—your commitment to decorum."

Harriet had to bite her lip to keep from laughing at how far from accurate this description of Virginia was. She managed to smile instead, but her eyes nearly watered from the effort of holding back the bark of laughter that threatened to break forth. "And I you, Mr. Brou—er, Andrew."

Mr. Brougham smiled placidly. "There now, Virginia. We are getting along famously already, are we not? I do like calling you Virginia. 'Tis a beautiful name."

Harriet's nerves were calmed slightly by Mr. Brougham's unflappably calm demeanor. Could *nothing* rattle him?

She inwardly managed a frown. She could think of at least one thing that would: finding out on his wedding night that he had married a woman he'd never met who had recently borne the child of another man.

"Virginia?" Mr. Brougham asked when he noticed she had clearly not been paying attention. She looked back at him.

"Forgive me, Mr.—I mean Andrew. I was lost in my thoughts. You were saying?"

He came toward her and knelt on the ground before her, grasping both her hands in his. "Virginia, will you do me the great honor of becoming my wife?"

Curzon Street, London

"And she looked about ready to lose her lunch, miss, pardon the expression!" Mandie crowed. "She could not speak for a full minute, I'll warrant. For when I came into the room all unexpected-like and surprised her, she finally hopped to it enough to say 'yes,' but not without what seemed a considerable effort."

Virginia and Harriet both laughed, but neither were at ease.

"Well?" Virginia forced a calm expression. "When is the wedding to be?"

"Mother arranged everything—the banns won't be read until April sixteenth, to allow plenty of time to plan the wedding party, and the announcement won't be published in the *Times* until then, either." At the look on Virginia's face, Harriet added, "I held it off as long as I could."

Virginia clutched her round belly, which appeared to be shifting again. Harriet was amazed at how much detail she could imagine while seeing the movements. "And today is . . ." she thought to herself for a moment, "March the twenty-seventh. Publication is more than two weeks away. I am surprised that my mother was willing to wait as long as she did to lock Mr. Brougham into a betrothal—I was afraid she would have you two married by special license tomorrow!"

Harriet shuddered at the thought. "Still, this doesn't give the baby much time to make its grand entrance. So, we may need to alter our plan."

"Ralph will come and this will all be for nothing. You'll see," Virginia insisted.

"Of course he will." Mandie sounded certain, and Harriet shot her a curious glance, but Mandie only shrugged and gave Harriet a pleading look.

"I am hopeful, too," Harriet's tone was unbending. "But I am not going to trust your baby's fate entirely to Ralph's punctual arrival, Virginia. I promised I would not!"

Virginia seemed a little surprised. "What are you suggesting, Harriet?"

Harriet buckled a little under the pressure of the two women's gazes, but she did not take long to recover.

"We will need to get both you and the baby out of the house before the duchess can make her move. This means that . . . if at all possible, we're going to need to keep the fact that you are giving birth a secret from your mother. Do you think you can do that, Virginia?"

Virginia's eyes widened. "I can *try*."

Harriet was only half-listening. She paced the room, thinking aloud. "It is likely to be difficult. In case the duchess learns of the child's imminent arrival before we can safely hurry you away, we'll need to think of another place to hide you, or at the very least, the baby."

"Why don't I just run away *tonight* if I'm going to do it at all?" Virginia moaned. "I'm not likely to feel like going on a hearty walk immediately after bringing a child into the world."

Harriet shook her head. "You need to remain here for the present, Virginia. To allay your mother's suspicions, and to give Ralph the best chance of coming for you himself. The plan I am considering, at its very best, can only buy a little time for us, but it ought to at least keep the baby safe."

Virginia smiled and managed a light chuckle. "Harriet, you really are something. I do not know what your plan is, but if you are the one coming up with it, it just might work."

Chapter Twenty-Nine

Curzon Street, London

Harriet read the note from Mr. Desford for the seventh time, just be sure she wasn't inventing things. "Lady Virginia," it read, "Although it has not yet been formally announced, I wish to congratulate you most warmly on your engagement to my friend Mr. Andrew Brougham. I wish the two of you very happy."

The duchess had been pleased when she had read it that morning. "Well, at least that's some evidence that a bit of good breeding has survived in his family."

But Harriet had felt worried about the missive's unusually polite, formal tone. Virginia had noticed her nerves and tried to quell them. "Harriet, dear, what can he do? Even if he did have power to harm you, why should he wish to? You know that men do not like to share women with other men. Perhaps he has simply given up."

"You did not see the look in his eye that night," Harriet insisted, chafing her own arms to stave off a sudden chill.

"Harriet, love, I never noticed him look me in the eye at all, let alone with the terrifying glare you seem to describe. Isn't it possible that you are worrying over nothing?"

Harriet reread the polite note for the eighth time, remembering the pleasant times she'd spent with Mr. Desford, and allowed herself to be comforted by Virginia and Mandie's continual insistence that the man was powerless to harm her.

As much as Desford frightened her, he wasn't the only thing she was worried about. Stephan was never far from the front of her mind. She had wondered time and again if she ought to write him and assure him that she returned his affections. To thank him for any efforts he may have made to look for Ralph. What if he refused to wait for her? What if he had already begun courting another? More than two months had flown by since their passionate conversation in the library, and it was growing easier to fear that Stephan was no longer hers.

She could not believe that she had asked him to help them by looking for Ralph. He had said that he would, but surely it was a difficult task, and perhaps even a dangerous one! And they were not even courting. But he had openly spoken of marriage—surely some would say they were already courting? It did not matter—she would hang her usual conventions and write him a letter. If he was still hers alone, he deserved to know that she was his.

But she wouldn't have a dowry. Her stomach twisted and she closed her eyes against the pain of the fact that she was back where she'd started—without a dowry. Now that she had a plan to turn directly against Her Grace and help Virginia escape, her hopes of being granted a dowry were all vain. Surely the duchess would not count her charade a success unless Virginia was able to eventually fulfill her role in public life once more.

Harriet bit back the fleeting temptation to betray Virginia's trust and earn her dowry by fulfilling the duchess's hopes and expectations. It was not a difficult temptation to resist. She simply *couldn't* betray Virginia. She couldn't stand by and allow the forceful separation of a mother and child—or of a missing father who may be trying to return. Not while she could stop it. The dowry was not worth having if it came at the cost of Virginia's little family. She would simply have to find another way to prove herself of worth to Stephan and his mother.

Her worries moved on to the only thing left to be concerned about: her impending nuptials to Mr. Brougham. How could she deceive such a nice young man in this way? To become engaged to a woman he's never even met without realizing it, and one who would, god willing, jilt him before the ceremony had taken place? He had done nothing to deserve this, but Harriet knew of no way to stop it from going forward, so she pushed it from her mind. Surely someone as steady and kind as Brougham would have no difficulty finding a suitable wife.

Harriet indulged herself in the few minutes of spare time she had by walking out on the balcony and staring down at the streets below, letting the slight breeze jostle the curls on either side of her face. The white morning dress she wore that day was still finer than any she had owned in Somerset, but far more simple than any of Virginia's other gowns.

Soon, all of it would end—for better or for worse. Mr. Brougham would more than likely be jilted, poor man. But if he weren't, Virginia would be married to a man whom she had never met and whom she did not love. Harriet would either enter a blissful marriage state with Stephan or return to the monotonous, invisible life of a governess, living in constant fear that Mr. Desford could arrive any day to threaten her good name.

And Virginia's baby . . . Harriet stood up straight and tall on the balcony, daring the breeze to muss her hair. The child was the one thing that gave her courage instead of fear. She could not allow anything bad to happen to that baby. She could not allow Virginia to be separated from her own child. She would need to fight to keep their little family together, and she was prepared to do so at all costs.

She said another silent prayer that Ralph would arrive in time, and forced the hope of a dowry from her mind. She could worry about her own story once Virginia's had a happy ending.

Stepney Manor, Cheltenham, Gloustershire

It was a lovely wedding. Stephan had needed to blink back a few tears, and surreptitiously touch the corner of his sleeve to his eye. He'd never considered his foolish cousin Frank a romantic before, but the way he'd looked into Frances's eyes at their wedding was considerable evidence to the contrary.

Once the mercifully brief ceremony ended, the happy couple exited the church in the warming weather on that rare sunny day in Cheltenham to the cheers of dozens of neighbors, friends, and family members. What seemed to be several pounds of rice were thrown, and the happy couple embraced a handful of friends.

One of the few that Frank embraced was Stephan. "When I return from my honeymoon, I expect to hear that you are betrothed," and the look in his eye did not look ready to accept an argument.

Stephan had smiled weakly. "I hope I shall be."

Frank had left his side only to look back and shout a moment later, far more loudly than Stephan would have preferred, "Go and get her, man!"

Stephan watched his cousin help his new wife into the carriage before climbing in himself. He felt a twinge of envy. He'd never thought that Frank would beat him to the altar. Not that it had been a race.

Instead of joining the festivities, he immediately made for the inn in Cheltenham where he was staying. He asked for his bag to be packed and for a post chaise to be procured immediately. It had been over a week since he had last ascertained that Harriet remained safe from Mr. Desford, and he was not willing to risk waiting much longer.

He had to see her again. They had not spoken in months, and he had remained fairly patient until her note had found him the day before, and now he could not wait any longer. Her brief note, in addition to making him miss her more than ever, had given him the sinking suspicion that she was in more trouble than she wanted to admit. Not an hour later, he was climbing into a carriage headed back to London. He had no time left to lose.

Curzon Street, London

"What do you think of this, Harriet?" Virginia held up a little white nightgown, fit for a baby and edged in lace.

"It's darling!" Harriet carefully took the little garment and turned it over in her hands.

"Hmph," grunted Mandie.

Harriet turned to glance at Mandie through narrowed eyes. It was very rare that Mandie got into one of her bouts of true ill-humor. Harriet always found out what caused them sooner or later, because Mandie tended to hold onto things until she spoke her mind about them. She handed the little nightgown back to Virginia and walked over to sit next to Mandie.

"Is there something you wish to tell me, Mandie?" Her voice was soft, but she hoped Mandie caught the significance to her tone.

Mandie glanced over at Virginia, already busy at work once more. She nodded, and flounced out of the room, pulling Harriet out of the room with her by the wrist. They went down the hall and entered Virginia's bedchamber, now occupied by Harriet.

Once the door was shut, Mandie sighed and pulled a piece of paper out of her pocket.

"I've heard from Ralph," she blurted.

Harriet's mouth fell open. "I . . . He's really responded? Is that the letter? May I read it?"

Harriet's fingers twitched toward the paper Mandie held.

"Go on, then." Mandie relinquished the paper. "There'll be no talking with you until you've seen it yourself."

Harriet eagerly unfolded the letter, greedily drinking in its contents.

1814 March 22

Dear Mandie,

I am more relieved than I can say that Virginia continues in good health. I hope that you do, also. I am a simple man, and I do not excel at writing letters, but I must address the charges you have laid against me.

You ask why I had not the decency to marry her. This surprises me, as we are already married. Virginia and I were married in St. Ann's church in Radipole village, the banns read weeks before, and an announcement published in the Dorset Echo. I am surprised she did not tell you herself.

Harriet gasped. "*Married?*"

"Right under her parents' nose, too, in a humble village church. Apparently, moving about in the lower circles of society grants invisibility."

"But . . . surely she would need permission!"

"No, she didn't—she is of age, remember." Mandie growled again. "But I cannot *believe* she did not tell me so herself! It is unpardonable!"

Harriet patted Mandie's arm in what she hoped was a reassuring manner. "We don't know her reasons, Mandie."

"Well, *I* can't think of any decent ones."

Harriet bit her lip. Her curiosity was driving her mad, and so she allowed Mandie to continue stewing while she finished reading the letter.

I did not jilt my wife—nor would I ever do so. Though I am guilty of marrying without the appropriate means to support a wife and family, and I am not certain I shall ever forgive myself for it.

When we first married, we were happy enough trespassing on my sister's kindness. When Virginia became with child, however, my sister wished for us to leave. I hadn't a farthing to my name and needed to either sell out and work as a laborer or continue military service, leaving Virginia alone in wretched circumstances. She was unaccustomed to hard labor, and so I thought Virginia's staying safely with her family for the time being was for the best. I knew I had little enough time before the baby came to make my fortune.

I sold out and set sail on the first available ship and volunteered for the most dangerous and potentially lucrative position I could find as a privateer. I did not want Virginia to worry, and so I did not tell her. Our crew was fortunate and we captured several wealthy French vessels. In a matter of a few months, I had a tidy enough fortune to secure a small home of our own. Soon after my return to England, however, I learned of my great-uncle's passing. He was not a wealthy man, but was dear to me. He has a widow with no children and had worked a long life as a farmer not far from Brighton. My uncle's landlord asked me to take up his position, lease, and home, as I am his nearest living relative. I accepted, and as I write this, I am leaving Portsmouth for Brighton to settle my affairs before coming to collect my wife.

I hope that Virginia shall enjoy being a farmer's wife. It is far from the glamorous life she has previously led, but I hope she will be happy. She led me to believe before I left that writing her was not safe—her mail would surely be read by others. I have refrained from writing on her order. However, I pray you will give her notice of me. You may expect me no later than April the 15th, and I shall hope to find her, and the child, if it has already arrived, safe, well, and ready to join me at our new home.

Sincerely,

Ralph Clifton

Harriet bit her lip. "Mandie, but it is so romantic! I must confess, I did not really believe that he would come. Oh, I am so happy to have misjudged him!"

"I am too," Mandie admitted.

"The fifteenth . . . that is in only three days! How glorious! And not a moment too soon. The wedding is set for May first! Oh, but I could cry from happiness!"

"He did say he may be sooner." Mandie had begun pacing the room. "But what if he is later? And what about the baby? If it should arrive before Ralph does, how shall we keep the baby safe from the duchess? You must help me, miss!"

"Calm yourself, Mandie!" Harriet clasped Mandie's shoulder. "We can and *will* think of a plan. For now, shouldn't we go and tell poor Virginia about this letter?"

"Poor Virginia, indeed," Mandie grumbled, going from anxious to annoyed in a heartbeat. "I still cannot *believe* she didn't tell us!"

Chapter Thirty

Curzon Street, London

Harriet urged Mandie to think carefully about how to broach the subject to Virginia, but Mandie's impertinent spark made her tongue sharper than ever. Mandie rolled up her sleeves, armed with confidence from her conversation with Harriet, and marched into Virginia's quarters, Harriet following close behind.

"Virginia!" Mandie stormed into the room. Virginia nearly dropped the little baby bonnet she had been edging.

"What is it, Mandie? You frightened me half to death!"

Harriet slipped through the door behind Mandie before Mandie slammed it shut.

"Why didn't you tell us you were married?"

Virginia's eyes widened and she blinked several times in silence. "I . . ."

"Mandie, please," Harriet urged Mandie over to the sofa, where she could relax.

It gave Virginia a moment to gather her thoughts. Harriet held her breath as she waited for the explanation.

"You're right—I should've told you." Her voice was little more than a rueful murmur. "But I could not bring myself to at first. I think . . . silly though it is, I was afraid that talking of it would cause what already seemed a dream to disappear entirely. If I'd told you of the marriage and he *didn't* return for me, someone may have forced him to. After all, my father . . . once when my father came to speak to me, he asked me about Ralph. He said the most awful things about him, Mandie! That he was a scoundrel and a cad for leaving me the way that he did." She wrapped her arms around herself as if to stave off a sudden chill.

"But the truth is . . ." she continued, "I never deserved Ralph, and I think a little part of me wondered if he'd only married me out of pity, and escaped at the first chance."

Harriet's jaw dropped open. "No." Her denial was swift and sure. "No, he *loved* you, Virginia. He felt unworthy of *you*."

A flush rose in Virginia's cheeks and her hands roved over her swollen belly. She shook her head as tears streamed down her cheeks. "He deserves a woman with work-worn hands and good sense. Who can make a little go a long way. Who won't . . . introduce unnecessary stress into his life. I am equally useless whether I am a lady or a sailor's wife."

Mandie hadn't responded yet, but Harriet noticed that her own irritation had swiftly drained as Virginia spoke and been replaced with sympathy and hurt. "But Virginia, you still could have told us. You did not need to bear this burden by yourself."

Virginia's eyes were closed, and a tear slipped from the corner of one eye. "I know I ought to have told you. But you know my mother's mind, Mandie—she would never have allowed me to return home if she had known I am married. She likely would've forced me to seek an annulment or divorce before coming home! And by the time I felt you could have borne the secret, the doubts had already slipped in."

"But you've always insisted Ralph would return," Harriet pressed, puzzled.

Virginia sniffled. "As much to convince myself as anyone else."

Harriet shared a glance with Mandie and walked over to sit next to Virginia and pull her into a comforting embrace. "And so he shall, Virginia. I am certain of it."

Mandie pulled the letter out of her pocket as she settled onto the sofa next to Virginia, clearing her throat. "He *will* come," she echoed, "And I am glad you are already sitting down, Virginia, since this might come as quite a surprise."

Audley Street, London

Virginia and the midwife expected the baby to arrive any day. Her ankles were so swollen she could barely walk, and her once-slender form sported a midsection larger than Harriet could believe was possible without looking at it herself. She could have sworn there were *two* babies there, but the midwife insisted there was only one.

The wedding was set for a mere two weeks away. The engagement had been formally announced in the *Gazette*, the banns read, Lady Virginia's wedding clothes chosen and made, flowers arranged to be delivered, the church decided upon, and even a honeymoon location selected. With each day that Virginia had not delivered, however, the duchess grew more and more snippy and anxious that she would not shrink small enough in time for stays to hold her into the dress, in spite of the dress's being made far larger than Harriet's frame required. She simply prayed that no one would notice the difference on the day of the wedding.

"Perhaps it would be better for Virginia to take her rightful place *after* the wedding," the duchess said. "Perhaps we should have a dress made for *you*, instead."

Harriet's eyes had widened in horror at this suggestion.

"That wouldn't be a legal wedding, Your Grace," Mandie interjected.

Harriet gave a silent sigh of relief.

"I suppose you are right," the duchess had complained, "but let us be sure to choose a suitably thick veil!"

Harriet attended a ball at number forty-four Audley Street only two weeks before the wedding was to take place. After dancing much of the evening with Mr. Brougham, someone else approached and asked her to stand up with him.

"Lady Virginia," the silky voice of Mr. Desford murmured in her ear. "Please do me the honor of dancing the next with me. After all, it may be my last opportunity before you become a married woman."

Mr. Brougham was by her side in an instant before Harriet could find an excuse to refuse. He had been looking far more pale and haggard in the last couple of weeks. He greeted Mr. Desford politely before turning to Harriet.

"Is something the matter, Virginia?"

Harriet shook her head. "No, no. All is well."

"Could you spare your betrothed for a single dance?" Mr. Desford asked with exaggerated politeness. Harriet could hear the barely concealed irritation oozing through his words.

"If my lady so desires."

Harriet smiled weakly at Mr. Desford but her insides writhed as she accepted his hand. He led her into the dance with a stiff arm and they danced in tense silence. He did not say a single word until the dance was coming to a close.

"Meet me in the library at half past eleven. *Please*," he finally said when he did speak. Harriet did not respond. Her heart was hammering too hard from the vigorous dancing and from her not knowing what to say.

"I beg of you," he urged. "I ask only a few minutes."

Harriet hardly knew what to say. That dark, threatening look she had seen before was gone and he seemed so desperate to talk with her that she couldn't bring herself to refuse him. She only hoped that he wasn't misleading her.

"All right," she reluctantly agreed, allowing Mr. Desford to lead her back to Mr. Brougham's side.

"Would you like to dance the next, dear Virginia, or are you fagged enough to adjourn to the music room?"

Harriet smiled. "The music room sounds lovely . . . Andrew."

He led her in as a duet was beginning. There was a clock in the corner of the music room and Harriet stared at it as the music played, growing more nervous by the minute. Finally, at one minute to half-past ten, she excused herself from Mr. Brougham's side and went to meet Mr. Desford. As she nervously roamed the nearly empty hallways, she wished she could take back her promise to meet him.

The library was empty when she arrived. Or so she thought. She called for Mr. Desford in a half-whisper a few times and was about to leave when he stood up from a chair hidden behind a shelf near the door and, without looking away from her, closed the door behind her, barring her escape.

Her heart felt ready to pound right out of her chest.

"Harriet," his tone was husky. "I hardly know what to say."

Harriet regretted, not for the first time, her sharing her real name with Mr. Desford.

"I . . . would rather you didn't call me that."

"Just this once." He walked toward her, grasping her hand and bringing it to his mouth for a kiss. "Harriet," he whispered.

She swallowed, and could have sworn he could hear it. Harriet pulled her hand away as soon as Mr. Desford's grip loosened.

"Harriet, I . . . you aren't really going to marry Brougham, are you? Just to be *comfortable*? Wasn't it . . . wasn't it *I* that you cared for, not so very long ago?"

Harriet's mind raced. He thought she was going to be the one marrying Brougham instead of Virginia? Perhaps it was for the best if he believed that.

"My life is not my own to give to whom I wish at the moment," she said quietly. Stephan's face flashed in her mind and she reveled in the momentary thought of him.

"So, you admit that your heart belongs to me?" Mr. Desford snaked an arm around her waist, but she quickly maneuvered away from him before he could pull her closer.

"I do *like* you, Mr. Desford," she said nervously. "It's only that—"

"But a wedding under Lady Virginia's guise . . . It would never work. The moment he discovered the deception, you would be left disgraced and alone."

She leaned away from him far enough that she lost her balance and took a step backward, closer to the door. "Of course I'm not going to—"

"You needn't continue this charade any longer." He took a step closer. "You can run away with me."

"What?" she snapped.

"Come away with me." He took both her hands in his. "Please. Harriet, I don't think I can bear life without you."

She tried to tug her hands away, but he held them firmly, his eyes pleading. That look in his eye—the dark, dangerous glint bordering on madness—was back, and she bit her lip to hold back the scream she felt like releasing.

"I cannot," she finally insisted.

"Please," he whispered back. He leaned in until his lips were mere inches from hers and then paused. Her back was pressed against the door behind her and she could not go further. She leaned away from him, but he closed the gap between them with a small moan.

Harriet gathered all her strength to shove Mr. Desford away from her, wiping the taste of him from her lips with disgust. His nostrils flared with anger and there was a spark in his eyes. She wanted to run away immediately but knew that he could likely overpower her long before she could reach help and there was no telling what he would do in a mood like this. It was time to *really* put her acting skills to the test.

"I cannot run away with you." She swallowed her distaste and made her tone as gentle as she could. She reached up and softly stroked his cheek. "I have duties to attend to."

"Thoroughly admirable, Harriet," he chuckled, relaxing again. "But you ought to think of yourself, and what *you* desire. It does not matter to me that you are a governess. I shall make you mine all the same if you will have me."

Harriet's curiosity got the better of her. "What do you mean?"

"I mean that you shall be very well cared for, dear Harriet."

His mistress. As soon as she realized his meaning, she fought back another wave of revulsion and anger. Harriet's heart beat more quickly, and she somehow managed a smile. He was in earnest—she knew that he was—but he no longer seemed the genial, handsome man she had whiled away so many innocent hours with months before. She could not believe she had allowed herself to be so deceived in him.

"Poor or not, I am a Christian woman, Mr. Desford," she said, trying to sound shy and modest instead of disgusted. "And I must return." She tried her best to look regretful. It was difficult.

After a pause long enough to make her nervous, he finally nodded, but first tightened his grip on her arms. "I . . . shall not keep you now. Only I beg you to reconsider. Mine is an offer far better than any other you are likely to receive."

Her teeth were clenched behind her sweet smile. When she remained silent, he finally squeezed her arms before letting go with a sigh. "Come." He finally led her to the door and opened it. "If you do change your mind . . . I shall be eagerly awaiting word from you at my home in Bond Street."

After opening the door for her, he released her hand and let her depart, following her with his eyes until she turned a corner.

Chapter Thirty-One

Curzon Street, London

That evening, as the carriage pulled up in front of the palatial house on Curzon Street, Harriet immediately felt that something was different. As soon as they entered the house, Mandie met them on the upper landing. "Harriet, you're back! It's begun," she said breathlessly. "Help me!" She shot a nervous glance at the duchess before sprinting back up to Virginia's guest quarters.

Harriet's eyes widened and she started running up the stairs behind her.

The duchess narrowed her eyes. "Dickson!" she called, and the steward appeared. "Please inform all household staff that they shall have this evening and all of tomorrow off to visit with their families and loved ones."

Dickson seemed startled. "Which members of the staff, Your Grace? The chamber maids? The grooms? Surely not the kitchen staff?"

"*All* of them," the duchess snapped. "I don't want another soul in the house tomorrow apart from Virginia's and my personal maids. And I should prefer it if everyone would leave the premises immediately, returning no sooner than tomorrow evening."

Dickson nodded, and managed to swallow some of his shock by the time he responded. "It shall be done, Your Grace."

Harriet barely heard the end of this exchange on her way to Virginia's room. *She knows*, she fretted to herself. She barreled through the door and there she saw Virginia leaning with her back against a wall, looking flushed and miserable. She only managed a weak smile at Harriet before something came over her. She squeezed her eyes shut and her breathing became shallow.

"Breathe in *deeply*," the matter-of-fact midwife reproved Virginia. "It'll hurt less that way."

Virginia gritted her teeth and shot an annoyed look at the woman, but she tried to comply.

Harriet ran over to her and grasped her hand, which Virginia promptly squeezed so hard that Harriet needed to bite back her own yelp of pain. After a minute, the wave passed and Virginia took a few deep breaths, managing one of her bitter little smiles and even a slight laugh.

"This is much more difficult than anyone ever told me it would be."

Harriet could think of nothing to say, so she rubbed a gentle hand on Virginia's back.

"Come over here and crouch like this." The midwife led her across the room. "It may help things move along a little bit faster. I can tell already though, dear—this baby is going to join us *tonight*. No waiting around for tomorrow!"

Mandie was fluttering around like a nervous wreck, first running for some hot water and clean cloths, next attempting to sponge Virginia's brow with cool water, then simply pacing back and forth when there was nothing more she could do.

Between waves of pain, Virginia teased Mandie mercilessly, making both Harriet and Mandie laugh in spite of their nerves. It couldn't have been easy for Virginia to make light of her struggles while in the midst of them, but she did. Virginia was nothing if not incredibly strong.

After about half an hour of this, the duchess tentatively poked her head in, but made a shocked, disgusted sound at the first glimpse she caught and closed the door once more. A moment later she came back in, a handkerchief pressed over her nose, pointedly looking away from Virginia, who was prostrate on the bed, legs splayed.

Harriet was overcome by a sudden desire to slap the duchess for her behavior, but she simply marched over to her, as it was clear she had something she wished to say. "What *is* it, Your Grace?" she snapped impatiently.

"Oh, but I feel ill," the duchess groaned. "This reminds me of when Virginia was born. It was horrible! I cannot stay—can't stand the sight. Harriet, I shall enlist your aid. As soon as the child is born, bring it straight to me—once it's cleaned, of course!—and under no circumstances allow Virginia to hold it."

Harriet's blood ran cold.

"You will help me in this regard, will you not?" the duchess asked.

Harriet had not planned on needing to lie outright to the duchess, but she had no choice. Her heart was pounding and her stomach was churning, but she nodded, and forced a neutral expression onto her face. "Of course, Your Grace," she lied, dropping her gaze and bobbing a little curtsy.

The duchess seemed satisfied with this reply and nodded briskly, marching out the door.

Virginia sat up as soon as she had left. "That one was awful," she moaned. "I need to move about again."

"Try sitting up like this." The midwife positioned Virginia's legs and arms differently. "You're progressing quite quickly, Virginia."

"Feels anything but!" she groaned, turning to Harriet. "My mother was in here, Harriet," Virginia said, between deep breaths, "*Why?*"

Harriet wasn't able to respond before another wave of pressure took Virginia's breath away.

Mandie looked at her significantly. "Knowing her, it wasn't good," she said.

Harriet sighed and pulled Mandie off to the side. "She told me not to allow Virginia to hold the child, and to bring it straight to her."

Mandie's eyes narrowed. "I don't like the sound of that."

"Nor I," Harriet whispered. "I hadn't bargained on needing to act so *quickly*. I thought the baby wasn't going to arrive until next week! Virginia will not even have a chance to recover, and if we move them too soon, it risks the child's life, as well."

Mandie's breaths started coming more and more quickly, until Harriet realized Mandie's lips were turning purplish. She made Mandie sit down and lean forward, taking calming breaths. "Mandie, breathe!" Harriet scolded gently. "We need your help!"

Time passed. Harriet was not certain how much. She did not allow herself to think of *what* would happen as soon as the baby arrived but remained quietly determined to disobey the duchess's last order in any way she could. She would bar the door and fight the duchess with a frying pan if she had to!

Virginia seemed comparatively calm between the overwhelming waves of pressure, but as the night grew long, the calm became less calm and the pain grew more intense. After a few hours, Virginia, exhausted, closed her eyes and remained silent as she breathed and shifted and worked.

"At least you're getting your exercise, miss! You always complained that—"

"Oh, do shut up, Mandie!"

Harriet and Mandie's words were all either ignored or swiftly rebuked as Virginia pressed on. Harriet hurried back and forth, keeping Mandie calm, supporting and encouraging Virginia, and fulfilling the midwife's requests. By the time dawn was tickling the horizon, Harriet was so exhausted that she dared not take a rest for fear she would never wake again. And so she soldiered on.

"Nearly here, now!" the midwife cried.

Virginia smiled, although it looked more like a grimace, and pushed once more.

Harriet let out a little "oh!" of surprise as a slimy, bluish-gray creature slid into the midwife's hands.

Harriet stared, fascinated, as the midwife deftly wiped the crying baby's face and covered the baby in a bit of flannel for warmth.

"A fine boy." The midwife smiled fleetingly, but hesitated. "Should we invite the duchess back in?"

Harriet shook her head. "Let Virginia hold her child," she commanded.

The midwife smiled and placed the baby on Virginia's stomach. Tears were leaking out of Virginia's eyes as her arms greedily embraced the little bundle before her. As soon as the child was pressed against her bare chest, he stopped crying. She kissed his little head a dozen times and held him close, murmuring lovely things into his little ears.

Harriet was blinking back tears and when she glanced at Mandie she saw that the maid was sniffling and wiping her face with a spare cloth. Harriet squeezed Mandie's hand and smiled, giving a sigh of relief.

A few minutes passed before the midwife returned them to the present. "There, now. Finished. He's ready for a bath now." The midwife handed the child to an awe-struck Harriet, who reverently took the baby, and, with Mandie looking over her shoulder with mingled admiration and fear, gently washed the little boy's tiny pink body with some warm water and swaddled him in a napkin, clout, and a large flannel blanket.

"Harriet," Mandie suddenly came to herself, sounding nervous, "What are we going to—"

"I don't know, but we're *not* taking him to the duchess," Harriet pushed a loose tendril of hair from her forehead with her shoulder. "And it isn't as though she has armed footmen hanging about— I'll fight her off myself if I must." She gently returned the child to Virginia's waiting arms.

Virginia kissed his nose. "He looks just like his father."

Mandie tried to sound flippant and failed. "I've not met Ralph, but I imagined him a bit larger than this little soldier."

Virginia laughed, never taking her eyes off her baby. "Two Ralphs in one family would be confusing anyway, do you not think so? What say you to Raphael?" she asked the baby. "Will you answer to that?"

The child gave a yawn, then, and the three women laughed— mostly in relief—that the most daunting task ahead of them that day was past. They hoped.

Curzon Street, London

The midwife left plenty of instructions for Virginia's recovery before slipping out of the house and disappearing into the early morning light—so many instructions that Harriet had needed to scramble for pen, ink, and paper to write them all down. Only a few short hours after the baby was born, everyone was asleep: Harriet on the sofa, Mandie in a chair in the corner, and Virginia in the bed, with the new baby sleeping peacefully in the crook of her arm.

As they slumbered, the door swung open with a vengeance.

At the sound of the slamming door, Harriet's eyes popped open and she sat bolt upright, just in time to hear the duchess's furious monologue.

"How *dare* you—all of you! How dare you disobey me? Harriet, I had expected better of you. You have broken your agreement, and I'll be hanged before I'll honor ours!"

The duchess stomped over to the bed, where Virginia was finally waking up herself, and not looking too happy about it.

"What is happening, mistress?" a gnarled voice said behind the duchess. Harriet wrinkled her nose. The dirty middle-aged woman following the duchess smelled odd and did not seem like respectable company at all. She made the hair on the back of Harriet's neck stand on end.

Harriet leapt off the couch as quickly as she could and rushed over to stand between the duchess and Virginia. "What do you plan to do with the baby, Your Grace?" Harriet asked breathlessly. It had taken her barely a moment to recognize the threat. She could act as boldly as she pleased now that the duchess was no longer planning to honor their agreement. She stood tall as she faced the noble woman.

"Harriet, get *out* of my way," the duchess spat.

Harriet's nostrils flared and words she'd been holding in for far too long finally spilled out. "Your Grace, if you keep coldly demanding perfection from others without supplying it yourself, you'll soon find yourself alone and friendless, even in a sea of pleasant acquaintances!"

The duchess did not seem to quite understand what Harriet was saying. She puffed up a bit like a rooster about to attack. "*Move!*" she demanded.

"What are you planning to do with Virginia's baby?" Harriet asked, unyielding.

"That is none of your concern!" the duchess snapped.

"But it is *my* concern," Virginia said before Harriet could reply. "You shan't touch my child, mother. He's not going with you, or with this *woman* you've brought, either."

Mandie came and stood beside Harriet, looking terrified but determined.

The duchess appeared to silently size up the situation.

"I . . . Virginia, do be reasonable," the duchess finally pleaded, forcing a little laugh. "You are not able to care for an illegitimate child on your own!"

Virginia sat up taller, with fire in her eyes. "He is *not* illegitimate!" she shouted. "He is mine! *My* son! And he is every bit as legitimate as I am!"

The duchess maintained a suspicious calm, but her gaze was poisonous. Before she could reply, however, a loud knock was heard on the front door below—a knock that could not possibly be from a polite social caller.

"Could that be—" Harriet breathed to Mandie.

"Perhaps!" Mandie bounced where she stood.

"I shall go and see," Harriet said determinedly. "Hold the fort, Mandie!" She hurried past the duchess and was a little surprised when the duchess did not try to stop her. Then she disappeared out the door and down the stairs.

Chapter Thirty-Two

Curzon Street, London

"Legitimate," the duchess spat derisively.

"He *is* legitimate," Virginia insisted, "Ralph and I were married, Mother. I didn't dare tell you at the time, but it's the truth! And if the vicar at St. Ann's church in Radipole says we're married, that ought to be good enough for you too, Mother!"

The duchess paused long enough to show that she was rattled. "*Your* child could never be legitimate! Who is his father? Who is his father's father? Who are his uncles and aunts? With such connections as his, he would never be accepted in polite society! You may as well have *died* as married such a low-born scoundrel!"

Virginia's angry grimace didn't diminish, but as she blinked, a couple of tears fell. When she did speak, it was with exaggerated clarity. "Ralph's connections, whatever they may be, are better than *mine*!"

The duchess took a step back as though she had been slapped. The baby awakened and began to make himself heard. Virginia hurried to calm him, bouncing him gently in her arms and murmuring softly to him.

"You'll allow me, miss," the dirty woman said, finally stepping forward from behind the duchess. "The brat's just 'ungry." With no preamble, the woman sat on the bed next to Virginia, bared one large breast, and reached for the baby.

Virginia pulled the child closer and edged away from the woman with a look of extreme disgust, shooting her the angry look she normally reserved for the duchess. "You shall not *touch* him," she hissed.

Mandie stood up a bit taller, though she was still too frightened to defy the duchess outright. "Th-there, you see? Virginia and Ralph were married—legally! And y-you may not like it, but the child should be with his mother and father."

"With his father?" the duchess questioned dangerously.

"Yes!" Mandie seemed to grow in confidence, "and he ought to be arriving any moment! In fact, that may have been him at the door!"

This gave the duchess pause. "That *sailor*? Here?" She spoke as though she'd just discovered a mouse in her wardrobe.

"Yes! And th-they may be coming up the stairs now! Any moment!" Mandie's voice squeaked, but she only cleared her throat and stuck out her chest.

"We shall see." The duchess seemed a little shaken, as though she hadn't bargained on needing to deal with not only three determined young women, but a strong young naval officer, as well. The three of them looked toward the door, as if Harriet, Ralph in tow, would be turning up on the other side of it at any instant.

When the door did not reopen immediately, the duchess calmed and Virginia and Mandie grew more frantic. "Where *is* she?" Mandie moaned. "She ought to have returned by now. It isn't as though she could get lost on the way to the door and back!"

Virginia slipped a shoulder out of her gown and began to feed little Raphael as the midwife had shown her how. The duchess's nostrils flared at the sight, and her mouth withered into an angry line. The wet nurse was clearly annoyed at having her sagging breast spurned, and promptly covered herself.

"I am certain she will return soon," Virginia soothed, but she sounded nearly as worried as Mandie.

"I . . . what if something has happened to her?" Mandie asked. "Should I . . . should I go and see?"

"Yes," the duchess spoke swiftly, "Yes, Mandie, *do* go and see where our dear friend Harriet has gone off to."

Mandie bit her lip at the look in the duchess's eye and turned back to Virginia. "I don't want to leave you, miss."

"Then don't, Mandie," Virginia's eyes were wide. "I-I am certain Harriet shall return soon."

"Perhaps this, er . . . new friend of Your Grace's could go and see to it," Mandie suggested, giving a sidelong glance at the dirty wet nurse the duchess had brought to them.

The wet nurse grunted an assent as she stood and left the room.

There was an awkward silence as they heard the woman's heavy steps fading away down the stairs. After another long moment waiting, the woman called back up the stairs. "Oy! No one's 'ere! But the front door's gappin' in the breeze right enough!"

The duchess frowned at Mandie and a second later they were racing one another down the stairs.

"*Gone?*" the duchess cried, "Impossible! Where would she have gone off to? She cannot simply be *gone!*"

"Harriet?" Mandie called, running out the open door as she cried out, "Harriet?" She panted as she looked left and right down the posh street—barely showing signs of awakening for the day—and could not see a trace of her. "Harriet!" she called again.

"Shut up!" the duchess cried out to Mandie, gesturing furiously for her to reenter the house. "Quit shouting out that nobody's name! I still need her to be Virginia!"

Mandie turned around only to glare at the duchess. "You already said you'd not honor your agreement with her—why should she help you now?"

"Oh, you heard that, did you?" the duchess said carelessly. "I was only angry! I did not really *mean* it! I . . . oh, do come back in, Mandie!" she wheedled desperately, hugging the doorway as if afraid to be seen.

"Oy," a small voice said near Mandie's waist. She turned around again to see a small boy standing up, appearing from behind a decorative plant. "You looking for a young woman come from this 'ouse not two minutes ago?"

"Yes." Mandie gave her full attention to the boy. "Where has she gone? Is she all right?"

"Dunno if she's a-right," he said, "but she got in the carriage with a gen'lman of quality, by the looks o' things. They drove off not a minute ago. That way," he gestured down the road.

"I . . . *what?*" Mandie shook her head. "She would not *leave*. Not like—"

"I might add, she didn't seem none too happy 'bout enterin' the carriage, by the looks o' things. The gen'lman *insisted* she would be a happy bride and right near carried 'er into the post."

"You . . . you must be joking," the duchess said faintly.

"'Fraid not," he said, "but if you could be so kind as to line me pockets a bit for the information?"

The duchess looked about frantically. "I do not have my reticule with me, boy, I—"

Mandie made a frustrated little noise and ran to a little sideboard near the door, jerked open a drawer full of coins and tossed a small handful of shillings at the boy. "Thank you, child!" A couple coins hit the boy on the head and he complained mightily—and loudly—until he saw what had hit him and immediately scrambled to collect all the coins. Mandie firmly shut the door.

"It was Mr. Desford."

The duchess ignored Mandie. "We must remain calm." She sounded anything but as she paced the entryway. "Where could she have gone? Was it with that . . . Stew. . . Stephan! That was her young man, was it not?"

"I—yes, it was, but no! It couldn't have been him. It *must've* been Desford!"

The duchess frowned. "The one whose father married that loose nobody of a woman? Shame. He really ought to have married better—he did no favors to the Desford name with *that* connection."

Mandie glared at the duchess. "Hang his father! It wouldn't matter if he were the *pope* if we don't get our Harriet back!"

The duchess looked as though she'd swallowed a lemon, but only glared silently at Mandie. Neither one of them had any further time to discuss the matter, however, as just then there was a thump on the doorstep and the door swung open.

The duchess groped at her chest when she saw who was on the other side. "Charles! I . . . what are you doing here?"

The Duke of Dorset paused on the threshold and frowned at his wife. "What am I doing here? Ruth, I *live* here. Or have you forgotten?" He chuckled and shook his head.

The duchess's cheeks were flushed. "Of course, dear. Of course. I was only . . ."

"Only what?" the duke asked, entering and depositing his hat and cane on the credenza. "I went out for a morning stroll, and I thought these were quite nice." He pulled a bouquet of long-stemmed red roses from behind his back and handed them to the duchess.

She accepted the bouquet with a shocked smile on her face. The flush remained. "Th-thank you, Charles. They are lovely."

The duke smiled and leaned in to kiss the duchess on the cheek when he caught sight of the dirty wet-nurse and frowned. "Who are you?" he asked her.

The woman looked more than a little discomposed at the naturally stern expression in the duke's eyes. "I, er . . ."

"She's the wet nurse," the duchess said breathlessly. "For Virginia's child."

The duke's eyes lit up. "She's had her baby, then? How is she? How is the baby?"

"Both are doing quite well," Mandie chimed in.

The duke thanked her with a smile and shot another look at the wet nurse before turning back to the duchess. "Surely we could find a nurse who's a bit more . . ." he glanced at the woman again. "Clean?"

The duchess did not seem to know what to say. "Of course, I . . . you are right, Charles. I do not know what I was thinking. Elsie, you are dismissed."

Elsie gave an affronted little gasp. "You're not like to find any others offerin' my *particular* services."

The duke's smile slid off his face. "What services?" he asked. "Ruth?" he spoke in a warning tone.

When the duchess refused to meet his eyes, the duke turned back to the wet nurse. "Why were you hired?"

The wet nurse pulled herself up a bit straighter, and she dove into what had to be her sales pitch, it was so well-rehearsed. "I take and raise unwanted children, sir. *And* I take good care of 'em until they's old enough to take on respectable work." She gave a brisk little nod. "And nuffin' illegal about it!" she added, as if as an afterthought.

The duke stared at the woman and slowly turned to look at the duchess, horror written on his face. "Ruth? What is this all about?" he asked. "Is Virginia's child not to live at one of our country estates?"

The duchess glanced at Mandie as if for aid, but Mandie was studiously avoiding her gaze. "I . . . well, we couldn't very well have an unexplained *child* about, Charles. Surely someone would suspect!"

The duke shook his head sadly and turned from her with a sigh. "I understand the implications, my dear. However, Virginia's health and happiness—and her child's—matter far more to me than her reputation. I've put up with this elaborate charade long enough. Elsie, you may leave. We will not be requiring your services. Not today, and not ever."

Elsie shot them both a dirty look and stomped out of the room, mumbling under her breath. The door closed behind her, leaving the duchess looking overwhelmed and humiliated. Her breath was coming in quick little gasps and she had begun gently pacing across the floor. "It is . . . it is a wonder to me that *you* are lecturing *me* about caring for our daughter, sir!"

The duke examined his left boot. "You refer, I suppose, to my . . . frequent absence. My penchant for seeking solitude."

The duchess let out an unladylike noise of frustration.

Mandie knew that the closer the duchess came to bursting into tears, the angrier she grew. Mandie came up to her and gently wrested the bouquet of roses from her grasp. "Let me put these in water for you, Your Grace," she murmured, escaping toward the kitchen.

The duchess hardly seemed to notice. "Solitude!" she spat. "Is *that* what people are calling it these days?"

The duke frowned at the duchess, his mouth falling open. "Then it's true," he said, "I had not thought it possible, but it's *true*. Harriet told me that you thought I had a mistress."

The duchess's cheeks turned fuchsia and she turned away. "How indelicate of her to mention such a thing! I shall have to speak with—"

The duke caught his wife's hand in his and pulled her toward him, meeting her eyes with his twinkling gray-blue ones. "My dear, please let me first assure you that I do not now, nor have I ever *had* a mistress. I beg you would believe me! Can you not trust me?" His eyes searched hers for a response.

Mandie had made it partway down the hall but stopped and risked a glance back at the couple. The duchess's breathing was ragged and heavy, and it had been a long time since Mandie had seen her even half so flustered.

When the duchess remained quiet, the duke lifted one of her hands to his mouth and kissed the back of it. "It pains me to see . . . this is not how I envisioned our marriage would be when we entered it more than twenty years ago. I am not blameless, I know. I have withdrawn, kept to myself . . . It has been so long that it almost seems too much to hope that anything can change. However," he stopped here to take a deep breath, "I wish that you would be more open with me, Ruth. And I am willing to try to do the same if you will let me."

The duchess tried halfheartedly to tug away, but failed. When next she looked back into her husband's face, it was up through her lashes, almost like a child. Her eyes were filling with tears. One slipped down her cheek and the duke reached out with a hesitant thumb to brush it away. At this, the duchess began crying in earnest. The duke's face mirrored her pain as he clutched her to his chest, holding her close.

Mandie could look no longer. She turned away from the tender scene, a hand flying to her heart. It wasn't until she was returning with a water-filled vase of roses that she heard someone pounding at the front door. With a little gasp, she hastily set the roses on a side table and sprinted for the front door. She arrived an instant before the duchess could and wrenched it open.

On the other side of the door was a handsome, though shabbily dressed, young man. He stepped through the doorway without hesitation, pulling off his hat as he did so. "My name is Ralph Clifton," he said, "and I have come to take Virginia home."

The duke's eyes widened before they narrowed below a thundering brow, his mouth drawing hard line across his face. "You *left* her, you pup! And now you have the arrogance to waltz back here and try to do it again?"

Pain flashed in Ralph's eyes, but he only frowned at the duke. "I have come to take her home," he repeated evenly.

"Where has everyone gone? And who was that at the door?" Virginia called loudly from upstairs. "Won't anyone tell me what is *happening*?"

Ralph looked up toward the source of the voice and wordlessly walked past the duke and duchess, who stared agape at him as he climbed the steps two at a time. A second later, they were at his heels, following him up the stairs.

"What do you think you are doing, young man?" the duke barked.

"My lady calls." He reached the upper landing and calmly continued heading toward the sound of Virginia's voice.

"Stop right there!" the duke said, wheezing after mounting the steps with such speed.

The duchess also tried to stop him but could not. "What do you mean, *your* lady?" she snapped a bit breathlessly.

"I mean my wife, Virginia Clifton." Ralph did not even glance at them before pushing open the door to Virginia's room. He smiled at her, nothing but love in his eyes. "I'm sorry I'm late, darling."

"Your . . . *what?*" The duke was beside himself.

Virginia smiled up at Ralph, tears in her eyes. "You came for me," she whispered.

"I always will," he replied.

Chapter Thirty-Three

The road to Gretna Green

When Harriet had hurried down the stairs from Virginia's room to answer the door, she had been fully expecting to see a dashing sailor when she opened it. However, it had only been Mr. Desford.

"Oh, *you* again," she was too tired to be frightened. "Now is not a good—"

"You are here!" Mr. Desford said, a smile lighting his face. He instantly seized Harriet's hands and pressed a kiss on the back of one of them. She'd stepped backward as quickly as she could.

"I had not . . . It's a bit early for a morning visit, is it not?"

"My darling Harriet, I couldn't wait another moment to see you again."

Harriet, confused, thought back to their last encounter only the evening before. It seemed an age ago. He had not seemed particularly happy then. He had seemed disappointed. Angry, even. Impatient. She took another step backward, and Mr. Desford crossed the threshold without an invitation.

"I still do not understand. Why are you here?" Harriet asked.

"I thought about what you said last night," he said, "and I thought . . . well, never mind what I thought. Come for a drive with me and I shall tell you all about it. My carriage is waiting outside."

Harriet shook her head in disbelief and dissent and tried to pull her hand from Mr. Desford's grasp. "*Now?* I . . . I cannot, Mr. Desford. Virginia needs me and I will not leave her side. Now if you'll please—"

Mr. Desford smiled at her but did not release her hand. The smile did not quite reach his eyes, and Harriet felt panic welling up inside of her as he stepped toward her again. "Harriet, my love, I am certain . . . I *know* that I shall make you happy."

Harriet's eyes widened and she tugged harder against his grasp, trying to step away. It was no use, however, and he pulled her toward him with a vise-like grip that only grew stronger the more she struggled. Before she knew it, her back was toward him, his other hand covered her mouth, and he was dragging her out the door.

She kicked and pushed against him, trying to scream, but the sounds that made it past his hand were muffled and practically inaudible. She cursed the fact that the duchess had sent all the servants away from the place.

"Harriet, you need not resist any longer!" He ignored her screams as he pulled her into the carriage, only a little breathless at the effort. "No one can see you, and very soon now we shall be married! Isn't it wonderful?" He closed the carriage door behind them and whistled for the driver to set off.

Harriet's eyes widened at the sound of this, and her fists pounded at the carriage door, roving for the latch.

He attempted to pull her into an embrace in the carriage, "I realized my first offer was not enough for such a lovely young lady as yourself. I have decided to commit myself entirely to you *and* to matrimony. There, you see? Perfectly respectable. Now you no longer need to hide your affections for me!" He finally sounded breathless at the end of this monologue and leaned in to attempt to kiss her.

Harriet pushed away from him as hard as she could and landed with a thud on the other end of the carriage. "Don't *touch* me!" she screamed.

Mr. Desford looked at Harriet, seeming surprised and a little deflated for the first time that morning. "I had thought you would be pleased." His voice was blank, emotionless.

Harriet looked at him in disbelief, still panting for breath, leaning as far away from him as she could. "What have I said that would lead you to believe that I would be happy to be pulled into a carriage against my will, kicking and screaming?"

Mr. Desford began recounting to her all the times they had spent together laughing at balls, walking the park, and visiting at various parties and social gatherings. He told her of how his affection for her had grown throughout all this. As he continued, he became more and more animated, and grew gradually angrier, as though he were surprised all over again that Harriet did not seem pleased at being kidnapped by him.

Harriet's mind was whirring as he talked. She knew she would have no chance of getting away safely should she simply leap from the carriage—even if she could manage to open the carriage door without awakening his suspicion. She knew she would likely need to wait until they had stopped to exchange horses. She mentally swore, biting her lip until she nearly drew blood, and wishing desperately that she could be at Virginia's side, where she was needed. She looked out the window, steeling herself for the role she knew she would need to play. When Mr. Desford finally finished speaking, she had a warm look waiting for him.

"There, there," she moved toward Mr. Desford and willed herself not to grow physically ill. "You have saved me from my own reservations. And I am here now, m-my love." She smiled and swallowed hard before patting Mr. Desford on the arm.

Mr. Desford looked up at her, hope in his eyes, his manic expression calming. Harriet continued to speak with him, bringing him down from his frenzied state and back to the more or less charming Desford she'd always known. She knew though, as she talked to him, that she could not keep up this charade forever.

Curzon Street, London

Stephan mounted the steps of the palatial house in Curzon Street with a small bouquet of flowers and his heart on his sleeve. He was not even certain that he would be allowed in but took courage from the fact that he had been formally introduced to "Lady Virginia" and had an encouraging letter from Harriet in his pocket. He had stopped in Palace Court the day before, and finding that Harriet was not with the Donahues, had steeled himself to visit Curzon Street that morning, before he could lose his nerve.

He knocked at the heavy, carved door and was surprised that no one answered. Surely, he thought, the very wealthy always have *someone* or other ready to answer the door. He frowned. The more he thought about the potential reasons that no one would answer, the less he liked any of the options he came up with. He knocked harder, pounding at the door with stubborn persistence until it finally cracked open to reveal a small, frightened young maid.

"I b-beg your pardon, sir, but her grace is not accepting morning callers today." Her voice was even smaller than she was.

Stephan swallowed nervously. He was not sure what possessed him, but he said, "I am not here to see her grace," as he pushed gently on the door, opening it a little further, "I am here to see Lady Virginia."

The maid's eyes widened and she shook her head. "She is not receiving callers today, either."

She tried to close the door again, only to have him stop the door with his foot. "I am terribly sorry!" He pushed the door open and slipped inside the hall, closing the door behind him. "Please excuse me, but I cannot leave! Not until I . . ." he stopped himself and took a deep breath, "I am *really* here to see Harriet," he corrected, in barely more than a whisper.

The girl's eyes widened and wordlessly she glanced about her for any listening ears. "How did you know Harriet Shore was here?"

"My name is Stephan Grimsby, and—"

The girl nodded, cutting him off, "Yes, that's right—Mandie told me about you. You're Harriet's young man and you already know everything, don't you?"

Stephan colored. "I . . . well, Harriet did tell me that Lady Virginia was in, er . . . in confinement."

The girl rolled her eyes. "That's putting it lightly. Well, I'll fill you in, but I can't stay long. Virginia's husband has come for her—"

"Ralph is her *husband*?"

The maid nodded impatiently. "And he and the duke and duchess have been locked together in the east drawing room for over an hour now. Now and then I'll hear one of them shouting, but it doesn't sound physically violent quite yet. But that's not the worst thing. It's Harriet. You see . . . she's *gone*."

Stephan felt his veins run cold. "Tell me everything."

The Rose and Pony Inn, Bedfordshire

Harriet had been grateful when she had feigned sleep and Mr. Desford had finally left her alone after her modest insistence that they were not yet married and must not sit too close. Pretending to be fond of a man whom she'd like nothing less than to push out of the carriage and into the mud was more taxing than her already exhausted body could stand.

She awoke when they stopped to change horses. When she learned they had gotten clear to Bedford, she knew the time had come.

"I must alight as well." She started stepping down from the carriage, but Mr. Desford blocked her path, a hard look in her eye.

"I see no call for that, my love," he insisted, suspicion entering his gaze.

Harriet shifted, and swallowed the temptation to hit him in the face as hard as she could. *It'd never work, anyway,* she told herself—she didn't have a chance of physically overpowering him. She needed to blush. She closed her eyes and imagined Stephan finding her with Mr. Desford. What would he think of her? When she felt the inevitable heat rise in her face at the thought, she looked back up at Mr.

Desford through her lashes and spoke in a small voice. "Mr. Desford, I . . . I have some private matters to attend to. Pray forgive me. I shall return in only a moment."

Mr. Desford nodded, slightly embarrassed, and allowed Harriet to pass by him into the small inn. As soon as the door closed behind her, she hurried to what appeared to be the busiest part of the establishment.

"You must help me!" she cried as she ran into the kitchen.

Several serving maids and a cook yelped in surprise and dropped things.

"What's this?" an authoritative woman entered the room, seeming dismayed at the sudden uproar.

She looked like she could be the proprietor of the establishment, or his wife. "Ma'am," Harriet pleaded, "That gentleman outside with the post chaise has kidnapped me and is taking me to Gretna Green!"

She raised an eyebrow. Harriet may have been bedraggled after her night helping Virginia, but she was still undoubtedly a young lady of quality. "Is he now?"

"At least he intends to marry her," one of the serving wenches muttered.

Harriet ignored the young woman and allowed one of the frightened tears she'd restrained to finally fall. "I am in earnest!" she cried. "I *must* get away from him, ma'am. You see . . . he wishes to marry me against my will, and against my family's wishes, and I am underage . . . and I am promised to another!" she wailed dramatically, giving a pathetic sigh. She winced at the little untruth, but reminded herself it was *half*-true. She hoped.

The woman tutted angrily. "Indeed?" she asked. "What a monster! I thought p'raps you was trying to run from yer father or another relation just now. But you say this fellow isn't yer kin?"

Harriet shook her head emphatically.

"And you say yer betrothed to another?" the woman's eyes narrowed in suspicion. "One as yer family approves of?"

Harriet swallowed a lump in her throat as she thought of Stephan and nodded. She thought *her* family would, even if his did not.

The woman gave her another hard look, but when she heard Mr. Desford's voice in the taproom calling for Harriet, and saw Harriet's exaggerated expression of terror, she nodded. "Aye, I'll help you, girl. You can call me Mrs. Burbadge."

Harriet dropped a curtsy, and Mrs. Burbadge called to a maid to help Harriet hide in the larder behind a few sacks of potatoes before going out to speak with Mr. Desford.

Harriet ignored the smells of rotten cheese and cured meats and focused on remaining silent and unseen. She listened closely to the mild uproar in the taproom, and breathed through her mouth to avoid the odd smells of the larder. Mr. Desford was fast becoming impatient, and if he refused to give up, they might be forced to reveal her position. The minutes dragged by like hours.

"That young man of yours," Mrs. Burbadge entered the kitchen once more in a huff. "He's tryin' to turn out the whole place lookin' for ya! He sounds bloomin' mad, but that's the quality for you— beggin' your pardon, miss—to act like they own every place under their feet!"

Harriet nodded meekly. "Th-thank you for helping me hide."

The woman thought for a moment, and seemed to have an idea. "You know, Miss. Didn't say nuffin' earlier 'cause you's quality, you see, but old Farmer Johnson been by and has his 'orse at the stable, nigh ready to leave. He's got a cart not fit for a dog, but is headed for London this minute. Pr'aps you could go with 'im?"

Harriet burst into grateful tears—she didn't need any acting at all to bring them about—and allowed herself to be calmed by Mrs. Burbadge. Harriet's pockets were empty and she had nothing of value on her person, but she promised herself to one day repay the woman.

"Oh, *thank you*. Thank you!"

Mrs. Burbadge opened the large, low kitchen window and assisted Harriet as she climbed out of it. She gestured toward the stables and the cart in question and Harriet thanked the woman once more before sprinting toward the little cart.

When she drew near, she hid behind a small outbuilding and peered about her to make sure she was not seen. Her heart was pounding. But no Mr. Desford came charging out of the inn after her, so she tiptoed forward.

"Farmer Johnson!" she spoke in an exaggerated whisper.

The man looked up and looked about him. "Who's there?" he said, clearly unsettled.

Harriet gave another nervous glance toward the inn. "Shh!" she said as she crept around the side of the cart facing away from the inn. "I have heard you are traveling to London."

The old man looked down at her with some confusion. "Hello, there, Miss! I had not seen you there."

Harriet glanced at the inn. The door looked like it was opening. She tucked herself against the outbuilding and prayed she would remain undiscovered. Farmer Johnson seemed a bit hard of hearing. She glanced around the corner and, to her relief, the only one who exited the door was a scullery maid sent to gather lettuce from the kitchen garden.

"Farmer Johnson," she said, a trifle louder than before. "I have heard you are leaving for London shortly. Might I ride with you?"

The old man glanced at her and raised his eyebrows. "With *me*? I'm only taking turnips, not young ladies!"

Harriet's face fell. "*Please*, sir. I need to find my way back to London immediately."

The old man looked flustered. "I haven't a . . . I've only bags of turnips, you see. No seats, and no blankets or—"

"I would be eternally grateful!" Harriet insisted, growing hopeful. "I do not mind sitting among the turnips!"

"It's not that I mind assisting you, miss, but where is your father? Why London? Who's waiting for you there?"

As soon as he said he did not mind assisting, Harriet glanced about her once more before climbing the wheel to the carriage as though it were a tree from her childhood and hastening to hide behind a bag of turnips.

"My mother and father are in Burnham-on-Sea. I am a governess to a respectable family in London, but I have been kidnapped and my captor is within the inn. I do not wish to alert him to my departure, though, so I pray you will *please* pretend I am not here!" she said. She nestled deeper among the turnips and used the bags they were wrapped in to shield her from the chilly wind. "I am ever so grateful!" her muffled voice chimed.

Farmer Johnson shook his head at her story, but mercifully remained quiet until he finished loading his cart and began driving southward.

The ride was bumpy and dirty, and the already exhausted Harriet was anything but comfortable, but she still sighed in relief as they rolled down the road. She had successfully evaded Mr. Desford and was on her way back to London where she needed to be.

Chapter Thirty-Four

The Rose and Pony Inn, Bedfordshire

Stephan had never ridden so hard for so long. He was beginning to tire, and he was more than a little concerned for his horse when he came up to the first posting house on the main thoroughfare to Gretna Green. He did not give the order to slow down, but his horse nevertheless slowed a bit and gave a whinny of complaint when it saw the nearby stables and smelled the fresh hay. With a groan, Stephan realized he had no choice and led his horse to the house.

"There we are," he reluctantly allowed his horse to plunge its muzzle into a waiting trough of water.

He dismounted and instructed a young groom to care for his horse before walking into the tavern to seek further information. He was surprised, upon arriving in the taproom, to find it nearly empty, apart from one very loud, very upset Mr. Desford.

"And to think I *believed* her! I . . . fool that I am!" He slammed his rough tankard of ale on the table. Given the broken glass on the floor all about him and the angry looks the man of the house was shooting at him, Stephan surmised that a battered old tankard was all he could be trusted with. He walked over to his host, casting a wary eye at Mr. Desford as he did so.

"I am, er . . . I am looking for a young lady taken against her will toward Gretna Green," he said in barely more than a whisper.

"Gretna Green, ye say?" the man said, glaring at the drunk young man, "This one 'ere 'ad a girl with 'im not 'alf an hour ago."

Stephan raised his eyebrows and shot another glance at Desford. *He certainly doesn't take long to get drunk as a wheelbarrow, does he?*

"Where is she?"

"Me sister says the lass was right frightened and hid from 'im, so she sent the girl back toward London in the back of old Farmer Johnson's cart."

She's already escaped, then. Clever Harriet! Stephan was filled with relief and allowed himself to relax long enough to accept a cup of tea. He thanked his host and arranged to take a fresh mount back to London as soon as possible.

Stephan was finishing the last of his tea when a couple of fingers tapped his shoulder. "You there," Mr. Desford stumbled as he spoke. "You're that fellow that wants to marry Harriet."

"I'm afraid you are mistaken." Stephan avoided eye contact with Desford. He drank the last of his tea and wiped his lips, placing a few coins on the counter.

"No, no, I'm sure I—you're that friend of Harriet's!" he insisted as Stephan stood. "You *fought* me at the academy and ran away scared!"

Stephan heaved a sigh and finally met Mr. Desford's eyes. His voice was flat. "It must be a great comfort to you to remember it that way."

Mr. Desford's eyes burned angrily as he grasped Stephan's wrist. "*You* . . . where has she gone?" he finished lamely.

Stephan froze. "Unhand me. Now." His voice was like iron. When the drunk man's grip only grew tighter, Stephan deftly shifted out of his grasp, twisting Mr. Desford's arm until he cried out in pain. "She clearly had no desire to go with you to Gretna Green, and you, sir, are fortunate that our excellent host has not already carted you off to Bow Street to the authorities!"

Mr. Desford let out an angry growl as Stephan released him and began walking toward the door. Mr. Desford started toward Stephan with his fists up, but before he caught up with him, Stephan turned to face him again with a sigh, pulling a small pistol from the inside of his coat as he did so. He began inspecting it calmly. Mr. Desford stopped when he realized what it was. He was unarmed.

"Oh no, my dear fellow—go ahead and attack." Stephan lazily cocked his loaded pistol and casually pointed it directly at Desford. "I believe I can defend myself."

Mr. Desford's face was beet red with anger, but he remained silent, leaning heavily on a rough-hewn table.

"You are a gentleman," Stephan reminded him. "But you have not acted as such today. Hear this now. If I hear a word—*one* word—of your so much as *considering* approaching Miss Shore again, I shall call you out."

Stephan fired his pistol then, causing Mr. Desford to jump backwards and land on his rear end, scrambling to ascertain that he had not been hit. The table Mr. Desford had stood behind had a bullet lodged in it, inches from where Desford's hand had rested not one second before.

"And I shall call you out with the sword," Stephan said calmly, "for I'm a terrible shot."

Mr. Desford's eyes widened as he watched Stephan toss a few coins onto the counter for the damaged table before walking from the room without so much as a backward glance.

The road to London

Harriet was already tired of the scent of raw turnips when she thought she heard a male voice calling in the distance. As her ears pricked, listening, the voice slowly grew louder until she could make out what it was saying.

"Harriet!" it cried.

She gasped. Could Desford have discovered her deception so very soon? Had Mrs. Burbadge given her away?

The man calling had to be on a galloping horse, he was drawing near so quickly. Harriet tucked herself away tightly among the turnips, willing the rider to leave her alone.

"You, there!" the man's voice said, presumably to Farmer Johnson. "Have you a young woman in your cart?"

The farmer sputtered a little in disbelief. "A young *woman?*" He sounded affronted at the very suggestion.

Harriet brightened as she recognized the familiar voice. She popped her head up from between the sacks of vegetables.

"Stephan!" she cried.

"Harriet!" Stephan dismounted and ran to the side of the cart to help her down. As soon as her feet had touched the ground once more, he embraced her, and she threw her arms around his neck.

"Stephan, you *came* for me!" she sighed into his neck, "I did not dare dream that you would come for me!"

"Darling Harriet, how could I not come after you sent that lovely letter? When they told me you were missing, I set forth immediately."

She pulled away to meet his eyes. "*They* told you? Have you been to Curzon Street?"

"Yes, and——"

"How is Virginia? Is she all right? How is the baby doing? Did Ralph arrive in time?"

Stephan nodded with a slight chuckle. "The maid mentioned that a man named Ralph had been there arguing with the duchess for over an hour. She said next to nothing about Virginia or the child, but I would assume she is all right."

"Oh, *good*!" she sighed. "I am so happy he has come. I am certain all will be well now, but still . . . I ought to return to help as soon as I can."

Stephan stared at her in silence for a long moment, until Harriet grew a little embarrassed. "What is it, Stephan?"

"You've just been *kidnapped*." He shook his head in disbelief and let out a light laugh. "And you are still more concerned about Virginia than you are about yourself."

She could feel warmth rise in her cheeks and she suddenly realized that she was still clinging to Stephan in a most indecorous way. She quickly released him. "I . . . excuse me."

Stephan frowned as she moved. "I am sorry, Harriet." He stepped backward with hands raised. "Was I overstepping my bounds?"

Farmer Johnson chuckled, "There are few enough to witness you two on the side of a quiet country road. And I won't tell." He winked at them.

They both looked up at the old farmer and laughed a little.

"I take it you'll not be needing any further rescuing from me, milady?" Farmer Johnson asked, with a twinkle in his eye.

Harriet laughed and looked up at Stephan adoringly. "I do not believe so, sir!"

The farmer tipped his hat at the two of them and was off once more.

"Oh, Stephan," Harriet walked with Stephan toward his horse stopped on the side of the road, her arm cradled in the crook of his. "It seems an age since last we met."

"Indeed." He squeezed her hand. "And I am sorry not to have visited or written more, but I was terribly busy, you see."

"I am certain you were." Her expression was rueful. "I left such a heavy charge on your shoulders. It had been so long that I imagined you must have been so *angry* with me for doing so. I thought you had given up on me."

"*Never*," he reassured, stroking her cheek with his thumb. "But between addressing some affairs of my estate, attending Frank's wedding, searching for Ralph Clifton, and trying to keep Mr. Desford from giving you trouble, I scarce had time for any visits. I lost track of him for a bit at the end, there, but it will be far easier to protect you from him once we are married."

Her eyes filled with tears. "Oh, Stephan. You would do all that for me?"

Stephan nodded, pulling her close again. "That and more, Harriet."

Harriet sniffed as her tears began to fall. She reached up and wrapped her hands around the back of his neck, pulling his lips down to meet hers. His hands pressed into her back, drawing her closer.

It was with a little laugh that Stephan finally pulled away. "This whole adventure has been a bit more exciting than I'd imagined it would be when I first left Burnham-on-Sea."

Harriet smiled as she played with the lapels of his coat. "What *did* you imagine, my love?"

"That I would charge into London on a white horse, win your love, and rescue my lady fair from the dull life of a governess."

Harriet giggled. "I haven't exactly been *bored*, Stephan, but I was certainly in need of rescuing! So, am I your 'lady fair,' then?"

Stephan met her eyes, and the emotions that she read in them nearly overwhelmed her. "You always have been, even back when we were climbing trees together." His voice dropped to a low murmur. "And you always shall be."

Harriet felt warm down to her toes and looked away. "I could not tell you when we last talked at that ball how *very* dearly I love you, Stephan. I hadn't the courage, nor the proper words then. I have much to apologize for," she mumbled.

He nearly cut her short, shaking his head. "You have nothing to apologize for."

Happy tears sprang to Harriet's eyes as she looked up to meet Stephan's gaze.

He smiled tenderly. "I love you, Harriet. With all I am. Please say you'll have me."

Harriet grinned through her tears. "Of course!"

Stephan gave a small whoop and leaned forward to kiss her swiftly before she could protest. Her cheeks colored and she struggled to recall what she had been about to say. Then she remembered.

"There is no one I would rather marry than you, Stephan," she told him when they broke apart. "Only . . . I remain terribly unworthy of you."

Stephan turned away and started examining a nearby tree, trying to hide a smile. "Let me reassure you that *I* am the undeserving one, Harriet. If you only knew how much, you might never forgive my audacity."

Harriet laughed and shook her head, even as her cheeks flushed prettily. "I . . . I *will* marry you, Stephan. Because you really want me to. But what does your mother say to all this?"

Stephan laughed. "My mother could do nothing to stop me even if she wished to. She is aware of my intentions toward you, however, and I believe she begins to warm to the idea."

Harriet raised an eyebrow at this.

Stephan smiled guiltily. "All right, I'll admit it—she might not yet be *entirely* aware of my intentions. But my mother has some very specific, narrow-minded ideas of what would make me an appropriate wife. And she is wrong. There truly is no one for me but you, Harriet. And she will simply have to grow accustomed to that."

Harriet smiled and stood on tiptoe to kiss Stephan yet again.

Chapter Thirty-Five

Palace Court, London

Harriet had let out a sigh of relief when Mandie had opened the door of the grand house on Curzon Street. Seeing the duchess again was the last thing she wanted. After slipping in to kiss Virginia and the baby and congratulate Ralph the lease of his new farm, Harriet had been all too willing to allow Mandie to shoulder the burden of cleaning up the rest of the mess.

"We shall be off tomorrow," Ralph had assured her. "Virginia is already feeling remarkably well, as is little Raphael. We will travel slowly, but to Brighton we shall go."

Harriet had sighed with happiness and relief.

"Go and be with your young man, Harriet! Leave everything else to me," Mandie insisted.

Harriet was already nearly out the door when she suddenly remembered something. "But what about Mr. Brougham?"

"Poor fellow. He can finally know the truth about it all."

Harriet gave Mandie a warning look. "I know you can be blunt, Mandie, so do be sure to let him down *gently*. And thank him for being a perfect gentleman."

Mandie had laughed, but Harriet allowed herself to feel reassured as she climbed back into the hackney coach Stephan had hired.

His hand clasping hers gave her all the courage she needed, but she was astonished at how quickly this bravery evaporated once she found herself, hair askew, dress dirty, standing before Mrs. Donahue in her private sitting room with her jumbled explanation of the latest turn of events.

"And, well, Stephan has proposed to me and I have accepted."

"Ah," the lady said once Harriet had breathlessly finished her narrative. She looked up at Harriet through tight lips, but a smile forced the corner of her mouth upward before too long, and soon she was shaking her head and laughing.

"Harriet, you are the most unreliable, inconstant, and *unusual* governess I think I've ever heard of!"

Harriet flushed, but she could not argue with that assessment. "Indeed, you are right, ma'am. You deserve a great deal better." She plucked up her courage and sat a little bit taller as she continued, "That is why, a couple of weeks ago, I wrote to a friend of mine from school—a Miss Wallbridge who, I must admit, has always been a great deal more accomplished than I."

Mrs. Donahue frowned. "*Weeks* ago?"

Harriet nodded sheepishly. "I . . . well, yes, ma'am. You see, Mr. Grimsby made his intentions known months ago, and because Virginia's baby was expected any day, I wrote to my governess friend."

Mrs. Donahue sighed and rested her forehead in her hand. "You might have told me about all of this sooner."

"And she has responded," Harriet said quickly. "She writes that she would be exceedingly grateful for the position here with your family, and that she will set out for London immediately upon receiving a favorable response from you."

Mrs. Donahue listened begrudgingly, her eyes narrowed in exasperation. At the end of Harriet's speech, she took the proffered letter and read it herself. As she read, her frown softened into a slight smile. "She has a pleasing mode of address . . . and a very elegant hand."

"She is far better at the pianoforte than I and she sings like an angel. I am certain you would be very well pleased in her should you offer her the position."

Mrs. Donahue pursed her lips for a moment. "I shall write to her directly." She looked at Harriet once more and shook her head with a little smile. "Will you remain until she arrives, at least?" When Harriet nodded, Mrs. Donahue continued, her face relaxing. "Well, I can't say that *I* shall miss the adventure you brought to our household, but I know my daughters were fond of you."

"And I of them, ma'am." Harriet felt tears stinging the backs of her eyes as she thought of leaving dear little Katherine and Susan. "May I have permission to write to them when I go?"

"I'd be disappointed if you didn't!" Mrs. Donahue exclaimed. "They need to practice their penmanship. I hope that you will not disappoint me in *this*, Harriet—at least no more than you already have!"

Curzon Street, London

The next day had dawned and felt surprisingly ordinary to Mandie given all that had occurred the day before. Less than twenty hours before, Virginia and the baby had left with Ralph, Harriet had gone to the Donahues', and the rest of the household staff had returned and settled back into their various routines.

The only real difference between this day and any other was that the duke and duchess had sequestered themselves in the duchess's rooms and were refusing to welcome any visitors.

Mandie had just finished writing a missive to Harriet containing directions to write Virginia in Brighton when she was privy to a slight uproar on the upstairs landing. Mr. Brougham had come to call, and one of the footmen was arguing with the duchess's personal maid.

"Their graces are *not* accepting callers today," the maid said. "You'll need to send him away."

"But where is Lady Virginia? A man really ought to be able to see his own fiancée!" The footman was indignant.

The duchess's maid was completely overcome. She was one of the few who had known Virginia's true condition, but she was not about to tell this nosy footman the whole story. "I . . . I . . ." she stuttered, flushing.

Mandie hurried to her aid. "Is it Mr. Brougham come to visit Lady Virginia?"

"Yes!" the footman said, "and I should hate to send him away if they're to be married in less than two weeks! I know *I* could never stand to be turned away like that."

Mandie nodded and started down the stairs. "I will go and speak with him."

The man wrinkled his nose. "Why should he wish to see *you*? You had much better run along and fetch Lady Virginia!"

Mandie rolled her eyes at the footman. "My, but you're behind the times. Lady Virginia is not here."

"Not here? Well, where else would she be? And why aren't the duke and duchess taking callers?"

Mandie laughed. "Perhaps I'll tell you when you're older," she said with a wink.

When she opened the door to the drawing room that Mr. Brougham had been shown into, he immediately leaped to attention. But when he saw that the young woman opening the door was *not* Lady Virginia, he seemed puzzled.

"I'm afraid I *must* speak with Lady Virginia. It is rather urgent." He fiddled with the edge of the hat he held in his hands.

Mandie gave Mr. Brougham a smile laced with sympathy as she closed the door behind her. "Mr. Brougham, you are a fine chap. But you've been caught in the middle of . . . an unusual set of circumstances."

He frowned. "Is something the matter with Lady Virginia?"

Mandie grimaced. "Not exactly. To arrive at the point—Lady Virginia *cannot* marry you."

Mr. Brougham surprised Mandie by grinning, and he let out a sigh of relief. "Really? Oh, that is *capital* news!"

Mandie blinked a few times. This was not the response she had expected. "You . . . aren't upset about this?"

"Upset? Why, I'm delighted! And relieved, ecstatic . . . I only courted Lady Virginia to make my mother happy and to prove to her that it would never work." He let out another little sigh. "I was worried Lady Virginia would never call it off and that I would be forced to go through with it."

Mandie burst into helpless giggles. "That is the best news I've had all day, Mr. Brougham! I am so happy to hear you aren't disappointed."

"Far from it, I assure you. In fact, I must be off directly. I have a . . . a friend I need to visit."

Mandie raised an eyebrow with a smirk. "Mr. Brougham! *Already?*"

Mr. Brougham flushed. "Is that so very terrible of me? I suppose it is. But . . . you say Lady Virginia is well? Is she happy?"

Mandie smiled. "Very much so. Married. And with a beautiful baby boy, too."

Mr. Brougham looked confused for a moment, but could only shrug slightly and smile again. "I wish her very, very happy indeed."

"Harriet is happy, too. She's engaged now."

"Who is *Harriet?*"

"Harriet is—"

Brougham held up a hand to stop her, laughing. "No, no! I . . . I have heard enough. I am not entirely sure *what* drama was playing itself out in this household, but I am happy that it all appears to have ended well."

Mandie smiled. "You, of all people, are entitled to a full explanation, Mr. Brougham. If you won't sit and hear it, I shall write it to you in a letter."

Brougham chuckled. "Very well. Thank you very much, er—?"

"Mandie."

He nodded and turned to walk out the door, but Mandie stopped him again. "May I be so impertinent as to ask what *friend* you are off to visit right now?"

Mr. Brougham smiled broadly. "I hope you'll see our engagement in the society papers soon enough." He tipped his hat, gathered his cloak, and tripped cheerfully down the front steps with an added bounce to his gait.

Palace Court, London

Harriet giggled at the picture Mandie painted in her letter. It had taken the duke and duchess several days to recover from the initial shock of Virginia's leaving. Mandie said that, at first, the duchess tried to convince the duke to tell all of their acquaintance that Virginia was dead, but he quickly pointed out it would never work and suggested they instead surrender and acknowledge Ralph as their son-in-law.

When the duchess finally left her chambers, she initially wore somber colors, to reflect her feeling that Virginia was lost to her. However, Mandie wrote, it did not take very long for the duchess to declare that all was useless and switch once more to her usual bright silks and jewels. It helped that the duke purchased her a gold silk turban trimmed with ivory feathers.

Harriet laughed until her side ached—Mandie was always droll, but she was especially diverting when making pointed remarks about the ridiculous behavior of others. Apparently, while passing hours and hours in her private sitting room with the duke, the duke had begun fondly remembering holding Virginia when she was a tiny baby. The duchess mourned the fact that she had not been able to look properly at Virginia's new son to see if he had the Sackville nose or not. Mandie was beginning to suspect the duchess had finally gone soft, for when all was said and done, she hadn't received a whisper of a punishment for all of her defiance.

"I'll wager it's the duke," Mandie wrote. "The two of them have been inseparable since Virginia left. The duchess has hardly gone out in public or accepted callers at all! She's practically a schoolgirl again. It's equal parts beautiful and revolting."

Harriet thanked the stars and laughed again.

The doorbell rang and Katherine and Susan looked up from their lesson books eagerly, the slightest distraction serving as an excuse for them to stop reading early. Harriet sighed, but gave them leave to close their books. They had likely read enough for the day and she was tired of arguing with them.

"Miss Shore, shall we go down and see what it is?"

"Yes," Susan whined, "I do so long to stretch out my stiff legs."

Harriet forced herself to keep a straight face and gave a little nod to the girls. "Do not disturb your mother!" She called to their retreating backs, but she doubted they heard her.

Not two minutes later, the girls came scurrying back into the schoolroom. "Miss Shore! Miss Shore!" Katherine sprinted into the room with Susan on her tail, waving a small billet in her hand. "You've another letter, Miss Shore!"

"And the lady who brought it says she *won't* leave until you come down!"

Harriet frowned as she examined the seal. It was from the duchess. Her stomach twisted with nerves and she ripped open the letter.

Miss Shore,

You have not yet spoken with my solicitor to settle the affair of your dowry. Had we agreed on ten thousand pounds? No matter—it shall be ten thousand and not a penny more! And it is to be given only on condition of your marriage to a respectable gentleman. Please ask the bearer of this letter to escort you by coach to meet with Mr. Lenville, my solicitor, upon receipt. I wish to have the matter well settled by Saturday.

Cordially,

Ruth Sackville, Her Grace the Duchess of Dorset

P.S. Virginia writes to say she is well, and that her son appears to have the Sackville nose, after all. I am quite relieved to hear it.

Harriet stared at the letter in her hand. Her heart was pounding. "I . . . I do not know what to say." She was breathless. "I had not thought . . . but there must be some mistake—we had originally agreed on five thousand, but this . . ."

"The woman is still waiting downstairs, Miss Shore!" Susan called, after having run to the landing and back to ascertain this fact.

Harriet nodded, in a daze. "I will simply have to make clear that . . . but I thought she had changed her mind!" she said to no one in particular.

Katherine tugged impatiently at Harriet's arm.

Harriet turned around and gave the girls a shrewd look. "I suppose you two will be wanting an outing in the park while I am gone."

Susan nodded eagerly, and even Katherine tried to contain her excitement at the suggestion.

Harriet smiled at their enthusiasm. "Mind your nursemaid until I return." She hastily put on and tied her bonnet. "And if I hear one word from her that you've misbehaved . . ."

They shook their heads. "We shan't!" they chirped as they ran off.

Harriet put on her spencer and bonnet and walked downstairs to meet the messenger.

"Mandie!" she cried as soon as she saw her. Harriet nearly ran into Mandie's arms. One would think it had been weeks, not days, since they had seen one another.

"Harriet! It's lovely to see you again."

"B-but, I only asked her for five thousand, Mandie, and she unmade our agreement! You heard her, didn't you?"

Mandie waved a hand. "She didn't really *mean* it, Harriet. Besides, the duke and duchess have decided together to publicly acknowledge their daughter and son-in-law. To thank you for your assistance she has said the dowry is the least she could do."

"No. I cannot believe it. What produced this great change? I half expect to wake up tomorrow and find it had all been a dream!"

Mandie chuckled. "If I had to guess, I'd say that the change stems from a bit of perspective. Your words at Raphael's birth had an effect. Her Grace was finally forced to recognize that protecting her heart by holding grudges is only another way of breaking it. And she has recognized that romantic love has a place in her life, after all."

Harriet laughed. She was too happy to speak for a moment. "She and the duke are reconciled? Oh, I am so happy. It is too much, Mandie, it's—"

Mandie clucked to make Harriet stop talking and started steering Harriet out the door. "Oh, if anyone deserves such a happy ending, you do. Also, did I mention that I'm to change employ to Virginia's home in a fortnight?"

"Capital news, Mandie!" Harriet cried eagerly.

"Now, tell me all *you've* been up to in the meantime, my dear," Mandie took Harriet's arm like a sister and led her to the waiting carriage. "And don't leave out a single detail of what has happened with that handsome Stephan fellow!"

Chapter Thirty-Six

Palace Court, London

Stephan returned to Burnham-on-Sea at least a full week before Harriet was able to, and she was not sure how she would survive without his morning visits. When Maria finally arrived in Palace Court to take her place as governess, Harriet was ready to sprint out the door and into a hired carriage.

"Harriet, really. I don't know what to say!" Maria embraced Harriet as soon as she arrived.

Harriet returned the embrace impatiently. "If anyone deserves a position this lovely, it is you, my friend." Her gaze flitted to the door. She was already wearing her spencer, and her valise was waiting in the hall.

Maria glanced about and laughed at Harriet. "You *are* anxious to leave, aren't you? You have said that Stephan has proposed, but I cannot help but notice you have not yet said that you are engaged."

Harriet sighed as she subconsciously edged toward the door. "That is because he has not yet consulted my father. For until he does, the announcement cannot be published!"

"Well, I see where your mind is. Not so much as a how-do-you-do!" Maria teased.

"Oh Maria, I *am* sorry, only I am just so very excited to return to Burnham and see my family, and—"

"And fall into the waiting arms of your fiancé?"

Harriet's cheeks turned rosy and she laughed. "Well, there is that," she admitted.

Maria laughed again. "Fine, then. Off with you! I'll expect a letter within the week with the rest of your story, my dear. And as you can't stay long enough to have tea with me now, promise you'll come and visit the next time you find yourself in London!"

Burnham-on-Sea, Somerset

Harriet could not contain herself. Her head bobbed out the window of the post carriage as Burnham-on-Sea loomed before her, looking every bit as lovely and familiar as ever. She had not been home since she'd left in September, and while the seven months had passed quickly, she had never been away from her parents for such a long period in all her life.

"Careful there, miss!" The driver had caught a glimpse of Harriet leaning out the window again.

She ducked back in with a rueful smile, but she had already seen the fence on the edge of her father's farm, and knew they had only minutes to go.

The carriage had scarcely stopped by the time Harriet had leaped down from it and into her parents' arms. She felt a slight twinge of disappointment that Stephan had not been here to meet her, but she shoved it away.

"I've missed you so much!" Harriet said with a sigh.

"And we you, my dear." Her father kissed her forehead and released her from his embrace. "It would appear you have quite the adventure to relay to us."

Harriet feigned innocence. She had told them nothing about her masquerade as the duchess's daughter, figuring that her mother would have had a fit of the vapors if she found out. "A governess is not exactly the most *exciting* occupation, Papa."

Her father chuckled and her mother gave a little sigh and shook her head.

Harriet's face fell. "What is it?"

"It's no good, my dear." Her father ushered her into the house. "Stephan already told us everything. We know your adventure had more to do with the Duchess of Dorset than the Donahue family."

Harriet's eyes bulged, but her first glance was to her mother, who was perfectly composed. "I . . . I did not want to tell you about the charade, Mama, because I knew that you would worry."

Her mother scowled at her as she steered Harriet into the house. "And so I did! But knowing that Stephan was keeping an eye out for you allowed me to rest a bit more at ease. And it's been so long since I've known of it now that my anger has quite dissolved and now I wish to hear *exactly* what happened."

"And so you shall, Mother."

A surprise greeted Harriet on the other side of the door—a flurry of activity captured her attention. The furniture had been rearranged, the stairs carpeted, and a maid she did not recognize was polishing a large silver urn that she could not remember being there before.

"My goodness. The house is . . ."

"Different?" her father finished for her. He nodded. "Quite a few things have changed around here, Harriet. I am quite willing to tell you the whole as soon as you have finished *your* story."

Harriet smiled and tugged her parents to comfortable seats in the parlor to listen. "Then I shall begin directly!"

She told her story with eyes wide, pacing back and forth, mimicking voices, and gesturing dramatically until her parents' laughter shook the furniture and tears formed at the corners of their eyes. They were a delightful audience. They laughed, sighed, and gasped in all the right places. It was a most satisfactory performance for Harriet, and after a quick bow, she flopped breathlessly onto a chaise lounge that she did not remember having ever seen before.

As her parents' laughter died away, Harriet sat forward eagerly, awaiting *their* story.

"Well?" she pressed. "Now you both know the whole of the sorry adventure I was embroiled in, and the happy results of it. It is *your* turn to tell me what has happened here since I have been away!"

Her parents glanced at one another before her mother started in.

"Your father has always been prudent, Harriet, and we have always lived modestly and well within our means," Harriet's mother was careful to emphasize the moral lessons she had tried to teach her daughter.

Harriet smiled. "I'm certain he could never have arrived to this point without *your* sage advice, Mother."

Mr. Shore patted his wife's hand as he started in. "Well, Harriet, I did not know the extent of the Grimsby estate's debt, but I did know that I'd saved enough to pay a fair price for our farm and try my hand as a yeoman farmer. When I finally did meet with Stephan about purchasing our parcel of land, he was in such sore need of ready money for their debts that he willingly sold me not only *our* farm, but the Browns' next door, as well as those smaller properties on the outskirts of the village—the ones that abut our farm to the southwest."

Harriet's head was reeling, but she quickly recovered, her eyes sparkling. "Do you mean to tell me you now have *tenants*? Father, it seems that now you're a gentleman in quite your own right! I am very happy for you."

Her father's cheeks turned a flustered ruddy shade and he grinned.

Harriet looked about the room and admired the changes she noticed in the parlor alone. New decorations, newly upholstered sofas and chairs, and new paper on the walls. And those were only the changes she saw in that room.

Their once humble home had had quite a few improvements made and another wing was being added. It was beginning to look quite a grand little thing. Harriet wondered how they had managed to keep all the changes at home a secret from her in their letters. Eliza Watson, their maid, had since become the housekeeper. There were now several more servants: a groom, a cook, a gardener, and three new maids—not to mention the farm laborers—who were all henpecked by Harriet's mother every bit as much as their smaller staff had been before.

Burnham-on-Sea, Somerset

A full week later, when Harriet arose in the morning earlier than she wished to, she stared at the ceiling and waited until the maid came into the room before climbing out of bed.

"Hello, Nancy," Harriet yawned.

Nancy set a cup of tea on Harriet's side table. "Hello, Miss. Will you be wanting any assistance with your hair this morning?"

Harriet sighed. It was odd having a servant able to wait on her in the mornings. "I . . . think I shall be fine on my own, thank you."

Harriet readied herself for the day quickly and carelessly. After a flavorless breakfast and a half-hour of irritated pacing, Harriet sought out the housekeeper.

When her first plea met with resistance, she considered dropping to her knees. "Put me to work. *Please*," she begged.

Mrs. Watson reluctantly looked up from her household ledger. "The only work suited for you, miss, and for one of your *status*, is to pick flowers in the garden an' it please you."

Harriet resisted the urge to roll her eyes at Mrs. Watson's pride in her new *status*. "Thank you, Eliza."

Moments later, Harriet was out the door in an old dress and an even older apron, with a bonnet to stave off the morning chill still on the air. She glanced about and saw a few flowers she could cut and dry, but noticed that one of the vegetable garden beds was full of weeds and had not yet been planted. She exchanged her floral shears with a rake and hoe she found in the shed and set to work.

Why had Stephan not yet come? That thought had been the only one on her mind for the entire week she had been home thus far. He had said he would come as soon as he could, and Harriet trusted him completely, even though it was hard to remain patient.

Two hours later, the sun had brightened and warmed the muggy air and earth and Harriet's forehead was glistening with a hard-earned mask of perspiration. The knees of her apron and gown were damp with dew and dirt. The weedy bed was ready for planting and the large cabbage bed was almost completely weeded. Harriet smiled ruefully, certain that Mrs. Watson would disapprove of her dirty, work-worn appearance. Still, though, as she worked, she felt better than she had in weeks. Idleness did not suit her—she was her mother's daughter indeed. She was humming to herself, intensely focused on her weeding, when he approached.

"Harriet," he said.

Chapter Thirty-Seven

Burnham-on-Sea, Somerset

The hairs on the back of her neck prickled a little and she slowly glanced behind her, not sure whether she wanted to jump for joy or hide her dirty face behind a bush. *Now* he comes?

"Stephan," she whispered. She whipped off her gloves and hastily wiped her face with the corner of her apron and tucked a stray lock of hair behind her ear. She turned to face him, praying she hadn't smudged dirt on her face.

Stephan walked toward her. "I am sorry to have kept you waiting."

Her heart pounded so hard at the sight of him that she wondered that she could still hear anything at all.

He took another couple of steps closer. "I stayed away at first because I wanted to be sure you had ample time to spend with your family."

Harriet shifted uncomfortably. She *had* enjoyed her time with her parents thus far, but had been so distracted by constant thoughts of Stephan that her father had teasingly accused her of being terrible company only the evening before.

"I also wondered if, now that you know that you are the daughter of a landed gentleman, you might wish to . . . seek alternate suitors."

Harriet could feel her cheeks flush with hurt. "Do you want me to?"

"Of course not!" he said quickly.

"I have only ever wanted *you*, Stephan." Her voice was quiet. "I've told you this. No one else, gentleman or not, has ever won my heart."

He walked forward and took both of her bare hands in his before shaking his head as his face split into a broad smile. "It never ceases to amaze me that I have somehow managed to capture your interest, Harriet." He stroked the backs of her hands with his thumbs, sending shivers down her spine. "And I shall never stop trying to deserve it."

Harriet sighed a little. Her heart was pounding cheerfully away in her chest and she thought she might burst from happiness.

"I also stayed away because I needed to . . . inform my mother of our hoped-for engagement."

Harriet wilted, nervous to hear about the largest hurdle she could think of between herself and Stephan. "And?"

Stephan grimaced slightly before smiling again. "She is . . . warming to the idea, as I said before. She had been hitherto uninformed of the recent business conducted between your father and I, and all of the, er . . . implications associated with it."

Harriet felt guilty for smiling. "And now?"

"She is well aware that your marrying me is the only way your father's wealth can ever again be a part of the estate. She is now openly supportive of our engagement. That is, if there still *is* an engagement."

She felt heat rush to her face again. "I have already accepted you." She was surprised at how shy she felt and sounded. "You have only to talk with my father."

Stephan sighed and pulled her into his arms, where he could easily whisper into her ear. "Harriet, what if your father will not accept me as a son-in-law?"

Harriet snorted involuntarily with sudden laughter. "Stephan!" she cried. "Why should they not accept you? Have you done something horrible they ought to know about?"

"Now that your father is an important landowner, I thought that perhaps—"

Harriet smiled and shook her head. "Stephan, you ought to know as well as I that he already sees you as the son he never had."

Stephan seemed relieved and smiled back at her, gathering courage. "Then I wonder if he'll honor me with a private audience in the course of the morning."

Harriet's heart thudded away happily in her chest and she could not keep a smile off her face. Stephan slowly lifted each of her hands to his lips for a kiss. Harriet bit her lip.

"I am certain he shall," her breath caught in her throat as she spoke.

Stephan allowed her to lead the way into the house herself. Harriet left him in the entryway and immediately ran to her father's study, still in her dirty gardening smock and half-boots, arriving at the door a bit breathless.

"Father!" she said, and he abruptly dropped his newspaper.

"What on earth is the matter, little Harriet?"

"Father, *Stephan* is here."

"Ah," her father said knowingly, giving her a sly look over the top of his little round spectacles.

"He . . . he wishes to speak with you."

"Wishes to apply for my consent, eh?" Her father smiled. "Shall I frighten him properly for you, then?"

Harriet gave a startled bark of laughter. "Papa, you *mustn't*!"

Her father smiled and settled back into his chair. "Let him come in."

Harriet led a nervous Stephan to her father's study and closed the door behind him. She paced up and down the corridor, too distracted to do more than remove her gardening smock and put her gloves away. When she heard the study door open once more, she rushed over to meet the two men.

"Well?" she asked.

Her father smiled and took her hand in his. "How does the first of June sound to you, Harriet?"

Fyne Court, Burnham-on-Sea, Somerset

Harriet's knuckles were white as she gripped Stephan's hand. They were nearly to Fyne Court, the main house on the squire's estate, to discuss wedding arrangements with Stephan's mother.

"Looking forward to seeing your new home? You will soon be mistress of all of it."

Harriet sighed, a cautious hope glowing in her eyes. "Home," she repeated. "Do you think I really belong here?" she mused aloud.

"I think you belong with *me*," Stephan said. "And everything I have will be yours."

Harriet thought on that. Everything he had. His name, his position, his home. A place at his side in society. A place where she could finally belong. It was too much.

"Harriet," Stephan said gently. She self-consciously relaxed her vise-like grip on his hand. He laughed a little at her reaction, but his expression quickly grew serious once more.

"There is something I have not yet told you," he said.

"Is it to do with my father? The land he purchased from you?"

Stephan tilted his head to one side as though a little surprised. "Er, yes and no. You see, the *reason* I had to sell such a large parcel of land to your father was that many of my parents' debts were coming due and had to be paid immediately."

Harriet frowned. "How bad is it?"

Stephan looked uncomfortable. "The debt left by my father was irksome but surmountable. It was the debt incurred by my mother that caused the most damage—the balls and parties she would host, her wardrobe, racehorses, and extensive redecoration projects. Two years ago, my father died, and as I was not yet of age to manage the estate myself, she . . . well, she *nearly* ruined me. I hope to heal the estate and make it thrive once more."

Harriet nodded. It sounded as though Stephan was arriving at his point, so she patiently waited.

He sighed a little. "However, I'm afraid that with quite a few debts left to pay we shall not have quite the *grand* life that you may have imagined for us. We shall need to economize for the next few years to pay back the rest."

Harriet nodded, trying to hold back a smile. "I understand, Stephan."

Stephan looked away from her awkwardly. "Now I see I should have told you all this sooner," he sighed. "Does it change your mind?"

Harriet scowled at him. "Change my mind? What nonsense. All it *does* is help me understand your mother a little better. No wonder she was so insistent that you marry a young lady of means!"

Stephan laughed nervously. "Yes! It was very wrong of her."

"Oh, indeed it is! Seeking a white knight in the form of a large dowry to rescue her from her own financial imprudence. What you had better do instead, Stephan, is marry a woman who knows how to wisely manage what she is given."

Stephan squeezed her hand. "I sincerely hope that you fit that description, Harriet, since you are the one I'm set upon."

Harriet laughed. "I could not have escaped my mother's home without learning the good sense of economy and hard work. Now," she added slowly, "if only you could marry a young lady of good breeding, sense, *and* fortune."

Stephan shook his head. "Let's not start that, Harriet. You are precisely the woman I want and need. Exactly as you are."

He kissed the tips of her fingers for what seemed the hundredth time, and Harriet bit her lip to keep from grinning at him. "Stephan, my love, perhaps I ought to have told you this before . . . but are you aware that I stand to receive a dowry of more than ten thousand pounds upon our marriage?"

Stephan's face reflected a jumble of emotions. Harriet laughed a little at his expression and placed her hand on his cheek. "I am sure you wondered when I did not tell you my reasons for willingly taking on the role of Virginia Sackville, along with all its risks. Well, *you* were my reason, Stephan. I was to earn the gift of a substantial dowry at the end of the charade, and I thought it might make your mother a bit more approving of me."

Stephan took her hands in his, admiration and concern in all his looks. "All that danger, that risk . . . it was all for me?"

Harriet nodded, biting her lip as she realized she hadn't been completely truthful. "Yes," she said. "Although . . . you know full well that once I befriended Virginia, I could not rest until I saw her safely reunited with her husband."

"Perhaps you are the real white knight," he whispered in her ear, kissing the edge of her jaw below her ear.

She grinned but flushed with a little embarrassment. "And I suppose that I did it a little for myself, as well," she confessed. "You know that I always yearned to be an actress, Stephan, and I thought the role of Virginia Sackville would be a fascinating one to play!"

He burst out laughing at this and pulled her close to him. "And shall you be anxious to find some new role after we are wed, darling?"

Harriet shook her head emphatically. "No, I have had more than enough of being anyone but Harriet Shore!"

Stephan smiled. "Anyone?" he asked, "Not even Mrs. Harriet Grimsby of Fyne Court?"

Harriet blushed prettily. "Well, anyone besides *that*!" And she leaned forward to melt into yet another perfect kiss.

November 25, 1814

Dearest Virginia,

I am so glad to hear that Raphael has grown so very plump! I am as happy as anyone ever has been. Stephan and I have been married nearly six months and it is every bit as wonderful as I had dreamed. He is even more kind since we married. He walks with me in the gardens every day and when we talk of the baby we expect next spring, we joke that if we have a little girl, she ought one day to marry little Raphael!

Sometimes I think of how I came to know you, and all that happened while I was in London, and I marvel that I have finally realized my dearest wish.

Virginia, I am so happy I can hardly breathe sometimes for the joy of it all. We have done tolerably well for ourselves, have we not?

Yours ever,

Harriet.

Virginia smiled to herself and grinned at little Raphael, who had just crawled underneath her skirts. She finished reading the last line of her letter and looked up as her mother and father entered the room.

"Mother, you'll enjoy reading this, I think," she handed the letter to the duchess.

Her grace the duchess of Dorset was wearing a plain muslin morning dress she would never have been caught dead wearing in London, and the duke could have passed for a local farmer. Their cheerful faces were likely the product of that morning's bracing walk together in the clean, misty air on Ralph's farm.

"Oh?" Her grace reached for the letter. She read it quickly, and her smile broadened. She passed it to the duke. "I am glad to hear Harriet has settled into her position so very well. And expecting a baby already! Yes, I am quite happy for her. She has done very well for herself."

"Indeed. I am pleased that she seems so happy," the duke added.

"I have done fairly well for myself, too, wouldn't you say?" Virginia asked slyly, pulling Raphael onto her lap and helping him clap his chubby little hands.

The duke tried to remain stern. "Ralph *is* a good man. Sturdy, dependable, upright . . . but how was I to know this? I only knew he—"

"That's enough, dear. We understand." The duchess tried very hard to wear a disapproving look for a moment, but gave in to the smile hiding behind it. She sighed. "Virginia, you pushed me *too far*—much too far! But I must confess . . . your husband has proved himself a capable, not to mention *handsome* young man. And you may only be a farmer's wife—but your chubby little boy with that delicious Sackville nose! I must confess, that somehow quite excuses all the rest." The duchess leaned over at this pronouncement to poke Raphael's nose, inviting rapturous giggles. "Yes, my dear, I will say that things have not turned out *nearly* so badly as I had feared."

Virginia sighed. "Mother . . . Father. I am not at all sorry I married Ralph. But I am sorry if I disappointed you in the process."

The duchess looked out the window. "I think I was a little too easily disappointed, my dear. I see that now."

Virginia reached for her mother's hand and gave it a squeeze.

"Now," the duchess said, shaking herself from her brief reverie and reaching for her plump grandson. "Come here, my little love, and give your grandmama a kiss or two!"